Rosemary Friedman's writing ⟨ success by her first novel *No* ⟨ *Doctor Stories* alongside Somers⟨ She has gone to write eighteen fu of *Affection* ('a classic of its kind', *Evening Standard*), which was serialised by the BBC. She has also written two popular children's books, *Aristide* and *Aristide in Paris*, as well as *The Writing Game*, an inspirational memoir for writers and readers.

She has written commissioned screenplays for both film and television in the UK and US, and her play *Home Truths* toured successfully in 1997. In addition, Rosemary has been a judge of literary competitions and a member of a number of distinguished bodies such as the Executive Committee of PEN, BAFTA, the Writers' Guild, the Executive Committee of the Society of Authors, and the Royal Society of Literature. She lives in London.

Rosemary Friedman

Rose of Jericho

HOUSE OF
STRATUS

This edition published in 2001 by House of Stratus, an imprint of Stratus Holdings plc, 24c Old Burlington Street, London, W1X 1RL, UK.

www.houseofstratus.com

Typeset, printed and bound by House of Stratus.

A catalogue record for this book is available from the British Library.

ISBN 1-7551-0123-5

FOR JUNE AND DERRICK

Let the bridegroom go forth out of his chamber
And the bride out of her pavilion.

JOEL II : 16

There is a dream which keeps coming back to me at regular intervals; it is dark, and I am being murdered in some kind of thicket or brushwood; there is a busy road at no more than ten yards distance; I scream for help but nobody hears me, the crowd walks past, laughing and chatting.

ARTHUR KOESTLER

One

Kitty did not like flying and the fact that she was on her own did nothing to mitigate her fears. Each time the keen of the engines diminished, her heart sank with it; each time the wide body of the jet swooped she plunged mentally earthwards, effaced for all time. She did not like to leave the safety of her seat, where she kept the belt fastened across her lap, for fear of confounding the equilibrium of the unnatural monster in which she had paid good money to be incarcerated, and was not at all happy when others walked carelessly up and down the aisles. It was not that she was afraid of dying. Since she had been a widow, since Sydney's death, she had looked upon herself as being totally dispensable, but when her time came she preferred to die comfortably – if possible in her own bed – surrounded neither by the marvels of hospital technology nor that of the cabin in the sky in which, from her window seat, she felt she had only to put out a hand to feel the substance of the passing clouds.

She had been up since six – although for all the sleep she'd had she might just as well not have bothered to go to bed – and the winter darkness had exacerbated the feelings of alienation with which she regarded the grisly pantomime of modern travel, with which she had difficulty in coming to terms. The railway, the car, the aeroplane – and now of course the invasion of space – had, as far as she could see, increased his mobility, but not made man any happier than when he had restricted his movements to the distance his feet could carry him. Other cultures, other religions, had made him dissatisfied with his own.

She had been getting ready for a fortnight. Trying on and sorting, selecting and rejecting, washing and ironing, making lists – on paper and in her head – and sorties to the cleaners. While others prepared for the siege of Christmas, with which she had neither affiliations nor patience, Kitty packed her case for Israel and Eilat. Her anxieties about flying, about abandoning *terra firma, terra cognita*, for that megalith in the sky, manifesting itself by its vapour trail by day, and its lights on wing and tail in competition with the stars at night, displaced itself on to her clothes. Should she take the thin white cardigan or the thicker blue? If the white one were thicker or the thicker one not blue there would be no problem. She would resolve the matter in the evening by putting them both on the pile in the spare bedroom, from which she would remove one next morning, only to substitute it for the other before the end of the day. Closing her eyes she tried to transport herself to the Red Sea; to test the hot sun tempered by the desert wind upon her arms. All she could feel was the warmth of the Magicoal fire in her sitting-room penetrating the sleeves of her winter dress. She turned to the weather report in the newspaper – through the window she could see fat white flakes of snow, in no hurry, making their way to the ground – Singapore, Tangier, Tel Aviv. It was no help. She accepted that somewhere the sun was shining but could not imagine it. Sydney would have advised her. He would have packed for her too. Always had. She'd put her dresses out, and he'd transform them into neat rectangles, interspersed with the virginal tissue he'd brought home from the showroom – where it was used to wrap gifts – before putting them in the case. Sydney was not here. She had learned over the long months, like a newly-born foal, to stand on her two feet. She had staggered and stumbled and little by little succeeded in remaining upright, to manage on her own. At moments like this she saw Sydney by her side so clearly she could almost touch him. There were fewer and fewer of them.

Josh had taken her to the airport. He was a good son. At Shepherd's Bush she wished she could go back for her old, comfortable sandals: pride had made her pack the new ones not yet broken in. At Chiswick she swore she'd forgotten the passport she'd placed meticulously into a compartment of her handbag, undoing the zip to peep at it a dozen times. Josh took her hand reassuringly in his. He carried her case to the check-in, where she watched the needle on the scale anxiously for overweight, bought her a magazine she would read but not see, kissed her and waved as she entered the departure lounge where she was alone. She put one foot in front of the other as she had learned to do.

The voice of the captain – *'your* Captain', *noch* – came across the tannoy: "In a few moments those of you sitting on the left-hand side of the plane will have a good view of the Bavarian Alps."

Kitty was sitting on the left-hand side of the plane. Her palms were sweating and her mouth dry. She looked straight ahead at the brown curls of the man in front of her, his knitted skull-cap secured with hair clips. What did she want to see the Bavarian Alps for? All week she had been slithering and sliding in the High Street – up to her ankles in slush each time she crossed the road – in the worst snow for thirty years. Each time you went out in the street you took your life in your hands, and the central-heating boilers in the flats had proved no match for the untoward exigencies of the weather. She had put extra blankets on her bed at night and in the evenings sat in front of her electric fire which seemed to glow with scant enthusiasm. When Addie Jacobs' invitation came to spend the festive season in Israel, Kitty was not sorry, but she had no desire, en route, to look out of the lozenge of a window at the Bavarian Alps, Sarajevo, Salonika, Rhodes or Cyprus. When they touched down safely at Ben Gurion, then she would look.

3

It was her first holiday since Sydney had died. She did not count Godalming, where she had gone to stay with Carol and Alec and the children whose closeness had emphasised her own isolation, nor even Majorca where she had spent a week in their flat with Freda and Harry who had done their best to include her in the convivial rounds of endless drinks on endless sun-soaked balconies, and where it was almost home from home. Had it been Mexico Addie had suggested, or China or Brazil, she would not have accepted. In Israel, Kitty felt, *Eretz Yisrael*, she would not be betraying Sydney.

She had been on her own for eighteen months now and to her amazement she had survived. After Sydney's death she had wanted to die too. There was nothing to live for. She had, at a stroke, lost childhood sweetheart, husband, lover, confidant, friend, and been herself allotted the part-time role of mother to children who no longer needed her, grandmother to grand-children whom she rarely saw.

Despite the black terror of the days, and in particular the nights, immediately following Sydney's death nothing, surprisingly, had proved wholly insurmountable.

People had been kind. Their comfort was trite. 'You must pull yourself together.' 'Never mind.' Never mind! 'You'll be all right.' As if you could be, after almost forty years of marriage. They talked about 'losing your husband' as if she had mislaid her purse. Addie Jacobs, a widow herself, from the flat across the way, had put her arms around her, let her cry. It was what she needed. She had made a friend of Addie who was not her type. The children had of course helped. Josh with his practical support in dealing with the tide of paperwork which referred coldly to her darling Sydney as 'the deceased'; Rachel with her impulsive hugs and kisses, burying her mother's anguish in her wild hair; and Carol offering the unfailing panacea of the grandchildren. There was the family too, Sydney's family. They tried to sustain her but when she looked into their eyes she saw

Sydney beckoning her back into the past when she knew, with every fibre of her being, that her salvation lay ahead.

It was after Sydney's stone-setting that Kitty decided there was a time to cry and a time to stop crying. The ache in her heart was no less than it had been but, realistic as she was, she saw that the moment had come to tidy it away – as she tidied her thoughts when she had finished with them – and refer to it only in the privacy of her head. No one was interested anyway. A cheerful face begot a cheerful face. From now on the plaster of her smile would cover the hurt she doubted time was ever going to heal.

The 'stone-setting', eleven months after the passing of the deceased was, according to Josh, customary rather than obligatory, *minhag* rather than *din*. On the way back from the cemetery, inhaling the newness of Josh's Rover, and remarking wryly the renewal of life in the pink blossom of the almond trees that lined the road, Kitty felt it not wholly desirable that the wound, that afternoon, had been so cruelly opened when she had worked so hard during the past months to come to terms with her bereavement. The custom should be reassessed; to perpetuate it in its present form was, she felt, an insult to the memory of the dead person. A quiet moment of prayer at the graveside with the children would have sufficed. Sydney's family, in particular Beatty, had been horrified when she had tentatively suggested it and Kitty had been inveigled into the whole razzmatazz. At the insistence of Beatty she had not only sent out printed cards of invitation to the ceremony but inserted an announcement in the *Jewish Chronicle* (Tombstone Consecrations) so that every scarcely remembered acquaintance had felt obliged – at the expense of previously arranged outings and rounds of golf – to turn up to 'show respect' to the family who would secretly have preferred to be alone.

Because it was a Sunday ('must make it a Sunday', Beatty said), the stone-setting stakes at Bushey seemed to have got completely out of hand. They were marked up on the board, one every fifteen minutes like a railway time-table, and with as much feeling. The headstone, which Kitty felt had little to do with Sydney and which she had selected from the catalogue while her grief was still raw, had shone achromatically in the pale spring sun. The text she had chosen: 'In my children I speak clearly with the eternal', was Sydney's well-earned epitaph; a marble heart – 'a token of love from his grand-children' – his testimony from Debbie and Lisa, who had adored him, and from Mathew whom he scarcely knew.

When it was over, the prayers and the address and the infiltrating of the fashion parade among the grave-stones (many darting off at tangents along the paths to visit their own loved ones), they had gone back to the flat. Kitty had been against a big 'do', but Sydney's relatives, spear-headed by Beatty, had prevailed. Glasses in hand, as if they were at a cocktail party, the company spoke of holidays, the recession, mutual friends, and carefully avoided any mention of Sydney's name. Like a sea anemone the visitors swallowed Kitty into their protective midst while the waitresses, in their white aprons, with smoked salmon and with tea, laid balm upon the freshly opened wound. Afterwards, with their well meaning words.of consolation, they left her on her own again.

She had filled the days.

She worked in the Jewish Day Centre caring for those older and less fortunate than herself. In easing the pain of others she discovered an analgesic for her own. Her head was occupied if not her heart and she tried to keep it like that. It took her mind off the other; off the deep, empty, cold, dark chasm that had been left by Sydney. She worked mainly in the kitchens, finding an appreciative and extended family for her boiled beef and carrots, her *latkes* and her biscuits with the jammy port-holes. She had taken over from Sophie de Groot who with *gazpacho* and *crème fraîche* had tried to introduce some *haute cuisine* into the place and was *broigas* when the old people complained in disgust that the soup was cold and the cream sour. She had become a member of WIZO, throwing herself into the work for the welfare of women and children in Israel – regardless of colour, race or creed – and played bridge, two afternoons a week, with other widows in the flats. In addition there was the synagogue Ladies' Guild to which Kitty was now able to devote more of her time.

The evenings had been harder to fill. She had discovered that she was no good on her own. At Josh's suggestion she had enrolled in an evening class and ventured out each Tuesday into an alien world. In 'Listening to Music', she stuck out, she felt, like a sore thumb. Apart from the fact that she had never heard of, and certainly could not spell, Messiaen, there was something else. Her shoes were smarter, her clothes better and her outlook narrower than the rest of the class, who had for the most part come straight from work, bringing with them an aura of tube trains and the evening newspapers. They were friendly enough, but in the canteen during the coffee break she was unable to contribute to the conversation about the labour leader of the GLC (whose name she did not even know), the new bus fares, or arguments concerning the means of production. She was a fish out of water and knew nothing of rent and landladies, football matches and launderettes, concerts in Smith Square and Saturday morning shopping. She stuck it out and was delighted when on the records Josh bought her she could distinguish flute from piccolo, harp from cymbal, tuba from trombone. There was a world out there, she realised, which not even Sydney with his erudition and his Torah had discovered, a world one tiny corner of which she had started to explore. But she was no Columbus. She found the Evening Institute with its hard chairs and dusty classroom quite a strain and was happy and relieved to get back to the flat with its deep pile carpets, its polished, reproduction furniture and its memories.

Its memories. Apart from the 'keeping busy' at which Kitty had become adept, it was all she had. She could not erase

Sydney from his chair in which no one else had ever been allowed to sit, from her heart where he was always secure. Alone at night she spoke to him but there was no reply. That was the worst part. Telling him of the children, of Josh and Carol and of Rachel as she had been wont to do, discussing the bits and pieces of her day. Now, her voice reverberated from the rag-rolled walls, its echoes losing themselves in the velvet drapes. There was so much to tell. Sarah, Josh's gentile wife, was being converted to Judaism – how Sydney would have liked that; Rachel and Patrick were getting married, what a carry on there had been about the wedding too; Carol and Alec were looking for a bigger house and she wouldn't be at all surprised if Carol weren't pregnant again, she recognised the signs. Most important of all, she was herself taking a big step. She was going to Israel. It was as if she needed Sydney's approval before she could be allowed to enjoy herself. She had been going with Addie. It had been Addie's idea. They had booked up at the last minute, a cancellation. Then Addie had slipped on an icy kerb breaking her ankle and Kitty, encouraged by Rachel and by Josh, had elected to take the trip alone. Looking round the plane at friends, at families who seemed to be enjoying themselves together, she was already beginning to have qualms.

A 'hassid' with beard and sidelocks in the long silk coat – tied with its *gartel* separating the spiritual half of his body from that which was not – and the black hat of the ultra orthodox Jew, left his aisle seat and walked to the front of the plane. When he reached the curtain that segregated the first-class passengers from the hoi polloi he turned and faced the cabin, glancing nervously from side to side. Kitty watched as his hand reached across his chest and inside his coat. Her heart stopped. A hijacker. It was her punishment for coming away without Addie. For enjoying herself without Sydney. She wondered whether they would make a silent toast to her at Rachel's wedding. Whether her grandchildren would remember her. She wanted to say something to the woman who was sitting on her left, but her tongue was fastened to the roof of her mouth; to press the button for the stewardess, but her limbs were immobilised with fear. There had already been an incident in the departure lounge where the X-ray machine had revealed a gun in a suitcase. Security guards had been called and amid excitement had discovered a toy pistol being taken to a child for Christmas. In the old days it had been better. When she had gone to Westgate, with Sydney and the children in the car. No flying at a mad 30,000 feet over Karlsruhe, Stuttgart and Munich. No hijackers either, threatening the lives of innocent hostages.

She heard the cheep of the tannoy and the captain, *her* captain, clearing his throat. He was going to tell them he was being forced at gun point to fly to Beirut, Damascus...

"For your information..." His voice was deliberately calm.

Perspiration covered Kitty's top lip.

"We shall be serving lunch in five minutes..."

The *hassid* withdrew his hand from his pocket and with it a black book. Swaying back and forth, blocking the path of the approaching drinks trolley, he began to pray. Kitty was no drinker but decided that if the trolley ever reached her she would ask for a large vodka, regardless of whether or not it would agree with the tranquillisers which Lennie had prescribed and which she had taken.

She forced her mind from thought of air disasters – 'Four Hundred Passengers and Nine Crew' – and hijackings – 'Deadline Passed All Hostages Shot' – and tried to concentrate on Rachel's forthcoming wedding.

Two

Sydney would have been pleased. For longer than Kitty could remember he had been talking of Rachel's wedding, looking forward to the day when he would lead her to the marriage canopy and deliver her safely into the arms of some suitable husband at which point – the forging of another link in the chain of Judaism – he would feel a great weight of responsibility lifted from his shoulders. He had not been so concerned about his elder daughter. Of course he had been pleased – delighted – when Carol had married Alec, but there had never been any doubt that she would do the right thing. Rachel was a different matter. The path had not been smooth. At eighteen she had left home for university and to the outward eye disengaged herself from the shackles of orthodox Judaism in which she had been reared and from the company of its adherents. She kept Kitty up to date with the cyclorama of unsuitable boyfriends who walked at regular intervals in and out of her life. Sydney did not want to know. He had designated a fund for Rachel's wedding; bought the champagne which lay waiting in Issy Miskin's cellar. It was as if by preparing the way he would, like Circe, entice Rachel along it. Sometimes by way of conversation, as if to prepare him for the worst, Kitty would tell him of the son or daughter of people they knew who had married 'out'. He was not interested. Not responsible. It was not his worry. He worried about Rachel. When she abused the Sabbath. Ignored the dietary proscriptions. Incorporated the Holy Days into the calendar of her secular year. Sydney had died before bringing his carefully laid plans, his hopes, his dreams, to fruition.

Before Rachel announced that she would marry into the Klopman family, Kitty thought often about this irony, the unfairness of the trick played by fate on Rachel's father and pondered, when she did so, on Sydney's whereabouts and the 'world to come' in which she could not whole-heartedly believe. If it existed, to be sure, Sydney would be there, 'a ministering angel' among the 'disembodied souls of the righteous'.

Unable to convince herself of any independent existence of the spirit, Kitty had taken her doubts to Rabbi Magnus. In an attempt to explain how the body, while of use on earth, was dispensable in the hereafter, he had employed the analogy of the moon traveller. 'While on the moon man is totally dependent on his space-suit. If it is damaged he will die. But once he returns to earth he can throw off its restrictions to move about as he pleases.' Kitty prayed nightly that released from the space-suit of his body, in which during his last months he had suffered so miserably, Sydney would have heard the good news about Rachel's wedding. There were, it was true, irregularities of which he would not have approved but then he had never been one for compromise. Toeing the line of his religious beliefs Sydney did not deny the importance of sex – the Torah (where the subject was dealt with frankly) spoke to real people with real passions – but considered that it had no place outside the marriage bed. More pragmatic in her approach, Kitty was able to turn a blind eye to the fact that Rachel and Patrick, though not yet married, had set up home together in a borrowed council flat. When she saw that he not only loved, but seemed able to curb her headstrong Rachel, she had taken Patrick to her heart and was able, although she did not condone it, to put the irregularity into context. It was not the same world. By holding rigidly to his beliefs Sydney had tried to make it stand still.

When the time came for her to meet Patrick's parents, Kitty should, she knew, have invited them to her flat. Sydney, a stickler for protocol, would have insisted. Not yet at ease however in the mantle of her widowhood, she had become so agitated at the thought of the hospitality she would have to provide, that when Hettie Klopman had telephoned her she had gladly accepted the invitation for dinner at the house in Winnington Road. Apart from her sister-in-law Dolly's funeral, when she had unwillingly returned to the cemetery whose ethos stirred the embers of fires she strove daily to douse, it was the first family occasion she had had to face on her own. She stood in front of her wardrobe. Since Sydney had died she had bought no new clothes. There had seemed no need. Sydney had left her comfortably off but it seemed profligate to spend money unnecessarily when none was being earned. There was the outfit she had had for Sydney's last Ladies' Night which had come out again for Josh's wedding; the black crêpe, which went on for ever but reminded her of the mourning she had left. She reached for the fine wool two-piece, which she had worn all winter, when her eye fell on the dress she had bought on the morning that Sydney had died and which she had vowed she would not wear. She had never got rid of it. Had let it hang there like a talisman.

It was light and coloured, like the spring, a breath of the year to come, an augury; a breach of faith. She took it out and held it in front of her. She had not put on any weight. She let the pleats swing. It was part of her life with Sydney although he had never seen it. If she wore it he would be there with her. And yet it was a new start. She could not explain the paradox.

The evening had gone well. Kitty was glad she had worn the dress with the pleats although it was no match for Hettie Klopman's olive silk (the initials of the designer woven into its threads), the matching shoes, the cabochon bracelet from which she extended her pink-tipped hand. From the moment Kitty had rung the bell at the side of the double oak front door and felt the eye of the security camera above her head she knew that she would be looking at the evening through Sydney's eyes, measuring her responses by his standards.

The welcome had been warm. Herbert Klopman, cigar in hand had opened the door wide.

"Mrs Shelton!"

"Kitty." She corrected him.

He hung her coat with care in a panelled closet on a hanger bordered with antiqued studs, took her arm – as if they were old friends – as he led her towards the drawing-room which opened off the hall, its heavy curtains embracing a room warmed by the glow of a gas-log fire.

"I can see where Rachel gets her looks!…" Hettie Klopman enveloped Kitty in a perfumed cloud, kissing her and appraising her at the same moment. "Patrick's told us so much about you."

An elderly woman in a black dress, her head angled unnaturally towards the floor, sat with a newspaper and magnifying glass beneath a lamp.

"This is my mother," Herbert said, pinching her cheek. "Mrs Klopman."

Mrs Klopman's head stayed where it was as she raised her eyes to Kitty's, took Kitty's hand in both hers.

"Rachel's a grand girl. She'll make Patrick a grand wife."

Kitty hadn't thought of it like that and realised that she was in 'their' territory when she was used to being on her own.

A bookcase, with books whose spines seemed all to be bound in tooled leather, covered one wall. At some signal from Herbert a section of it swung open to reveal a bar. He listed a choice of spirits in their jewelled bottles.

"Something soft," Kitty said, "…tomato juice."

"Ice and lemon?"

She could see the slices, concentric on a plate, speared, like a hedgehog, with cocktail sticks.

"It's a beautiful house…" Kitty said, while Herbert busied himself with the Worcester sauce, watching the drops like some dispensing chemist, and Hettie hovered with a silver hors d'oeuvres tray, its cut glass dishes filled with olives and pickled cucumbers and with nuts. Kitty was not a great conversationalist. Sydney had always done the talking. "We used to have a house," she said. "In Hendon…"

She had gone back to it recently thinking to resurrect her early life with Sydney. The monkey-puzzle tree in the front garden, with its spiny, evergreen tentacles, which had obliterated the light in the dining-room and which Sydney would never cut down, had been summarily ripped out, and red asphalt – providing hard-standing for two cars – had replaced the grass and the roses. The friendly face of the house – between-the-wars stucco – had been masked by a timber façade and the windows were swathed in pink nylon.

"Now we live… I live…in a flat."

"I'll show you round, if you like," Hettie said, obviously dying to, "after dinner."

"If we ever get any dinner…" Herbert looked at his watch. "Where are the children?"

"Sure they're enjoying themselves," Mrs Klopman said holding out her glass. "You can give me another little drop of whisky, Herbert. It wasn't enough to fill a thimble!"

Kitty wondered if they ate like that every night. The table on its own was something to see, its mirrored top like an oblong lake on which floated silver and crystal and posies of flowers and a dish of fruit with cherries hanging down like ribbons and foil wrapped mints and crystallised ginger and pastel coloured sugar-coated almonds. She was glad that on the first occasion she hadn't invited Herbert and Hettie to her flat. She sat on the high-backed, tapestry covered chair on Herbert's right, opposite Patrick, who looked exhausted from his day on the wards, and Rachel who hadn't bothered to change from her jeans or brush her hair, and next to Mrs Klopman who had brought the whisky decanter to the table with her.

Hettie served *kreplach* soup from a Rosenthal tureen which matched the china.

"Do you realise there's no singular for *kreplach*?" Herbert said as two of the small, meat filled dumplings were ladled into Kitty's plate. "Probably because nobody ever eats *one*. Did you hear the story of the American tourist who staggered into Blooms' and said to the waiter: 'I'm tired and I'm hungry. I never knew London was such a filthy place. The stores are crowded, the streets are filthy and I got off the bus at the wrong stop. So bring me a nice plate of soup with *kreplach* and just one kind word for a visitor.' The waiter brought the soup, put it down and was about to leave. 'What about the kind word?' the American said. The waiter bent over and whispered: 'Don't eat the *kreplach*!'

Kitty saw Patrick and Rachel exchange glances and realised that the story was not new and had been repeated for her benefit.

A roast chicken and accompanying vegetables were brought in by a maid.

Herbert poured wine into the glasses with the twisted stems and picked up his own.

"*L'chayim,*" he said, looking at Kitty. "To our new *mechutanista.*"

Kitty raised her glass to the family who were to become her relatives by marriage.

"Patrick!" His grandmother hissed leaning across the table. "Patrick!"

"What is it?" Patrick took his eyes from Rachel.

"Will you give her the ring?"

Patrick took a box from his pocket. Inside was a solitaire diamond flanked by diamond baguettes.

"It was my own engagement ring," Mrs Klopman confided to Kitty. "Patrick's grandfather, God rest his soul – Patrick never knew him – brought it over to Dublin from South Africa."

"I hope it doesn't have the Lipshitz curse," Herbert said. Kitty looked at him.

"A lady at a charity ball was wearing this enormous diamond. 'It's the most famous diamond in the whole world,' she boasted. 'The first is the Hope diamond, then comes the Koh-i-noor, and then comes this one which is called "the Lipshitz".' 'It's magnificent,' its admirers said. 'How lucky you are!' The lady shrugged. 'Nothing in life is all *mazel*. Unfortunately, with the famous Lipshitz diamond you must take the famous Lipshitz curse!' Her friends buzzed round her. 'And what is the Lipshitz curse?' The lady sighed. 'Lipshitz.'"

"Herbert!" Hettie said.

Herbert lifted his glass. "Rachel and Patrick!" He looked at Kitty. "You can't imagine how happy we are with our new daughter, we couldn't have asked for better."

"Bits of nurses from the hospital he was after taking out!" Mrs Klopman muttered.

There were tears in Hettie's eyes as she drank the toast, Kitty knew, because Rachel had told her, that after Patrick was born his mother had given birth to a second son who was brain-damaged and was spending his life in an institution which Herbert had funded. She had been unable to have more children.

Hettie got up to kiss Rachel, resting her cheek against hers for some moments, then Patrick who looked embarrassed at the whole thing.

"*Mazeltov!*" Mrs Klopman said, toasting Rachel and Patrick but looking at the chicken. "Will you give me the parson's nose, Hettie?"

Over coffee they discussed the wedding which was to take place the following summer when Rachel, hopefully, had graduated.

"You don't have to worry about the reception," Herbert said, lighting a cigar, "I'll take care of it."

"I'm not worried," Kitty said, "Rachel's father…"

"We'll have it in the King Solomon Suite." Herbert puffed intently.

"As long as the ceremony is in Sydney's *shul*," Kitty said. "Rabbi Magnus…"

The cigar was glowing. Herbert examined its lighted end and Kitty was aware of a *frisson* of tension making its way through the clouds of goodwill.

"It's better to have the *chuppah* and the reception in the same place," Herbert said reasonably. "It saves having to park twice…"

"It was Sydney's second home," Kitty said, meaning Rabbi Magnus' synagogue to which he had worn a path over the years.

"It's a lovely *shul*, Herbert's," said Patrick's grandmother, leaning towards her. "And Patrick's my eldest grandson. They'll make a grand couple!"

Kitty felt the ground shifting beneath her and called inwardly for Sydney who would not have given way. She looked for help to Rachel who with supreme indifference was reaching for a chocolate. Patrick was digging her in the ribs with his elbow.

Rachel looked at him. She removed the silver paper and took a bite from the bittermint to give her strength.

"As a matter of fact…" she said.

"The King Solomon Suite takes about four hundred," Herbert said. "We can have Unterman to cater if we book him early enough."

"As a matter of fact…" Rachel tried again.

"Let the child speak, Herbert," Mrs Klopman said.

Herbert took no notice. "Patrick finishes at the hospital at the end of June so what about the first Sunday in July?…" He took his diary from his pocket and removed the gold pencil. "No, wait a minute, that's the 'three weeks'." He meant the period before the Fast of *Av* which commemorated the destruction of the two

Temples in Jerusalem during which time no marriages could be solemnised. "It will have to be the *second* Sunday." He made a note.

Sydney had favoured Tuesday weddings because on that day, in the account of the Creation in the book of Genesis, God concluded his handiwork saying 'It was good' not once but twice. Kitty held her peace.

"Wedon'twantabigwedding!" Rachel said into the silence.

"Unterman doesn't cater under four hundred," Hettie said. "It's not worth his while."

"Rachel and I will just get married quietly," Patrick said. "We'll marry in a synagogue if that's what you want, but no jamboree. Lunch here if you like."

Hettie stared at him. "For four hundred people!"

"Mother, we don't want four hundred people! Just..." he looked round the table, "...us."

"*Meshugger*," Mrs Klopman said. "Did you put anything in the coffee, Herbert?"

Herbert stood up and took the apricot brandy from the sideboard.

Kitty did not protest when he poured some into her coffee cup. She had the feeling she was going to need it.

"Listen son," Herbert said to Patrick when he'd sat down again. "There are certain things one has to do in this life to please other people. You're our only child..." His eyes met Hettie's across the table, "...who'll be getting married, at least allow us some *koved*!"

"We're not having a big wedding," Patrick said. "Forget it!"

"What a way to talk to your father, Patrick," Mrs Klopman said. "Don't you think I'd like to enjoy myself before..."

"You're upsetting your grandmother," Herbert said.

"Look," Patrick said, "I'm absolutely serious. Both Rachel and I..."

"Sure he's talking like a bridegroom already," Mrs Klopman said.

18

"...Both Rachel and I greatly appreciate what you want to do for us but we're simply not interested. As I said we're willing to marry in synagogue and come back here for a drink, or lunch if you insist, but other than that..." He took Rachel's hand and looked round the table. "...I'm afraid it will have to be the Registrar's when no one's looking."

"What about a tour," Hettie Klopman said pointedly, looking at Kitty, "round the house?"

Kitty had not seen anything like it. Deep pile carpets, specially woven, swallowed their footsteps and muted their voices. Paintings, bought astutely by Herbert at auction sales, glowed beneath their lights on every wall. She admired the kitchen into which you could have almost put her entire flat, and the hi-tech, third reception room with its deep leather chairs. On the first landing Hettie opened a door.

This is my mother-in-law's suite," Hettie said. "It's self-contained."

"Does she live with you?"

Hettie looked surprised. "Ever since we've been married. Herbert wouldn't have it any other way."

The master-bedroom was, Kitty thought, large enough to house the wedding reception – never mind the King Solomon Suite – and Herbert and Hettie had a bathroom each. Herbert's was lined with wood – incorporating a sauna and mini-gym, complete with rowing machine and exercise bicycle – and Hettie's with rose marble, with rose silk blinds which Kitty would not have liked to keep clean. When she saw Patrick's bedroom, with its cedarwood fitments housing his books and his trophies, she couldn't imagine how he could be happy with the peeling walls and chill discomfort of the council flat.

At Hettie's suggestion, Kitty availed herself of the facilities, hardly liking to dirty one of the tiny, initialled guest towels laid out on the wash-basin. When she went downstairs again Rachel and Patrick had gone.

"Headstrong!" Mrs Klopman said. "Takes after his grandfather."

"He'll come round," Hettie said confidently, patting the sofa next to her for Kitty to sit down.

"He won't get a penny from me if he doesn't," Herbert said.

Three

The fight had been uphill. The message was conveyed to Patrick that, with the diamond engagement ring, brought back from South Africa by his grandfather and which he had accepted from his grandmother, went the quid pro quo that he would concede in the matter of the wedding.

Kitty tackled Rachel for what was not the first time.

"It's ludicrous," Rachel said. "People don't have big weddings."

"Why is the King Solomon Suite booked up almost a year ahead?"

"Some people!"

"*One* day," Kitty said. "That's all we're asking. You're being very difficult. I can't see your objection."

"It's a waste of money to start with…"

"Nobody's asking you to pay…"

Rachel sat on the floor in her tired cords. There were holes in the elbows of her jumper. "In the streets of Calcutta," she said, "children are *dying* from hunger. Carts come every morning to collect the bodies."

"There's a lot of trouble in the world," Kitty said. "Don't change the subject."

Rachel looked at her.

Kitty tried a new tack.

"Weddings are important. Something to look back on. A day to remember."

"Do you remember yours?"

Kitty cast her mind back with difficulty.

"I think it's very selfish," she said. "There aren't that many happy occasions."

"All those people we don't even know…"

"You'll have the rest of your lives on your own…"

"We've made up our minds," Rachel said. "It's out of the question."

Kitty examined her trump card. She did not like blackmail.

"For your father. God Rest his Soul." She touched Rachel lightly on her Achilles heel. "Do you remember how he used to talk about your wedding? His 'little Rachel'…?"

She watched as the tears filled Rachel's eyes; as she went to the window to hide them; as she wiped away the pear-shaped drop that stole down her cheek with the back of her hand that wore Mrs Klopman's diamond.

"…he put money aside for it. Told me to be sure…when he knew he wouldn't live to see it. Do you remember how he used to tease you?"

It was Sydney's greeting to Rachel when she came to the flat for dinner.

"When's the wedding?" A veiled reminder to her to stop getting involved with non-Jewish boys.

"He even bought the champagne," Kitty said. "It's in Issy Miskin's…"

"You've made your point."

Kitty held her tongue. In the silence she recognised the special rapport that had existed between Rachel and Sydney. She did not disturb it.

"I suppose you'll be wanting bridesmaids next." Rachel said into the curtain.

"Only Debbie and Lisa." Kitty's voice was gentle, acknowledging the tenuousness of her triumph. "If you give me that jumper," she said, "I'll darn it."

Kitty was glad that Addie had booked on El Al. To be asked to fasten her seat belt, extinguish her cigarette, in the language in which God had addressed Abraham and Abraham had spoken to his son, filled her with a sense of pride and of belonging which she was unable to put into words. Looking round the plane at the Jewish strangers from Minsk or Manchester, Safed or Chicago, who chatted in their seats or congregated in the aisles, she realised that she felt more at home with them than she did with many gentiles whom she knew more intimately.

A stewardess with the dark skin and deep liquid eyes of the Yemen stood motionless outside the galley with her trolley as the tannoy crackled above her head.

"Ladies and gentlemen would you kindly *return to your seats* so that our cabin staff may serve you with lunch…" The message was repeated in Hebrew.

The King Solomon Suite had been reserved. Hettie Klopman had telephoned to say so. After her holiday, after Israel, Kitty would have to start thinking about the wedding in earnest. Once into the New Year the time would soon go. There would be guest lists to compose, invitations to send out, decisions to make concerning dresses – she had already consulted Rika Snowman, who, at Cupid of Hendon, specialised in Bridal Wear (and had made Carol's), about Rachel's dress – and table plans, for which she needed Sydney to prevent her being swallowed without trace into the well-meaning maw of the Klopmans. Kitty had already ceded the question of the synagogue – Rabbi Magnus was to participate in the wedding ceremony, but at Herbert's *shul* – and recognised the matter as the first in what was to be a series of skirmishes. The second encounter had concerned the engagement notice for the *Jewish Chronicle*, and the Klopmans had won, hands down. Kitty, as the mother of the bride, had proposed a simple statement which had been approved by Rachel and Patrick. The Klopmans had suggested minor changes, and Herbert had offered to complete the text, and drop it into the newspaper on the way to his office. When the announcement appeared, heading the week's 'matches', it ran to twelve lines, encompassing Rachel's middle name 'Sadie' – which she hated – Patrick's medical degrees (he wanted to know why his mother had not included the fact that he had passed his piano exams – without distinction – to grade four), references not only to Rachel's late father, which was appropriate, but to Mrs Klopman senior, the late Meyer Klopman, and to Magda and Joseph Silver, Hettie Klopman's parents, complete with their retirement address in Miami, Florida. The only thing which her future in-laws had omitted to declare publicly, according to Rachel, was how often she changed her underwear.

Twice a week, when he came for dinner, Kitty discussed the wedding with her nephew Norman, using him as a sounding board. It gave her something on which to concentrate her mind.

"Ladies and gentlemen…" There was a hysterical edge to the captain's voice. "…if you do *not* return to your seats the cabin staff will be unable to serve you…"

The aisles were still full, the conversation animated, punctuated by gunfire bursts of laughter. It was like a Jewish wedding, Kitty thought. She had weddings on the brain these days, which was hardly surprising considering what she was planning with Hettie Klopman for Rachel and Patrick. She could not help comparing it with that, exactly a year ago now, of Sarah to her only son, Josh.

Their wedding had taken place in a Leicester Register Office. Josh's father would not have approved. Kitty did not approve either, although her disapproval was equivocal because she loved Sarah, who was not Jewish, and had come to feel a closeness to her greater sometimes than she enjoyed with her own daughters. It was Sarah to whom she had turned after Sydney's death, Sarah who had comforted her and sat beside her in synagogue on the holidays, Sarah who seemed to understand the shadow beneath which she lived and which had replaced the substance of her life.

At first Kitty had wondered whether she should go to the wedding after all. Sydney would not have done. Of that there was no doubt. She had allowed herself to be swayed by the pleadings of Sarah and Josh. Sydney's family had rallied round, more from curiosity, Kitty thought uncharitably, than anything else. In a convoy they had made their way through the winter snows up the freezing motorway to Leicester.

Deirdre MacNaughton, Sarah's mother who had brought the dogs with her in the back of her Land Rover, waited for them in her wellington boots in the Registrar's Office where the heating had broken down and breaths were visible on the gelid air. Kitty introduced Beatty and Mirrie and Freda – Sydney's sisters – and Freda's husband Harry, and Juda, Sydney's younger brother. Huddled in their fur coats (Juda in an astrakhan hat he had bought in Russia) they waited, rubbing their hands, silently – more like a funeral than a wedding, Kitty thought, for Sarah's Uncle Arthur, her mother's brother, and her only relative, who had flown in from Nairobi.

Watching Josh, who should by rights have been beneath a *chuppah*, standing in front of the Registrar's table with Sarah aglow in her red velvet suit, Kitty felt a sadness that her only son, whom Sydney had reared so assiduously in the ways of his faith, had forsaken his birthright. Standing, though full of love, next to Sarah, he was the jagged ends, the severed connection, in the chain which Sydney had tried so meticulously to preserve. She shed a tear, and it was not her customary wedding one, for the weakness of her child, whose weakness, looking at Sarah, she understood, and for her own complicity.

"I now pronounce you man and wife!" The Registrar, his nose red, was gathering up his papers.

"*Mazeltov!*" Beatty said.

Deirdre MacNaughton stared at her. When she kissed Kitty her cheek was cold.

Freda narrowed her eyes at her watch. "Five minutes!" she said. "Hardly worth coming."

In the smoking-room of the rambling house, the two sides eyed each other while the butler from the caterers, who had taken the precaution of insulating his insides from the cold, handed champagne. The refreshment seemed all to be liquid.

"You'd think they'd put something on a biscuit!" Beatty said.

Sarah's Uncle Arthur flirted with Rachel who seemed, Kitty thought, to be wearing four sweaters in an effort to keep warm. Beatty listened, transfixed, as Sir Timothy Armstruther, Sarah's godfather, discussed the perils presented by the weather to his sheep. Harry tried Majorca on Lady Jayne but she wintered in Monserrat and did not know it.

Kitty wondered how anyone could live in such a cold place. There was a fire in the grate, true, but Sarah's Uncle Arthur was hogging it. The air in the rest of the room seemed little warmer than that outside where the snow drifted steadily on to the lawns. There was no sign of any central heating and at one point Kitty wondered if there was to be any lunch. The butler was circulating with the umpteenth bottle of champagne and the Leicester party extended their glasses while Josh's family covered theirs with their hands, shaking their heads, and the women wished they'd worn cardigans over their flimsy dresses.

"Catch my death," Mirrie could be clearly heard saying. "I've only just got up after flu."

In the panelled dining-room the refectory table, which looked as if it had been in the family for years, was laid with place cards. The first course had been served. Josh's family looked at it with horror. Round the rims of crystal glasses, fat pink prawns were curled obscenely. Sarah whispered to her mother.

"Good Lord!" Deirdre MacNaughton exclaimed. "You *said* fish!"

There was an embarrassed silence while half the company addressed themselves to the prawn cocktails, Juda tried to explain to His Honour Judge Pinkerton across the table that the purpose of the dietary laws, which eschewed the eating of shell fish, was not to make Jews healthy, but, through self-discipline, to make them holy. His Honour seemed fascinated, and Juda, warming to his theme, was explaining how the taboos on food were not felt as primitive, but established an area of daily life in which a Jew recognised some things as pure and some as impure, when they brought in the quennelles, floating like clouds, on their suspiciously rose-coloured sauce. Juda realised that, as the head of the family now that Sydney was dead, everyone was looking to him. He picked up his knife and fork and isolated a shred of familiar looking flesh.

"Tomato!" he proclaimed.

Beatty was not convinced. She scraped the sauce ostentatiously to the side of her plate to make room for the new potatoes and the peas.

The Leicester contingent, floating merrily on a sea of Sancerre, did not notice the poor appetites of Josh's relatives and Josh himself had eyes only for his new bride.

Hungry, Beatty asked for two helpings of the *Crême Brulée*, but there was only just enough to go round. She was summoning up her courage to ask the Judge – who was sitting near them – to pass the After Eights, when Sarah's Uncle Arthur, exceedingly red in the face, champagne glass in his hand, got to his feet.

"...Been asked to propose the toast," he said, one hand jiggling the loose change in his trouser pocket. "...Sarah and Josh." A long silence covered the table protectively. "Sarah's a lovely gel. Always been a lovely gel. Poor Dickie would have been proud of her today." He looked round the table and caught Beatty's eye. Beatty nodded encouragingly. She liked speeches.

"As you are no doubt aware," Uncle Arthur said, "I have – unfortunately – no experience of the matrimonial state. It has been said that marriage is a lottery, in which the prizes are all blanks... I don't agree. There is no doubt in my mind that in this particular lottery Josh has won the jackpot..."

"Hear, hear!" Kitty said.

"...and Sarah – it would appear from my brief acquaintance with her bridegroom – has by *no means* drawn a blank!"

Beatty thumped on the table causing Judge Pinkerton, who was dropping off, to jump.

"...See you all agree with me. Up till now I've always been a contented bachelor; but I must confess that today I envy young Josh the visions that I know he sees. Can't say more than that I wish from the bottom of my heart that his hopes may be fulfilled..."

It was Uncle Juda's turn to cheer.

"...and that he and our lovely Sarah will live long and happily to prove to me the error of my celibate ways. Before speeding them on their journey I would like to welcome Josh to our tiny family and ask you to join me in drinking a bumper toast to the happy pair. As we say in Swahili, '*Heri*'. Sarah and Josh."

Josh replied to the toast. Then Uncle Juda, speaking from notes, thanked Sarah's mother on behalf of the London guests – "never mind the rotten lunch" Beatty could be heard muttering – and by three o'clock it was over.

Kitty went up to the comfortless bedroom for her coat. There were pictures of horses round the walls, and an electric kettle on the floor where Sarah's mother made her morning tea. Beside the bed, whose cover was strewn with dog hairs, was a photograph in a silver frame of a man in Court dress. Kitty picked it up.

"Dickie thought the world of Sarah," Deirdre MacNaughton said, coming in and startling her.

On impulse Kitty replaced the photograph and put her arms round her new *mechutanista*, although she doubted if the term applied.

Neither of them spoke but between them was the silent intercourse of mothers who had given birth and widows who had loved and lost.

"So sorry about the luncheon," Deirdre said. "Sarah did say fish."

Kitty looked in the mirror to put on her mink hat. "You weren't to know," she said. "As long as they're happy..."

Deirdre looked at her blankly, her moment was over – she wondered if the caterers had remembered to feed the dogs.

Four

The El Al lunch had not been bad. A roll of smoked salmon –
flanked by a lettuce curl, a translucent slice of lemon and three
black olives – braised beef in its gravy, with french beans and
tiny roast potatoes, and a glazed pineapple tart beneath a whorl
of *parev* cream. The rectangular plastic sections, topped by their
transparent plastic hats, in which it was served, gave it an air of
unreality, of playing at food, unless it was the flavour which
seemed to have been frozen and sterilised out of it. While not
exactly a gastronomic experience the meal passed the time. Kitty
extracted a knife, fork and spoon from their slim paper envelope
and made the food last as long as possible – savouring each
morsel as though her life depended on its despatch – in an effort
to allay her anxiety as she thought what *might* have been
provided with a little more imagination. Handing the carnage of
the tray to the stewardess, who came smilingly to collect it, she
brushed the crumbs from her skirt, folded her table away and
wondered, since the diversion of the meal was over, how she
would pass the remainder of the flight.

Need overcoming fear, she excused herself to the woman
beside her and waited while she collected up handbag,
newspapers and pad of airmail notepaper, and stood up to let
her out. Making her way through the crowded aisle to the
toilets, which were at the rear of the cabin, Kitty glanced at the
faces in the rows on either side of the plane. Sleeping – in

ROSE OF JERICHO

attitudes of abandon – reading, lost in thought, playing board games, idly returning her glance, each countenance was familiar, yet she knew no one. She recognised a Polish peasant, a renowned violinist, her grandfather; the haunted eyes of a concentration camp inmate, Carol at four reading a comic, the infant Josh in a baby sucking at its bottle. In a head of dark hair there was Rebecca and Miriam; in a brow the prophet Isaiah; her late Aunt Esther; Addie's nephew – recently *barmitzvah*; a Jewish comedian; a well-known industrialist; they were all there. With a muttered apology she eased herself past the broad back of a man in a homburg. He appeared to be praying but when she'd squeezed by she saw that he was punching a pocket calculator. The plane lurched suddenly, seeming to sink and taking her heart with it. Clutching the nearest seat, Kitty wondered, was she the only one bothered by the tenuous drone of the engines, by the alienation of the situation, high above the clouds in the slim cigar of metal at the mercy of rods and pinions, human calculation and aeronautics? Were there others cold with fear and tense with apprehension who would say a prayer when the undercarriage touched the ground? She knew the statistics. Josh had told her. One thousand deaths, in thirty fatal crashes, for the 750,000,000 passengers carried by the airlines each year. You were more at risk, Josh told her, each time you crossed the road. Kitty had her doubts. As she joined the queue beyond the galley, the sun disappeared leaving a thin red line along the horizon.

When she came out of the toilet the windows were dark. In London they would be lighting the *Chanukkah* candles. With no Sydney to perform the ceremony for her, no family party, she was glad to be away. Alec, in Godalming, would be kindling the first light for the children; Josh would be explaining the festival to Sarah, who last year had had a Christmas tree; Rachel and Patrick would not even know.

Back in the non-smoking section Kitty fastened her seat belt. The sign was not on but she felt safer with the webbing drawn

31

tightly across her lap. She smiled her thanks to the woman on the aisle side of her whose writing pad was now covered with spidery Hebrew script which crossed the page from right to left. "I hate flying," Kitty announced to her own surprise. Since Sydney had died she had been diffident about addressing strangers, feeling that she was imposing, thrusting the burden of her widowhood peremptorily upon others.

The woman shrugged, in an age old gesture. She was sun-tanned, small and dark, wearing a jersey suit.

"If it creshes, it creshes, I'm not so important."

Kitty recognised the lilt of the Israeli accent, the philosophical approach of its people. She wished she could be as dispassionate but everything seemed to worry her.

"You come from Tel Aviv?" Kitty asked.

"Jerusalem. I've been to visit my brother in Hendon..."

"We used to live in Hendon."

"Mayflower Gardens."

"Mayflower Gardens!" Kitty said. "We were at 26. The house with the monkey-puzzle tree." She remembered that it was no longer there. A thought struck her. "You're not Archie Bensons' sister-in-law?"

"Arieh Ben Zion!" The woman laughed, "I'm Ruhama."

"It's a small world," Kitty said. "Archie used to walk to synagogue with my late husband. Wasn't it you...?"

Ruhama helped her. "My husband, Moshe, was killed in the Mitla Pass in the sixty-seven war. He was a tank commander. Now they're giving back the Sinai." Her voice was bitter.

"I'm going to Sharm-El-Sheikh," Kitty said. The tour had been booked to the southern-most point of that 'great and terrible wilderness' which intruded itself into the head of the Red Sea.

"Ofira!" Ruhuma said, giving the reef bound bay its Hebrew name.

For Kitty it would be a day out along the coast of the triangle of land that lay barrenly, with its mountains and its desert, between Africa and Asia. For Ruhama there was blood on the sand.

"My oldest son, Baruch, was shot down in the Yom Kippur war," Ruhama said.

Kitty thought of Josh, safe at home.

"…my baby, Amos, is doing his army service."

Kitty was silent. In the diaspora they collected money for the defence of Israel. She tramped the streets for Jewish Women's Week, for their personal contribution. It was blood from stones. In the cold and in the wet she went from house to house knocking on doors. It was a thankless task. Sometimes, in the bigger houses, the au pair was instructed to tell her that no one was at home when upstairs she distinctly saw the curtains move. She wrote receipts, awkwardly, on windy doorsteps, for derisory sums when inside there were hothouse flowers and luscious smells of exotic meals wafted from the kitchens. Frequently there were excuses. She'd heard them all. 'I haven't been to the bank.' 'I've run out of cheques.' 'I'm late for an appointment.' She'd offer to call back but it was never convenient. Kitty didn't suppose it had been very convenient for Moshe Ben Zion to give his life defending the Mitla Pass, nor for his son Baruch to die at the controls of his Skyhawk. At the more humble homes she often fared better. Women surrounded by mouths to feed would reach deep into their purses, and pensioners, living on their own, were proud to contribute, secure in the fact that they would not be called upon to make the ultimate sacrifice like Ruhama Ben Zion.

"Arieh – Archie – sent my ticket," Ruhama said. "It was his ruby wedding. They gave me a week off from my job. I work in the supermarket six days a week, eight in the morning until seven at night. In the evenings I teach at an *Ulpan*."

The supermarket all day and English to foreigners at night! With the absurdly high rate of inflation in Israel Kitty knew that Ruhama's situation was not unusual. She felt ashamed of her soft life in unthreatened territory.

"It was wonderful," Ruhama said, speaking of the ruby wedding. "All the family. Do you have a family?"

Kitty took out the photographs she carried in her handbag.

"This is my daughter, Carol, her husband Alec, and the children; my daughter Rachel – she's getting married in the summer – and my son Josh…"

Kitty looked at Ruhama but she did not flinch.

"…with my daughter-in-law, Sarah. She's converting to Judaism."

Sarah's decision had been announced to Kitty on her birthday. She could not have had a better present. Much as she loved Sarah there was always at the back of her mind the displeasing thought that were she and Josh to have children they would not be Jewish. The Shelton name would, in Sydney's eyes, have been disgraced.

The catalyst for the decisive step that Sarah was taking had been her love for Josh. Although apparently not committed as his father had been, Sarah had come to realise that – despite his denials – Josh and his religious heritage were one; that his Judaism went deeper than the practices he did not observe; that its tenets were a component of his corpuscles, its precepts embodied in his bones. It was a part of Josh she had no access to. His mother, Rachel and Carol, his uncles and his aunts, had more right of entry to the core of his being than she. If Sarah was motivated by jealousy it did not invalidate her decision for which there was another consideration. By marrying Josh she had overnight become allied to Judaism although she had not embraced it. She was asked questions as if she had joined the rabbinate instead of just getting married to Josh. 'Why do they consider themselves the Chosen People?' and 'Why do they always wear little hats?' She felt constrained to answer the queries, which until she had consulted Josh, left her floundering for replies. In marrying him, she had, she discovered, become one of 'them' without becoming one of them. She wanted to be able to answer the questions, to be accepted by Carol and Rachel and by Aunty Beatty and Uncle Juda, who looked at her as if she was from another planet. She was. She knew nothing of Sabbaths that began on Friday, Festivals threaded like golden markers through the year, laws and customs whose origins and minutiae fascinated her. She wanted to understand where Josh came from, what was his creed. "I would like to become Jewish," she said. The resolution was her own. It echoed the prayer of the most famous proselyte of all. 'Where you go, I will go...' She wanted to share the fortunes of the Jewish people the darkness as well as the bright joys of their triumphs. 'Your people will be my people...' She would identify with national aspirations. 'Your God will be my God.' She was prepared to serve as a witness to Israel's religious commitment. '...where you die, I will die, and there shall I be buried.' She would defend Jewish beliefs and practices even to the grave. She went weekly for instruction to a Mrs Halberstadt but it was Kitty who took her by the hand.

In Kitty's kitchen Sarah was initiated into the mysteries of *kashrut* – forbidding the eating of certain foods, including animals that had neither cloven hooves nor chewed the cud – the prohibition against the blood which carried the life of the animal, and the injunction that the killing must be done in the most humane way. The laws, Kitty told her, had a deep moral significance which raised the trivialities of the daily round into a continuous act of worship. They could no longer be defended on grounds of hygiene, but must be regarded as a kind of spiritual calorie count, intended to prevent obesity of the spirit and insensitivity of the soul. They refined the character, raised man from the beast, and as such were perennially valid.

Sarah watched while Kitty soaked her meat for half an hour in water, drained it for a further hour sprinkled with coarse salt, on a special board. She listened while Kitty explained that the prohibition concerning the mixing of meat, or meat products, with dairy foods extended to cooking utensils and even the plates on which the meals were served. In Kitty's kitchen there were cutlery, china and saucepans for the 'meat' dishes and some, in different designs, for the 'milk'. There were two specially designated washing-up bowls, with their own cloths and brushes, and tea-towels in distinctive colours. By her side in the kitchen, watching her prepare for the festivals, listening, while Kitty explained that each commandment must be carried out as beautifully as possible according to one's means, Sarah discovered that around her was a world of warmth, affection and stability and that it was just such a home that she wanted to build together with Josh.

She did not ask Kitty for the formula for she realised there was none to give. The haven that Kitty had created with Sydney, and now strove to perpetuate on her own, was based on a practical code embracing both the highest level of human love and the most humble domestic chore – to which Sarah did not have the key. That some of the practices were irksome there was no doubt. Josh found them so. Looking beyond them, Sarah was aware that they represented a shared sense of purpose in what seemed the most commonplace things. The symbols were intangible. The rewards, in her mother-in-law's face, in her life, were visible. Kitty knew that her replies, in response to Sarah's increasing flood of questions, were inadequate. Sydney would have known the answers but he would not have spoken them. Not to Sarah.

The mayhem in the cabin presaged the end of the journey, which was confirmed by the captain, together with the information that the temperature in Tel Aviv was some eighteen degrees higher than it had been in London. After Kitty's internal flight south it would be higher still. A steward, picking his way through aisles awash with debris, handed out landing cards. Kitty took one. He did not give one to Ruhama who was going home. Looking at it – name, address, date of birth, place of birth, destination – she realised that there was no helpmeet, no Sydney, beside her and that she must fill it in. Sydney had always taken it upon himself to do these tasks, just as she had automatically carried out such chores as were necessary in the home.

Kitty knew that today things were arranged differently. Carol and Alec in Godalming shared the responsibilities of Peartree Cottage, the children, and their lives together equally. She could not imagine Sydney changing nappies and washing dishes as Alec did, and she had not herself adjusted to the endless filling in of forms with which her daily life seemed now to be strewn. Sometimes, in the case of shares and their allotment, or declarations for the tax inspector, they appeared to be couched in a language with which she was not familiar. She was doing her best to master it but found it hard, as beginnings always seemed to be. She discovered, in small things of which she knew nothing – insurance policies and paperwork relating to the car – how Sydney had sheltered and protected her and that every day there were new skills she must learn.

The pressure on her ears announced the plane's descent. A screaming baby demanded attention, and a sickening and prolonged crunch directly beneath her directed her thoughts once more to her morality, although she knew it was the landing gear. The other passengers, trussed into their rows like battery chickens, seemed unperturbed. Kitty, stiff with fear, could not understand it. She picked up the magazine from the fish-net pocket attached to the seat in front of her and with clammy hands and fingers which were not steady, flicked through its pages. The maps of the world criss-crossed by the thin red lines of the air routes, diminished her; Bordeaux and Bucharest, Addis Ababa and Alice Springs; she had seen so little of it, knew even less, felt her own insignificance in the pale blue expanse of the named and numerous seas. In less than five minutes, if – God forbid, which she doubted – the plane did not crash with herself blown to smithereens, she would be in Israel which boasted four of them. Next to her, her neighbour was chattering about the whereabouts of her passport, speculating as to whether there would be anyone at the airport to meet her. Kitty did not answer. She did not feel like talking. As if her words would fall like stones upon the fuselage causing it to shatter. She gripped the arms of her seat with knuckles that were white as the engines whined, and the magazine fell from her lap to the floor. She heard the sound of prayers and added her own silent one. Inadvertently glancing towards the window, she saw the white sands of the seashore looming towards her at an unnatural angle, the skyline of Tel Aviv beneath her gaze. She was convinced, as they descended, rapidly now, over the grey-green water, that any minute she would be with Sydney, all her troubles, all her problems would be over, and wondered would her children mourn. There was a jolt. She had been right. The plane glided swiftly, smoothly along the runway fighting a battle of opposing forces with the airbrakes. She dared to turn her head, amazed that round her there were smiling faces and that she was alive. Together with others, rhythmically, spontaneously, she started to clap.

Five

Norman picked up Kitty's postcard from where it lay on the mat. Unbelievable blue fishes, flat – like the plaice on the bone his mother used to grill for him – swam to and fro, their backs striped with broad black bands, through the lucid waters of the Gulf of Eilat. He had missed his aunt. Not only for the dinners which twice a week she enjoyed preparing for him – having no one else to cook for – but for the wise and sympathetic ear of his surrogate mother, not yet having come to terms with the death of his own.

It was five months to the day – he marked them off on his calendar – since he had as usual taken Dolly her cup of tea, and she had not answered his habitual morning enquiry as to how she had slept, what sort of a night she had had. He had not thought it strange. Had put the tea-cup on the bedside table, opened the curtains to let the daylight fall on the thin carpet. Dolly's sleeping pills – which sometimes she took late – had, he imagined, not worn off. He shook her arm. Since her stroke she had aged. Her skin was slack like an old woman's. Not that she was young. Norman himself was forty-two and his mother had been getting on for thirty when he was born. She had shrunk. He had watched the gradual process, his heart bleeding, daily. She had never been a big woman but as he helped her down the stairs, into her chair, into her bed at night, he had felt the bones through the flesh, the increasing lightness of her frame. He shook her again. There was no response. She usually woke with a grumble, about her heartburn (for which she blamed Norman who had brought her night-time biscuits), her aching back, her lack of sleep.

"Drink your tea before it gets cold!"

Often she sent him down to make another cup.

A tiny dart of fear, the first, entered Norman's mind. He looked at the sleeping pills. Perhaps she had taken too many. Her hand was on the coverlet. He took it, the knuckles thickened with rheumatism. It was cold.

"Mother!"

He had dreaded this day.

"Mother!"

There had been no warning. Nothing unusual. Death had come in the night and taken her. Away from Norman. He stood stupidly in the sun looking at the old woman whom, since the death of his father, he had cared for at the expense of his own life.

The family had taken over, Beatty, Freda, his Uncle Juda. Norman had done what he was told. Had played his part in the funeral – unable to accept that it was his mother in the simple elm box – the prayers, the tying up of loose ends with the solicitors. When it was over he had paced the rooms of the terraced house where – six foot tall and heavily built – he had always seemed too large, hoping to catch a glimpse of Dolly. He saw her often. In the kitchen before her illness, cooking his favourite food; in the sitting-room where she knitted his pullovers which were never quite right at the hem; in the garden, putting bread out for the birds. When he put the kettle on it echoed with her voice – as did the narrow bathroom where she did his washing. 'Where are you going, Norman?' and 'What time will you be home?' He missed the security of it, the structure which it had given to his life.

It was inevitable that he thought of Della, the fiancée he had surrendered in consideration of his mother. He had chosen

Dolly who had no one else. For weeks now he had mustered his courage, rehearsed the lines he had composed, in the car on the way to work, before the mirror as he shaved. 'My mother died…is dead…no longer with us…passed away. I'm free. I love you. Have always loved you. Will you marry me?' From the mirror Della's voice mocked him for deserting her in favour of his mother; her laugh scorned his proposal. The plan, which he found himself unable to put into operation, occupied his waking moments and bedevilled his sleep. At Bluestone and Blatt, the Estate Agent's where he worked, they put Norman's agitation, his abstraction, down to his mother's death. The turmoil in his head and in his heart presaged, he thought, his own. Unable to tolerate his self destruction he took his courage in his ungainly hands. Fortified by the large whisky, which since his mother had died had become an evening ritual, enabling him to confront it alone, he drove to Kingsbury.

Della's father opened the door.

"Norman!"

The flat had not changed. Della's mother, still dress-making, took the pins from her mouth to greet him. They had read of his bereavement and commiserated. Norman's eyes circumvented the neat sitting-room looking for Della. For a sign.

"Is Della here?" He thought he would choke.

Her parents exchanged glances.

"Didn't you know?"

Died. Dead. Della. He was being strangled. Thought he must fall.

"Are you all right Norman?"

"Open the window, Mother, it's very hot in here."

"Della's not here," her father said.

"I thought you knew," her mother said, pulling the net curtain aside to let in the breeze.

"She got married."

"Lives in New Zealand."

"We had a letter…"

"Ever so happy…"

"We're going in the winter…"

"To visit…"

"They've invited us…"

"Geoff, his name is…"

"She's expecting a baby…"

"New Zealand?" Norman said.

"Ever such a nice boy."

He didn't remember getting home. He had no recollection of finishing the whisky. In the morning he found the bottle on top of the television set. Empty. Nothing inside. There was nothing inside Norman as he went to work, came home, went to bed, went to work again, came home, went to bed…until Sandra came into his life; from South Africa. And Aunt Kitty. He told Aunt Kitty about Sandra. To verify it. He did not believe it himself.

She had been a voice on the phone like many others, looking for a flat on Hampstead Heath. From the selection he had sent her she had chosen one to view and Norman had taken the keys to let her in.

The appointment had been for eleven-thirty. At noon Norman, wandering moodily through the empty rooms, staring from the windows at the green expanse below which did not move him, decided to give her another five minutes. The estate agent's life was beset by time-wasters, plagued by clients who failed to show. It was the distasteful thought of going back to the office that had made him wait for her so long. He found everything distasteful. Pleasure in nothing. Since his mother's death. Measured out his life in a succession of uninviting days.

He had left the front door open and did not hear her come in.

"Am I late?" Her accent was South African. He recognised it. He looked at his watch.

"You wouldn't have believed the traffic!"

She was small and slim with tanned limbs, dressed in a tan suit. Her handbag and her shoes, which had very high heels, were made of some sort of skin. She jangled as she walked towards him, the gold chains round her neck knocking one against the other.

"Sandra Caplan." She held out her hand. "You'll be from the agent's."

Her perfume had preceded her. Norman breathed it in.

"This sounds just what I'm looking for. I have to be near the city – the boys go to school – but I like to smell the air."

Her hair was spun gold. Norman wanted to touch it. The desire shocked him. He put his hands behind his back.

"Where would you like to begin, Mrs Caplan?"

She was looking out of the window he had opened. Through her eyes he saw the delicate tracery of the trees, the undulations of the Heath.

She turned to look at him and her face was laughing. It was a long time since Norman had laughed.

"Just anywhere."

From her expression he guessed that the flat was sold. He could always tell. She had fallen in love with it and he with her. It was that simple.

He showed her the three bedrooms, admitting the inadequate size of two of them – which she said would be all right for her boys – the out-of-date work-tops in the kitchen which Norman bemoaned as if he personally were responsible for their design. He agreed that the situation of the dining-room was ridiculous and apologised, looking at her band-box appearance, for the runnel of rust on the bath which had not, he confessed with embarrassment, been used for some time.

Back in the hallway she made him an offer for the flat and Norman explained that the owner was abroad and would not be back for a few days.

"Meanwhile, perhaps your husband..." He wanted to see her again. "If you would like to make another appointment."

With half-closed eyes she was looking down the corridor. "I'd like to bring my decorator. The place needs gutting."

Norman suggested a time the following day.

"Great." She turned her face to him. "Fortunately I can see the potential. You couldn't sell an igloo to an Eskimo!"

Norman knew it was true. It had been true before his mother's death. Now it was more so.

"You need to adopt a more positive approach. Be more assertive. I'll bring you a book." She held out her hand.

"See you tomorrow." Had she not moved away he would not have been able to let it go.

"And just for the record," she turned at the door. "There is no Mr Caplan."

Later he found out that she was divorced. It was like a dream. The boys were called Hilton and Milton aged eight and six. One played the cello, one the violin. They came to see the empty flat, hurtling up and down the corridors, their feet echoing on the bare boards. Their mother – she did not look old enough – dressed next time in a yellow dress with a pleated skirt, bringing the summer into the empty flat – brought Norman a paperback as she had promised. It would teach him how to be more confident in his job, in his life. He was too old a dog, he told her, to learn new tricks. She berated him for his self-defeating attitude. He took the book home and read it at night in bed. In every page he recognised himself; in his relationship with his late mother, letting her trample on him; his subservience at work, where he had never progressed to the partnership he had envisaged; his castigation of himself for every defect of each property he showed; his habit of agreeing with his clients when they were patently wrong. It was as if a door had opened, a mirror held up to the middle-aged Norman he had never before confronted. Tentatively, he tried, on Mr Monty, what he had learned at night beneath the covers. It was his dinner night with Aunt Kitty. She was making the stuffed cabbage leaves which she knew he liked. A client, leaving next day for Bahrain, had wanted urgently to view a house. In the office the typewriters were covered. They were packing up, going home.

"Give it to Norman," Mr Stewart said automatically, looking at the gold watch beneath his white cuff. He had tickets for the theatre.

"Norman will do it," Mr Bluestone said to Mr Pearl.

Mr Monty put the details of the house on Norman's desk. As usual he was in a hurry to see his girl friend before he went home to his wife in Potters Bar.

It was six-thirty. Norman, his viscera dissolving, looked pointedly at his watch, which was neither gold like Mr Stewart's, nor digital like Mr Pearl's. They took advantage of him. Of that there was no doubt. He had been only vaguely aware of it before he'd read the book which Sandra had given him. He closed his eyes and visualised the chapter: 'Working Late'. When he opened them Mr Monty was waiting.

"I can't manage it," Norman said in a voice which seemed not to belong to him.

Mr Monty stared. Mr Bluestone and Mr Pearl turned round in their chairs. It was as if a strange presence had entered the office.

Norman swallowed. "I have a dinner engagement..." He hoped they would think it was a smart restaurant, a beautiful girl, and avoided the mention of his Aunt Kitty. "...I'm awfully sorry." He stood up as resolutely as he was able on his rubber legs. "But I really have to go."

He wasn't sure how he had managed to get to the door, out of it, along the street. He stopped in front of a shop, looked unseeingly at the underwear in the window. He had to reassure himself that he was more than forty years old. When he had recovered he could not hear his feet on the pavement. With every step his silent voice said: 'I did it. I did it.' He could not wait to tell Sandra.

When he entered the office the next morning he held his head high. He had ironed the shirt which had dripped dry all night over the bath. Mrs Treadwell the receptionist looked at him. The word had clearly got round. He detected a change of

45

attitude when she handed him the typed details of a new property. A strange and exciting world was opening up like a flower before him.

Because of Sandra.

She had bought the flat and taken him under her wing. He could not for the life of him understand why. She involved him in every aspect of its transformation, asking for his approval of every knob and knocker, his opinion on shades of broadloom and snippets of silk. They walked on the Heath with Milton and Hilton where Norman was surprised that Sandra didn't stumble in her high heels. Sometimes she drove him in her smart coupé on which he thought he would drown in her proximity, her perfume, the sound of her voice. Her movements, delicate but strong, had entered his being and threatened to shatter his rib cage. It was as if he had had no life before. His mother, Della, faded into the unremembered background. He was like a man possessed, a wild thing. At work he had become a giant, a force to be reckoned with. He no longer bothered to care, to cringe, to bow beneath the menial tasks with which they overwhelmed him, for fear they would replace him with a brighter, younger man. His commissions, week by week, increased, keeping pace with his new-found confidence. It was self perpetuating. Accompanied by Sandra, Norman had bought new suits, new shirts, new ties. She took him to shops he had not dared to enter, to have his hair cut at a salon whose name was a household word. His improved appearance – Sandra declared him handsome – had given Norman a new pride, a self esteem, which he had lacked but never felt the need of. Impressing himself he impressed his clients. They treated him with respect instead of as the 'boy' from the office. At Bluestone and Blatt they watched the metamorphosis with caution. He did not think it coincidental that they took on a school leaver for the chores, began to address him with deference.

There were other things. Sandra took him to the theatre to see plays for which he would not have dreamed of booking, asking for his opinion, which previously he would have been too self-effacing to give; to see paintings in galleries he'd not considered for the Normans of the world; to concerts where monumental music elicited unexpected responses in his soul. It was as if Norman had died and a new Norman risen from the ashes. There seemed no end to the transfiguration Sandra had brought about. She told him she had done nothing. Merely released his true self. He did not believe it. Was a slave at her feet. Once in a restaurant he had been served with steak which had bled beneath his knife, although he had asked for it well cooked. Sandra had told him to send it back. "It doesn't matter," Norman said. Looking into the laughing eyes, now soberly appraising him, Norman knew that it did. His heart in his boots, he called the waiter who saw only a customer within his rights. Norman explained gently but firmly, as he had learned, that what he had been given was not what had been ordered. Apologising, the waiter took his plate away. Norman was sweating. He found his reward in Sandra's eyes. Gradually it became easy. He expressed his anger when it was appropriate, declared his interest, stood up firmly for his rights. He was like a coil with the spring released, the possibilities were infinite. He was astonished how good it felt to have others respond to him attentively, day to day encounters he had not dreamed possible, to find situations, from which at one time he would have shrunk, actually going his way.

For all this he had to thank Sandra and paradoxically his relationship with her was the only factor in his new life which he did not find satisfactory.

She was friendly enough. That was the trouble. He wanted more than friendship. Wearing his new, cashmere sports jacket, he watched her at the top of a ladder as she arabesqued to measure windows, or busy with swatches of material on the floor, and thought that he had never seen anything in his life more beautiful than the graceful sight of her and mastered an urge to grasp the silken ankle, to run his hand up Sandra's shapely leg, to take her in his arms and make wild passionate love to her. He waited for a sign. That she cared for him. That he meant more to her than a pupil she had trained to assert himself, to realise his potential. What was the use of his changed behaviour, his new-found attitudes, if they could not bring him the object of his sleeping and waking desire. Once Sandra's foot had found a pot-hole on the Heath. Norman had put out an arm to steady her and thought that there must be a burn where her skin had touched his. She had thanked him, laughing, and run ahead after Hilton and Milton, leaving him unable to move, as if his entire body would be consumed.

They met only at the new flat which was rapidly nearing completion. Because of Milton and Hilton, he guessed, Sandra never asked him to her rented house. Bit by bit, Norman had pieced together the marriage to Arnold Caplan. He could not understand how any man, when he had this treasure of a wife, this honey-coloured rose, could lust after other women, needing to possess them all. The infidelities had been numberless – his secretaries, casual encounters on planes and trains, a succession of mistresses – the divorce uncontested. He had been generous with Sandra whose parents were dead and who had money of her own. She had come to England, where she had friends, to start a new life. Norman was puzzled. She seemed to like him, wanting to occupy more and more of his time, but only her perfume, with which he was familiar and which permeated his dreams, embraced him. He guessed that she looked on him as a brother, a new toy. He saw her as a gift-horse sprung from some South African heaven and – terrified less it bolted – he was careful not to look it too closely in the mouth.

When he'd picked up Aunt Kitty's postcard from the mat, he had hoped it was from Sandra, who had taken the boys to Capetown to see their father.

He stared, disappointed, at the pouting blue fishes, the other-world creatures, that swam in the Gulf of Eilat.

Six

Kitty stood on her sunlit balcony, poised between desert mountain and Coral Beach – on the very spot where according to local residents, King Solomon in all his splendour had come to welcome the Queen of Sheba – and looked out across the diamanté mirror of the Red Sea to the Jordanian port of Aqaba, clearly visible in the morning light.

On previous visits to Israel, together with Sydney, she had sat on the broad beaches of Tel Aviv, trampled the streets of Old Jerusalem – stopping while Sydney prayed at the Western Wall – visited Haifa where they had friends. Standing before the tombs of Absolom and Zacharia, Rachel and David, Herzl and Weitzman, they had traced the thin line of their history: at Joshua's Jericho and Abraham's Beersheba – where she had taken a picture of Sydney in a kibbutz hat – the Bible had come alive. They had been to the Golan Heights – looking down, through the gunsights of a disused bunker, on Syria – the Mount of Olives and the Shrine of the Book, which guarded the Dead Sea Scrolls; by the Sea of Galilee they heard the story of the loaves and fishes, and the walking on the water by the Lord who was not their own; from a rock at Banias, they watched black-coated Rabbis cupping their hands to drink the melted snows of Mount Hermon, and noisy schoolchildren washing their picnic oranges in the crystal waters of the Jordan. Together they had laughed at the taxi driver who pointed out territory which had been apportioned by the '*Leak* of Nations' after the First World War, and wept at the mute and painful witness to their people's unprecedented martyrdom in their own lifetime, the *Yad Vashem*.

This was Kitty's first time without Sydney, the *sine qua non* of her life. The first time she had been as far south in the country as Eilat. There had been no one to take her elbow as she negotiated the steps of the aircraft at Tel Aviv – where bearded passengers prostrated themselves, putting their lips to the tarmac – no one to help her with her baggage in the confusion at the carousel. As she stood in line to have her passport stamped, eight branched candlesticks, anomalously, on every airline desk reminded her that it was *Chanukkah*. A smiling girl with dark hair, who looked like Carol, offered a tray of traditional doughnuts to the waiting passengers. It was a welcoming touch. Kitty hesitated, thinking of her figure, then took one, the powdered sugar falling on her hand. About to put it to her mouth, she saw that the girl was waiting for her to pronounce the blessing. Sydney would have needed no prompting. "Blessed art thou, O Lord our God, King of the Universe, who createst various kinds of food." Kitty recited it in Hebrew. A Scotsman next to her put on the proferred skull-cap, and tutored by the girl with the tray and those queuing, both behind and in front of him, repeated, good humouredly, the words of the benediction. Her mouth full of doughnut, which was heavier and stodgier than it looked, Kitty handed her passport to the official who wished her *Hag Sameach*. She realised suddenly that she was in the land of her fathers, bound by the Law of Return, and had an impression of belonging, an acute sense of chauvinism, of being amongst her own. To her surprise, she managed the formalities attendant upon her internal flight and congratulated herself silently on her achievement as she found herself in the right place, at the right time, to board the plane for Eilat. It had been a long day, made longer by her anxieties, and she had been glad, at midnight, to reach the lobby of the hotel where a *Hanukkiah*, sculptured in margarine and donated by the chef and his staff, guttered proudly. '*Hag Sameach!*', the desk clerk greeted her. She would have a happy festival.

The iron of the balcony was cold to her morning touch. By the end of the day, as she hung her swim suit on it, the metal would be fiery. A painted sail boat, silent on the water, caught her eye. She followed its smooth progress across the straits. It did not seem that she had been away for a week. She had missed Addie. Being on one's own in a hotel, she had discovered, was a disability. One had to adapt to it, like deafness, or being lame and having to walk with a stick. In the old days, on holiday with Sydney, the day had been effortless: shared walks, tables for two, a brace of deck chairs in the sun. How wrapped up in themselves they had been, how inward looking in their contentment. She had had to learn new skills. Like a child. To hold her head up as she entered the dining-room, needing to decide whether to go down early – when the room would be empty and her feelings of isolation enhanced – or later, when her solitary condition seemed accentuated by the tightness and rightness of family parties in the noisily crowded room, and whether to take a book.

There were other decisions to be made. When she sat by the pool did she put herself next to a couple, or a crowd – who had obviously come away together – or pull a chair, in solitary seclusion, into a patch of shade? If she smiled at children – thinking of Debbie and Lisa at home in Godalming – might the parents not think she was trying to impose herself upon them? If she addressed strangers, passing the time of day, might they retrain from answering, rejecting her, for fear they would be lumbered with her company? She was learning, rapidly, growing new skins. In her weaker moments she was cowed, self-pitying, crying inside for her loneliness, at other times she managed to convince herself of her own right to exist. It had on the whole been a good week, a marvellous week even, despite the pungent reminders which struck, at unexpected moments, to emphasise her anchoretic state.

As she had sat on the beach or by the pool, watching the swimmers, and the children at play, or the exercise group swinging to music, a nasal call would come over the loudspeaker for 'Dahlia Jacobson. Dahlia Jacobson *b'va kashaî*', or 'Mr Ben Amon, Mr Ben Amon to reception please' and she would know with absolute certainty, that no one would call 'Kitty Shelton'. One night before dinner she had walked along the corridor which led to her bedroom to be stopped in her tracks by the strains of *Moaz Tsur*, the hymn of *Chanukkah* which came through a closed door. She stood outside, a stranger at the gates, she who throughout her life had been warmly surrounded by relatives, by Sydney, and listened while the family – she could distinguish the separate voices of mother and father and children – gave themselves enthusiastically, tunefully to the nostalgic melody. A tear, in remembrance of *Chanukkahs* gone by, escaped her eye and wet her face as she made her way with slow steps to her room. The beds suddenly looked lonely, hers and Addie's, the impersonal room foreign. Despite the sun-filled days and the swimming pool, the Reef – with its rainbow-hued fish, thickets of sea-plants and gem-tinted coral – she wanted to be home, where it was snowing. The mood did not last. She had a good cry, sitting on the dressing-table stool, then realised that she was weeping for herself when there was so much in the world to cry for. She blew her nose on a tissue and dried her eyes.

It had not been bad. She had exchanged experiences with a woman whose husband was convalescing after an operation, and who belonged to Manchester WIZO. She had been befriended, briefly, by a family from Solihull with four young children, who had now gone home. In the restaurant at night the head waiter sat her at a table near the kitchens, in a row, together with the other singles, against a far wall. Sometimes she chatted to a solicitor and his wife from Hampstead Garden

Suburb, who knew Hettie and Herbert Klopman. They took her for a Chinese meal – proscribed for her in London – at which she ate chicken chow-mein with chopsticks and kosher spare-ribs. As she eavesdropped on conversations round her, watched the kaleidoscope of the carefree vocational scenes, what she heard and what she saw was familiar to her. Lonely as she might be, in Israel for much of the time she felt herself at home.

A splash in the azure pool beneath her was made by an early morning swimmer, taking advantage of its desertion to do his solemn lengths. The silence of the sandy road that ran in front of the hotel between the pool and the beach – which could be crossed by the connecting bridge – was broken by the whine of an army truck bouncing crazily over the pot-holes. For the present, Israel was at peace but she was ready, like an old and practised actor waiting in the wings, for war.

In the 33 years that had passed since her independence she had already lost too many soldiers from her civilian army in a total of five confrontations. In England Kitty had fought vicariously the War of Independence (facing the menace of surrounding armies in the Negev and the upper reaches of Jordan), the Sinai Campaign, code name *Kadesh* (living with Israel her hundred poignant hours), the Six Day war (in which to be defeated meant annihilation), the War of Attrition and the war which had entrenched two new words securely in the English language, 'Yom Kippur'. No matter where one went one was reminded of the nation's struggle for survival, her tenuous hold on the changing map of the Middle East. A burnt out tank by the roadside; young soldiers hitching lifts. Underground shelters in schools, and operating theatres buried deep beneath hospitals, ate away at the defence budget and demonstrated the readiness of Israel's David to stand firm against the Goliath of the countries which surrounded her, with their open threats to nudge her into the sea.

"*Shalom!*"

Below her the pool-man, his shorts and tee shirt like a white skin on his bronzed body, greeted the swimmer as he turned, exchanging pleasantries in the language that to Kitty habitually meant prayer. Perhaps she would learn modern Hebrew. They held classes at the synagogue. There seemed to be so many things that she wanted to do – in the music class they were on to Bach now, the variations he had composed for the insomniac Goldberg – new vistas opening up. Out there was a world of challenging opportunities. She had not been aware of its existence when hers had been circumscribed by Sydney.

Looking at her watch, and at the swimmer who had completed his lengths, Kitty saw that it was time to go down to breakfast if she was to be outside the hotel at eight-thirty for the bus. The days had been lazy. She had sunned herself, and swam, and walked – as far as the Coral Beach where she bought postcards for the family, sitting down for coffee and cake as she wrote them – and now she was ready to tackle the sights. She had reserved her seat on the air-conditioned coach which, on the first half-day tour, would take her to Ein Netafim, Canyon of the Inscriptions, and to the flat plain, girded by barren granite rocks, of the Valley of the Moon.

She checked her room to see that there was nothing she had forgotten – sun hat, sun-glasses, scarf – locked her door and pressed the button for the lift. Bare-legged children in the corridor, with happy, holiday faces, towels and snorkels, pressed it after her, each thinking his the alchemistic touch.

Outside the restaurant there was the customary queue which forged ahead as tables were vacated. The Israeli breakfast, laid out appetisingly on buffet tables was the best meal of the day: *mitz* (juices of orange and grapefruit); eggs any way; sardines, sprats and herrings (marinated, chopped and roll-mop); grated carrots, tomatoes, cucumbers and olives, both black and green; milk, yoghurt, soft and hard cheeses; honey, and jam of at least two kinds; fruit compôte (usually prunes); fresh rolls, with sesame or poppy seeds, wholewheat bread or toast, and steaming jugs of tea and coffee. It was not uncommon for those who would be out for lunch to fill not only their bellies, but their beach-bags, whose contents would sustain them for the day. The line moved quickly with good-natured remonstrances to the *chutzpadik* children, in their flip-flops, who infiltrated its ranks.

Kitty filled her tray then sat by the window at a table for one – in the mornings there were no set places – listening to the cacophony, and finished her breakfast with five minutes to spare before the departure time of the bus.

In their shorts and in their sun hats, laden with bags – snacks for the children and water bottles, as if they were crossing the desert instead of penetrating a few miles into it – cameras and tripods, the group waited beneath the portico of the hotel, out of the sun which was now climbing swiftly into the cloudless sky. Fifteen minutes later – Kitty could, she thought, have had another cup of coffee – the blue and white coach swung recklessly into the drive. Before it had come to a halt the doors sighed open and expelled a harassed guide, his hands full of papers.

Kitty chose a window seat – this was not an aeroplane and she didn't mind looking out – and put her hold-all at her feet. She was on nodding terms with the others from the hotel. There was an air of expectancy as they settled themselves – stowing their bits and pieces on the overhead racks – and waited for the guide, who had gone with the hall porter to check his vouchers for the trip.

A boy of about ten whispered to his mother.

"Hurry up already," she said and watched with her people's endemic anxiety as he jumped down the steps of the bus and disappeared into the hotel.

Kitty looked at her watch. Ten to nine. Not that she had anywhere else to go. The child came out again, a smile illuminating his face when he saw that the bus had not left without him. The guide – good-looking enough for the films, Kitty thought – followed him and counted heads. The sun was shining through the little window on to Kitty's arm. She covered it with her scarf. The air was stifling. The guide said something she did not understand to the driver who had a rifle on the ledge beneath the steering wheel. The bus did not move. It was five to nine.

An elderly man with a walking stick and tweed hat, whom she had noticed round the pool, came, in his custom made clothes, carefully out of the hotel. They had been waiting for him. The guide gave him a hand up the steps, the engine sprang to life and the doors closed.

"Okay," the guide said. "*Shalom*, good morning, *guten morgen, bonjour, ciaou, buonas dias*…that's the extent of my lenguages," he clung to a strap as the bus took the corner. "I'm only joking… I do my best you must excuse me! My name is Avi and this is your very good driver, Zvi…" There were other hotels to call at. Others waiting – as in Israel they had grown used to waiting – in their holiday groups. Kitty watched as they climbed aboard and made their way, with their belongings, down the narrow aisle between the seats: an Australian girl with her broad frame and open expression bringing a touch of the great outdoors; a nubile lady from the Bronx wearing a star of David, trousers – tight over her bottom – tucked into boots, hair pulled back into a pony-tail from her fastidiously made-up face; French students; a large, colourfully dressed Nigerian lady, her plastic carrier overflowing with biscuits and with fruit, with three colourful Nigerian children; a couple from New Mexico, he plump, red faced and bearded, with an albino wife in an ethnic dress; a precise German with his precise camera; two strapping Swedes in sawn off jeans; an exuberant family from Golders Green; two *yeshiva bochers* – their ivory faces framed by side-curls beneath their broad-brimmed hats – standing out amongst the suntans; a grey haired American in flat cap and zippered jacket on his own. When he had his full complement, of excited children, husbands who'd wandered off to buy newspapers, and straying wives who'd gone to look for them, Avi verified his numbers for the last time, picked up his microphone and relaxed.

"Okay," he said, against the noise of the engine and the blast of dance music from the radio, which Zvi was tuning at the same time as he lit his cigarette and negotiated the bends. "...Maybe you think we are a little disorganised in Israel. A friend of mine was telling me how much better they arrange things in Europe, how efficient they are. 'In Paris,' he told me, you get a beautiful breakfast – croissants, good coffee – the tours leave on time. You visit the Louvre, get a marvellous lunch, fantastic dinner, night-club, dancing, cabaret. The hotel rooms are clean, the beds wide and comfortable, and when you wake up in the morning you find five hundred francs under your pillow!' 'Impossible!' I said. 'You saw that with your own eyes?' 'No,' said my friend. 'I wasn't actually there myself, but my wife was and she told me!'"

Avi waited for the laughter to die down then held up a hand for silence. "Okay, so this morning we visit Biquat ha Yareah – Valley of the Moon – in the Negeve, the Red Canyon, and Canyon of the Inscriptions. On our way we stop at En Netafim..." he enunciated carefully, "...where the water comes from a spring in the face of the rock. The Negev, in the southern region of Israel, stretches from the hills of Judea in the North to the Red Sea. The word 'negev' means dry..."

Kitty, listening with one ear and looking out of the window at the rises, crevasses and sudden, unexpected flat stretches of parched land, was beginning to enjoy herself as they followed the trail – used a thousand years before by caravans bearing the perfumes of Araby – between the Mediterranean and the Red Sea. Strange violet mountains, orange rocks, and contorted shapes, which she had thought belonged to the Wild West, unfolded before her gaze. Avi, swaying with the bus, did not stop for breath. Neot Hakikar, a collective farm in the Negev, was, he told them, where he lived. The desert was clearly in his bones. Kitty wished, as she so often did, achingly, that Sydney was with her, if only to see the colours, soft yellows now and pinks –which had come as a surprise, for she had thought the desert brown – to ride with her the rough ribbon of the road as the juddering bus traversed the galaxy of stone. She would not be able to tell it to anyone, except on a postcard where it would be stripped of its immediacy. 'Today we drove into the Negev.' Her pen was not lyrical. She would not recapture for the family at home the spirit of adventure that she felt – as if she personally had hewn out the dusty road between the jagged crags – the lure of the harsh and desolate terrain, unfolding, like a school contour map, on either side of the coach. She could not even discuss the excursion with Addie. She would save it up for her, but knew that the sights and sounds, the surprise glimpses of blue water across the dusty brown surfaces, would be lost.

At En Nefatim where they got out of the bus, the dry rock was scored with streaks of purple and brilliant green, the natural effect, according to Avi, of oxidation. Outsize coloured stones, like precious gems strewn by the hand of some profligate desert god, lay casually on the ground. Kitty put her sun hat on. They crossed the old Egyptian border, which in three months was to be restored, leaving the narrow landmass that was Israel exquisitely vulnerable once again. In a semi-circle Avi's group stood on the dry cracks of the barren plain, resembling the surface of the moon after which the valley was named. From the crevices Avi plucked desiccated blooms, like fossils, and distributed them to his party. "Rose of Jericho," he said, "when put in water it will open." Kitty was sceptical but folded the brittle flower carefully in her scarf before putting it into her bag.

At the Canyon of the Inscriptions they straggled after Avi, in his blue denim suit and his kibbutz hat, to the mouth of the ravine. A class of schoolchildren from the coach ahead of them had already descended the cleft and was making its way, noisily, some of them balancing on ledges, along its length.

"I'm not going down there!" Kitty said, horrified, looking at the sheer drop without hand or foot hold, "I'll wait in the bus."

Avi pointed to the children. "The kids are also afraid," he said shrugging. "What's the difference?"

"A good few years," Kitty said. She did not care for callisthenics.

Avi, like a mountain goat, jumped on the rubber soles of his sneakers into the ravine.

A bronzed *sabra*, he looked up, extending a helping hand to the members of his party, scrutinising each face in turn for their enthusiastic reactions and fearful exclamations. One way or another, slithering, sliding and finally jumping, they all made it. Kitty looked down at the waiting faces below and searched for her courage which was nowhere in evidence. She had no head for climbing nor for heights.

"Sit on the rock," Avi shouted up.

Kitty looked at the smooth boulder.

"Throw your bag!"

Kitty threw her hold-all into the ravine – where it was caught by the grey-haired American – and with it her opportunity to return to the safety of the bus.

"Now sit on the rock."

Easy to say. The rock itself was some three yards away over lesser boulders. Kitty teetered tentatively, wishing she had brought her old sandals which had rubber soles. She reached the boulder, collapsing on to it with both hands, inelegantly. Avi climbed to a point half way up the funnel, his feel almost at right angles to the rock face.

"Sit down!" he commanded.

Easier said than done. Kitty was making a fool of herself. Without letting go with her hands, she swivelled into a sitting position – if she'd known what was entailed on the tour she would not have worn such a tight skirt – and contemplated the ravine. There was no way she was going to jump down, to launch herself through space on to its obstacle strewn floor.

Avi extended his hand, but she could not reach it.

"Jump!"

He must be joking.

"Don't be afraid…"

Afraid! She thought she would die of fright. There was not now even any prospect of going back.

"…We'll catch you!"

The grey-haired American with her bag stood below with his arms out. "It's okay!" His voice was reassuring, his accent foreign.

Kitty closed her eyes. There was no one to advise her. No one to care. She would die here in the desert and in the desert they would bury her.

"One, two…" Avi extended himself towards her as far as he was able without relinquishing his own perilous hold.

Why did I ever come, Kitty thought, without Addie? I must have been mad.

"…Three!" Avi said.

Kitty threw herself from the rock.

Seven

"There's a postcard from Grandma," Carol said. "A camel."

She turned it over eagerly to see if her mother was well. She had wanted to invite Kitty to stay with them in Godalming over the long holiday but Alec had said no. Peartree Cottage was not large and they were bursting out of it. An extra guest in the cold weather, when the children would for the most part be confined to the house, would be too much. Besides, Alec said, he wanted a rest. Her mother would be no trouble, Carol had argued but it was not altogether true. She knew what Alec meant. He had worked hard in the general practice – its list of patients had grown to a size now necessitating three partners – and wanted to defer to no one over the Christmas period when he was not at the end of the telephone and was able to enjoy his own home.

Carol herself was ambivalent. There was no doubt that her mother was self sufficient when she came to stay with them – ousting Lisa from the room she shared with Mathew – she even cooked for all of them. But she came between herself and Alec as in the old days when they'd lived near to her. In any conflict of will or of opinion Carol would find herself siding with her mother – pulled by the umbilical cord she had almost, but not quite succeeded in severing. Kitty's presence affected the children too. Debbie and Lisa, unconsciously almost, would try their luck with unaccustomed boldness in issues where they were at odds with their parents, knowing that they had

Grandma on their side. Even Mathew, almost two, sensed in Kitty's presence an indubitable ally and exploited every situation to the full. From the moment she appeared on the doorstep there was a subtle, but unmistakable shifting of loyalties, which affected all of them with the exception of Alec who was not emotionally involved. Carol suffered most. She loved her mother and felt responsible; for her father's death, although she could not be; for Kitty, although she was not. She had lain awake at night worrying about her mother, alone in the flat over Christmas, and had almost jumped with joy and relief when Kitty had announced that she was going, with Addie, to Eilat.

When Addie had broken her ankle, Carol, not thinking it right to let her go alone, had had wild thoughts of leaving the children with Alec, and accompanying her mother to Israel. She felt it the duty she had been brought up to do unquestionably. Alec had pointed out that if duty were involved, her allegiance was to him. As if she did not know. She loved Alec, but had to do frequent battle with her father's legacy to her – the sense of obligation to her parents – which hung like a millstone round her neck and of which, no matter how hard she tried, she could not completely rid herself. A grown woman, middle aged almost, in any dealings with Kitty she was still the obedient child whose instinct assured her that whatever her mother did, whatever she said, was right. Her younger sister Rachel seemed to have no such problems, neither did Josh. They did not appear to suffer – as Carol suffered – where Kitty was concerned. She was, she supposed, unusually sensitive. Lately she had put her sensitivity to good use. She had begun to write poetry – for no reason that she knew of – when she was alone in the evenings, with Mathew tucked up, Alec at the surgery, and the girls doing their homework. She had sent one of her poems, secretly, to a woman's magazine. It was why she had leaped out of bed, although it was Saturday, when she'd heard the postman crunching over the packed snow.

On the floor in the hall Mathew, in his pyjamas, was playing with the red fire engine they had given him for *Chanukkah*. He held out his hand for the postcard: "Camel."

Shivering, in her nightdress, from the icy draught that whistled through the old front door and the letter box, Carol turned the card over, fearing the worst. That the holiday was a disaster without Addie; her mother lonely, ill. 'So far, so good,' Kitty's card read. 'Hotel very comfortable, weather hot. Next week am going on some tours into the desert. Love to Alec and hugs and kisses to the children, especially Mathew. Tell him not to forget Grandma and that I'll bring him back a camel like the one on the card. Look after yourself, Mummie.'

Alec had said that if she stopped calling her mother 'Mummie,' like a small girl, she might not feel so much like one.

An unexpected sensation beneath her ribs made her catch her breath. It was the first positive sign, the initial attempt at communication, from the child that she was carrying. "The baby kicked," she told Mathew, who had lost interest in the postcard and gone back to his fire engine. Carol had not told her mother, who had been the first recipient of the news – in the case of Debbie even before Alec – when she'd been pregnant with the others. Her reticence was, she imagined, a victory, a breakthrough in the battle she was waging with her dependence. She would tell Kitty about the baby on her return. Meanwhile, a larger house was an urgent priority, nearer if possible to the girls' school. They had looked at several. In all of them Carol heard Kitty's appraisal, her father's judgemental tones. 'What do you want such a big place for?' 'How can you live in a house with so many stairs.' She tried to shut out their voices but the echoes reverberated inside her head as she read the particulars of rambling, unmodernised mansions, and of cottages surrounded by what would have been to her parents – accustomed only to urban life – a terrifying acreage of land.

In the sitting-room, littered with Alec's journals and Mathew's toys, the silver *Hanukkiah*, a wedding present from

Uncle Juda, was streaked with hardened globules of coloured wax. Carol picked one off with her thumb-nail. Separated by some 40 miles from Rabbi Magnus and his congregation, Carol had not thought that, religiously, they would survive. It had been surprising. Having to try harder to make her children aware of their heritage had been unexpectedly rewarding. Alec conducted services at Peartree Cottage on every first Saturday, and at school, where Carol helped in the kindergarten, Debbie and Lisa and three other Jewish children had followed the concert of Christmas carols with a *Chanukkah* play with which the teachers had been intrigued. Removed by Alec from the ghetto of North West London, in which she had been firmly entrenched, Carol had learned that, as far as Judaism was concerned, there was another way than that she had learned from her father, and which she had imagined to be the only one.

As she tidied the sitting-room, she could see through the window the pristine fairyland of the orchard with its snow-covered branches. She took Kitty's postcard up to Debbie and Lisa who, wrapped in their sheets, were standing on their beds in front of the mirror, practising being bridesmaids to Aunty Rachel.

Aunty Rachel was in bed with Patrick when her mother's postcard rattled through the letter-box of the council flat.

"You go." She kicked Patrick.

"I'm asleep."

"So am I."

"Probably the gas bill. I had a strange dream. A penguin island. Hundreds and hundreds of them – as far as the eye could see. One of them was me. What are you laughing at?"

"Black and white! That's you in your dinner jacket."

"Do we have to get married?"

"It was your idea."

"Not choral and floral!"

"You inviting anyone from the hospital?"

"They'd think it was the 'Thousand and one Nights'!"

"I might ask my tutor. Sit him next to Aunty Beatty. Give him a taste of the 'real' world."

"Shall I tell you a secret?"

"If you like."

"My father's planning to take you to Paris for your wedding dress…"

"Rika Snowman's making it…"

"…one of the well-known houses…"

"…Cupid of Hendon. She made Carol's…"

"…He's quite excited about it…"

"…My mother will do her pieces…"

"…Once my old man gets a bee in his bonnet…"

"…My mother can be pretty stroppy too…"

"Let them fight it out."

"They'll do that all right. Do you think they'll put our photographs in the *Jewish Chronicle*, making sheep's eyes at each other? 'Rachel Shelton and Patrick Klopman…' Uncle Juda thinks you should change your name. He says you must think of the future…"

"Pinchas and Solly didn't do too badly with Zuckerman."

"…he says Klopman sounds like a meatball…"

"My grandmother would do *her* pieces. Honestly, Rache, I don't think I'm going to survive this. I'm sick of the whole thing already. Where are you going?"

"To get the post."

"Don't go…now that you've woken me up…" He pulled Rachel to him.

"Okay, meatball!"

In Bushey Heath, Rachel's Aunty Freda was making tea (which she would take up to Harry), and was looking out of the window at the golf course covered with snow, when she heard the postman. She did not hurry to pick up the letters – most probably nothing more exciting than the magazine sent by the credit card company or the monthly bulletin from the synagogue, bringing advance notice of a whist drive to raise funds for Israel, or reports of the children's *Chanukkah* party which Freda did not want to see. All her married life she had an ache in her heart. Some days it was worse than others. This was one of them. The black mood had descended yesterday. Harry had seen it coming. After twenty-six years he knew her. Could divine her thoughts almost. Ridiculous really. You'd have thought she'd got used to her predicament after so long. She never had.

Harry knew that it was her fault, although Freda wasn't responsible for her polycystic ovaries, her hormonal imbalance, her inability to conceive, but he had never blamed her. Not by a word. Not by a look. He didn't need to. She blamed herself. The canvas of her life was coloured by the dark brown wash of her sterility. The other colours which were painted on it had left few marks. She and Harry were one of life's more cruel jokes. They had met on a committee for under-privileged children. Become engaged on the beach at Birchington where they'd taken a coach-load of kids for the day. Harry had tied a piece of sea-weed round her finger by way of a ring as the boys pulled at him to play cricket. They would have hundreds of children. Well at least six. That was what they had agreed. They had bought the big house – in what was then country – at the start of their married life, intending to fill it. Although now they rattled in it, with its five bedrooms and the room Harry used for snooker and that was to have been the playroom, Freda refused to move. To do so would have been a public admission of the failure which she did not admit, even to herself in private. As if there was still hope. The family, her brother Sydney when he was alive, her sister Beatty, Leonora – Juda's wife – had been unstinting with their advice. Adopt. Move to a flat. Get a dog…or a parrot…or a canary. She took none of it. As if the pain that overwhelmed her, the utter sense of frustration, of humiliation – that would, she thought, some day unbalance her – could possibly be dissipated by a canary. She hugged her failure to her, mentioning it rarely these days even to Harry who was her light, her life; and she'd rid herself of the tensions that surged up within her with her driver or her five iron on the golf course.

As she waited for the water to boil in her spotless kitchen, Freda day-dreamed, as she often did. In the early days their doctor had referred her to a psychiatrist who had suggested analysis. Freda had refused. She wanted to keep her fantasies. She did not want an analyst to take them away. Today, as she looked out on the white vista of the ninth fairway, her kitchen was peopled with children. Her children. Four of them sat at the table eating the porridge she had made to keep out the cold. A toddler stared at her through the bars of his playpen. Upstairs a baby waited for her breast. She could see them clearly. They made a lot of work but she didn't mind. It was the Almighty's work. Life's purpose. Her imprint upon the sands of time. Like Mary Poppins she cared for her shadow family without tiring, without soiling her hands.

The click of the switch on the automatic kettle brought back the empty kitchen. Freda made the tea and left it to brew while she went to see what the postman had brought. A postcard from Kitty – an aerial view of the hotel against a backdrop of granite mountains, with news about the weather and her greeting to them both – and a mauve letter addressed to herself in unfamiliar green writing, her name mis-spelt, 'Goldstien', the 'i' before the 'e'. She put Kitty's postcard in the pocket of her dressing gown, opened the strange envelope and extracted the single sheet of lined paper. She read the two-line message then read it again. She looked out at the frozen garden, at the golf course to see if it was still there, for the kitchen, with its waiting teapot, was dissolving before her eyes. The writing was barely literate. 'Dear Mrs Goldstien, I think you should know that your husband Harry is the father of my child...'

Addie Jacobs limped to the door in her plaster cast and sniffed with self-pity at Kitty's postcard with its picture of the sun beating down upon the sail-boats and her message 'wish you were here'.

"There's a card from Kitty," Beatty shouted as she spooned baby cereal into the shaking mouth of her husband who sat at the kitchen table. Leon stared at her, the pap dribbling down his chin from where Beatty patiently returned it to his lips. She wasn't sure that he had heard her. She never was. There were so many ravages of the rapidly progressing illness which had hit the little household like a thunderbolt some eighteen months ago. Cancer of the lung to start with – Leon had always been a heavy smoker, coughing his way through the day – followed by secondary manifestations of the disease, which were affecting his brain. Beatty went on chattering. She liked to imagine that Leon understood every word she said and talked to him day, and often in the night, just in case. For Beatty, it was no hardship. Her late brother Sydney had accused her of suffering from verbal diarrhoea. Since Leon's indisposition her verbosity had stood her in good stead.

For years she had helped her husband in his fur shop. Now she had taken it over, her loquaciousness putting her customers at their ease and persuading them, with little subtlety, of their need for coats. When Beatty told her generously built ladies that they looked like film stars, like princesses, like a million dollars, they believed her. If they did not, she demanded that they bring their husbands into the shop where strong men wilted beneath the momentum of her salestalk, reached for their cheque books in an attempt to stem the apparently inexhaustible torrent of words that issued from Beatty's mouth. There was no subject, no person, no event, about which she did not have something to say. Her spinster sister, Mirrie, in her more bitter moments, said it was Beatty who, after thirty years, had finally silenced Leon.

"There's a picture of a swimming pool," Beatty said. "Kitty always was a good swimmer. A cocktail bar right in the water! *Meshugger!* Who wants cocktails in the water? There's tables and chairs out. Umbrellas. For lunch I suppose. Talking of lunch I'll bring you a nice fillet of lemon sole, you'll like that. You think it's easy knowing what to give you every day? Looks like a nice place, the hotel. *Nebach*, on her own. Should have taken Mirrie, not that she'd be much company. Think she's going a bit 'up there' if you ask me – never was strong – or one of the children. Rachel could have gone, or Carol, or Josh with his *shiksa*. One mother can look after three children but three children can't look after one mother. I suppose she'll find other widows to talk to. We're always the ones left. I'll read it to you: 'A bit windy but otherwise gorgeous. It's lovely to see the sun. Next week I'm going into the desert...' I can just see Kitty on a camel! '...It's a bit lonely without Addie but I'm managing.' " Beatty raised her voice. " 'Give my love to Leon...' Hear that? '...and hope the cold snap has improved business. See you soon, love Kitty.'"

Beatty put the postcard up to Leon's face. "See the swimming pool? When you're better we'll go to Israel – remember when we went to Netanya for *Pesach?* – somewhere warm! Will you eat a piece of toast if I make it?" She put the postcard on the top of the fridge against the *Hanukkiah* whose candles she had lit for Leon each night of the festival. "I'll show it to Austin and Charles when they come."

The Klopmans had been to Marbella. Kitty's postcard, stacked neatly with their other mail, was on the satinwood table in the hall.

"Kitty!" Herbert said, reading the signature but not the message, and handing the card to his wife. Hettie, her mind occupied as it usually was these days with weddings, looked unseeingly at the copper mines of Timna. "We'll have to start talking about numbers," she said, "as soon as she gets back."

Mirrie showed the picture of the palm trees and the straw shades – like sun hats – on the beach, to the other 'girls' at the knitwear shop where she had worked all her life.

Juda, in his Hyde Park flat, glanced at his sister-in-law's card propped up against the silver toast-rack, while opening a letter from an art dealer in New York with whom he was negotiating for a Dürer. He forgot to show it to Leonora who did not rise till ten.

Josh and Sarah were in the country. Kitty's good wishes and her love lay on the Bayswater mat together with their Christmas cards.

Norman put his striped fishes on the mantelpiece next to the clock which he had not wound since his mother had died.

Eight

"Four times a year," Avi said, "Flash floods come sweeping down the Canyon. How do we know that?" He looked round his group, pausing only a moment for the answer to the Talmudic sing-song of his question. He put his hand into a crevice from which a clump of green leaves sprouted. "Look the tumbleweed! This tells us there must be water."

He moved on a few paces and pointed upwards towards a small carving in the face of the red rock. "Can anybody tell me what this is?"

"A fish," the Australian girl said.

Kitty thought the rough drawing resembled a bird but she did not speak. She had got herself down into the canyon, catching Avi's firm hand and throwing herself into the arms of the grey haired American who was still carrying her hold-all, but there was no way that she could see that she was going to get out of it again.

"A bird," the youngest of the Nigerian children said excitedly, putting up her hand.

"A fish, a bird," Avi said. He was enjoying himself. "I'll tell you. It's not a fish and it's not a bird…"

Kitty had seen the ladder.

Perpendicular against the rock face, it appeared to be the only route out of the canyon. To go back the way she had come was impossible. Throwing herself from the boulder was the most frightening thing she had ever done; to climb it again – twelve feet of smooth surface – was out of the question. So was the ladder. The canyon was deeper at the far end and the ladder seemed to go on for ever, fastened insubstantially into the cliff. There was no way she was going to scale it. She still hadn't recovered from her jump.

"…It's a bucket!" Avi said.

Kitty did not care.

"And this is a rope." He picked up a stick to demonstrate its outline. "It was the Bedouin way of telling each other 'here is water' when they travelled through the desert. Like today we might write 'Ike was here'…" he pursued his point, "…the Bedouin wrote, *Salaam*. Here is water!'… only by picture!"

Kitty looked about her to see if there was another way. The granite stretched threateningly over her head. Sometimes she fell even if she stood on the step-stool in her kitchen. Once she had had to have stitches in her head. She put a hand involuntarily to the scar. The schoolchildren were clambering up the ladder. Those who had reached the top looked like flies.

They left the representation of the bucket with the rope and walked on a few paces, joining the photographers of the party who had gone ahead to take pictures of the group on the floor of the rock-funnel. Avi picked a pod from a spiky plant, broke it open to exude a single drop.

"Used by the Bedouin women to make the beautiful eyes. Who is going to tell me the name?"

The grey-haired American in his zippered jacket stood at the edge of the group, Kitty's bag behind his back. "Belladonna."

"Absolutely!" Avi said. "In Italy they make from it a cosmetic. The leaves and the root are poison, from it is made 'atropine'. Don't touch please!"

Kitty, her heart pounding with apprehension at what lay ahead, had no intention of touching. She longed for Sydney. He had always looked after her.

The couple from New Mexico sat entwined on a rock while the German photographed them together.

"*Danke!*" the albino lady said.

The German didn't quite click his heels. "*Bitte!*"

The American with Kitty's bag walked on ahead. Avi stopped by a bush.

"The Tamar tree. There is a beautiful story. The Bedouin man, as he goes by on his travels, ties the leaves in a knot..." He took hold of a bunch of spikes to demonstrate. "This is his way of saying to his beloved 'I love you.' Later on, is coming by his very dear one. If she does nothing, she is turning him down. If she opens up the knot..." he untied the leaves again... "she is telling him she accepts already!"

Never mind the Tamar tree, Kitty thought, never mind the inscriptions and the belladonna, the flash floods and the tumbleweed, she wished she was back at the hotel sitting safely by the pool. Avi looked at his watch and guided them deeper into the canyon – there was already another group behind them – nearer the ladder.

They stood in a semi-circle at its foot. It was cool in the canyon. Up above the sun had almost reached its zenith. Kitty could see the bus driver, a smallish dot, on the cliff top. The Nigerian children went up first. They thought it great fun. Their mother followed, holding up her long cotton skirt. The girl from Australia went next, calling encouragement. The Bronx lady made a song and dance about it but started to climb, her bottom straining against her tight trousers, followed by the family from Golders Green, admonishing the children – 'Pay attention Harvey', 'Marilyn, be careful Sharon's feet!' – the French students with many '*mon dieu*', and the couple from New Mexico, the frail blonde followed by her husband's red-faced bulk.

Soon they were all on the ladder. Strung out like coloured insects. At the top Zvi was helping them on to the cliff. Only

Avi, Kitty, and the American with her bag, remained in the Canyon.

"Go ahead," Avi said.

Kitty was sure that a pair of the clamps was coming away from the rock. Somebody should tell them – the tourist department or whatever it was. There'd be an accident. She could see it in the newspapers. They were always happening. 'Holiday Catastrophe.' 'Three Perish in Ravine!'

"I can't," she said. "I just can't."

"It's all right," Avi said. "I'll be behind."

The last of their party was almost at the top. Even when she just looked up Kitty felt herself swaying.

"Like stairs," Avi said. "There's nothing to be afraid of."

Kitty looked at him, doubting if he had ever been afraid of anything in his life.

The grey haired American touched Avi's arm. "You go on ahead, I'll follow."

His accent was German, Kitty thought. American German.

Avi stepped on to the ladder and hopped up a few yards.

"*Shema Yisrael*," Kitty said silently and put her sandal, with its slippery sole, on the first rung.

The ladder would fall. She knew it would. Break away from the cliff, to which it was so tenuously fastened, and crash into the canyon. She was surprised that it hadn't happened before, the way it was fixed. They'd no right to expect you to climb it at all – should have warned you at the beginning of the trip – she would most definitely not have come. 'Stout shoes', the brochure said, 'for walking short distances.' Kitty didn't have any stout shoes with her, only the sandals and her sling-backs for the evening. The French students had worn heels three inches high. She didn't know how they managed at all; couldn't believe that she was the only one bothered by the jump to get into the canyon, the ladder to get out of it.

Avi was making encouraging noises. Kitty seemed to have been on the ladder for hours but had only made half a dozen steps. She looked behind her to see how far she had climbed.

"Don't look down," the American below her said. He probably could see up her skirt but she didn't care. About anything. She was about to die. "Just look straight ahead and concentrate on what you're doing, on the ladder. That's fine. Nothing can happen. Just like a staircase. That's all it is. A staircase…"

A staircase, Kitty told herself, I'm going up a staircase. But she was not. She felt sick. Ill. "…One foot in front of the other. Like a staircase…"

His voice was soft, hypnotic.

"Come on, come on," Avi was saying.

Kitty followed the blue and white of his sneakers which were level with her face but she did not listen to him. She hung on to the words of the American behind her with his European accent.

"…You're doing just fine. People get scared of heights, it's not uncommon. There's nothing to be scared of…the scare is in your head, the ladder is quite safe, they take people up it all day…"

"Old people, fat people!" Avi said.

Kitty felt that she was both.

"…just in the mind…" The reassuring voice went on.

Kitty looked at the crags before her nose.

"Am I nearly there?" Her voice was shaking. She felt an impulse to release the metal of the ladder from the grip of her hands, to let herself fall back into the abyss. The worst part was putting her sandal up on the next rung, feeling its smooth sole slip on the slim crossbar. Her arms ached. As if they would give way when she pulled herself up following Avi's feet. She felt she had been on the ladders for hours, for ever. A few pebbles crumbled from the rock face in front of her eyes. She froze. She could not go on. They would have to bury her in Israel, a martyr, at the Canyon of the Inscriptions. 'British Tourist killed in Cliff fall!' She would land amongst the belladonna.

"It's nothing." The voice from below did not change its soothing pitch. "A little sand. Keep going. One foot in front of the other. Nothing can happen to you…"

He just be joking.

"…wait till you tell them back home. You got kids?"

Kitty lifted the lump of lead that was her foot. "Three. Carol and Rachel and Josh. Rachel's getting married…" She didn't know why she was telling this to a stranger. She could feel the sun now, hot, on the back of her neck. She was in prison, doomed to see nothing but the granite through the bars of the ladder.

"Tell me about the wedding."

"It's ridiculous," Kitty said. "Two hundred couples."

"I guess you know a lot of people."

"It's not me," Kitty said. Her arms were really getting tired. "It's the other side."

"Rest a minute. They'll wait for us. Take your time."

Kitty held on to the ladder with one hand and wiped her brow which was damp. She knocked her sun hat into the canyon.

"Don't look!" The voice was soft, authoritative. "You'll buy another hat."

"Okay," Avi said. He had waited for her. "Let's go."

She would have to get a new hat. For the wedding. For the *Shabbat* when Patrick would be called up, a prospective bridegroom, as was customary, in the synagogue to the reading of the Law. A straw, she supposed since it would be summertime, to go with the new dress and jacket she would buy. A pastel, she thought – something pale – she was better, now that she was older, in soft colours.

"Nice guy?"

"Patrick," Kitty said. She could, she thought, hear voices now at the top of the cliff. "He's Jewish."

"*Gott sei dank*. It's always good news when the kids stay in the club."

Kitty hadn't thought of it like that. Avi's feet suddenly disappeared. The rungs were empty above her nose. All she could see was rock. She felt the panic return, remembered the canyon and how far it must be now below her, with its Tamar tree, its tumbleweed...

"You're doing fine..."

She could never have got so far without the voice. She doubted if her arms could hold her for much longer, her efforts would all have been in vain.

"Come on, come on..."

"Almost there, honey!"

Kitty recognised from above her the accents of the Bronx.

"Five more steps." The voice from below was steady. "Take it easy...take your time."

One... Kitty said to herself. An off-the-face hat, she thought, trying to concentrate on the wedding. Two... And they would have to start thinking in earnest about Rachel's dress. Three... She had already rung Rika Snowman with the good news. Rika had told her it was a big year for lace. Four... She liked lace. It was delicate, and would suit Rachel with her slim figure. Her waist had been slim like that when she'd got married. Five... Sydney had been able to span it with his two hands.

"Give me your hand!" It was Zvi talking. "Don't worry. Just give it to me. Straight ahead here. I won't let go."

There was a gap of about a yard between the top of the ladder and the cliff on which Zvi squatted.

"Oh my God!" Kitty thought. "I've still got to scramble up there. All that way, only to fall at the last moment."

"You'll have something to tell the three of them." The voice from below was confident, as if there was not still the obstacle ahead to overcome. Kitty gripped Zvi's outstretched hand for dear life. She had run out of rungs.

"Now the other hand."

He must be crazy.

"Lean against the edge and we'll pull you up."

Kitty closed her eyes.

It was half scramble, half pull. She grazed her shins, she did not care. She was lying on the ground.

"Okay," Avi said briskly. "Nobody left in the canyon?"

Kitty did not think it funny.

"Everybody in the bus please. Those of you who are coming with us to Ofira tomorrow please let me have your names."

Kitty dusted herself off. From the safety of the cliff she looked down into the canyon, at the ladder along which the group who had followed them was strung, at the buses ahead of her, parked neatly in a row.

The grey-haired American was standing next to her.

"Maurice Morgenthau – Morning Dew!" He introduced himself and handed over her hold-all. As if nothing had happened, as if she had not scaled Everest, reached the Pole, he walked ahead of her towards the bus.

Nine

"Listen to this…" Rachel shouted from the bed to Patrick who was in the bathroom.

There had been other letters with Kitty's postcard, as there were every day. Hettie Klopman re-addressed them, as did Josh from his mother's empty flat.

"Dear Miss Shelton, We would like to congratulate you on your forthcoming marriage…and take this opportunity to invite you to see our beautiful bridal collection…wedding dresses, toiles, and designs for bridesmaids and attendants…ideas for head-dresses and other garnishes for the whole entourage.' Garnishes! Or we could get married in a marquee." Rachel picked up the lurid colour photograph which fell from an envelope on to the duvet. "It looks like something out of the Arabian Nights. '…draped, spun-glass satin in a variety of colour schemes…' My Aunty Beatty had a marquee in the garden when Austin got married. We all sank into the mud!" She opened the next envelope. "This looks good! 'A Reception Beyond your Wildest Dreams. A Banquet under Rabbinical Supervision…"

"Talking of banquets," Patrick called, "any chance of some coffee?"

Rachel did not answer. "How does this grab you? 'Coupe Florida, Smoked Salmon hors d'œuvres with Egg Mayonnaise,

79

Kreplach Soup, Braised Ox-Tongue with Blintzes and Stuffed
Neck, Grilled Tomatoes, Green Beans, Tangerine Sorbet…' "

"I'll settle for a cup of coffee and one of those stale bran
muffins."

"Where was I? Oh yes, 'Tangerine Sorbet, Roast Poussin,
French Potatoes…' What's a French Potato? '…Garden Peas,
Asparagus tips and Mushrooms'…"

Patrick came into the bedroom drying his hair.

"…Hot Cherries with Kirsch…"

"Seen my socks? I'm supposed to be assisting with a hernia
at nine…"

"…Hot Cherries with Kirsch…"

"Stop it. You're making me feel ill at this hour in the
morning."

"Ice Gateaux Surprise…' I'm sure there shouldn't be an 'x'
on the end of gateau, or if there is it should be '*iced* gateaux'…"

"I've only got one," Patrick held up a sock.

"Look under the bed. 'Petits Fours…' "

"Rachel will you shut up!"

"Nearly finished! 'Nougatine Baskets… Coffee…!' "

"Thank God for that!"

" 'Selected Fresh Fruit.' "

"That's *all*?"

"Certainly not. Later on you get 'Dainty Sandwiches and
delicious Continental Pastries…' "

"Not to mention indigestion!"

"These menus can be varied'," Rachel went on, " 'to suit
your own particular requirements!' "

"My particular requirements at the moment…" Patrick said.

Rachel threw him a shiny leaflet. "This one's for you."

One arm in his jacket, Patrick's face grew black. 'Morning
and Evening Dress Wear – Individual Service for the Discerning
Man'.

"They don't want a big wedding at all," Kitty said to Maurice Morgenthau as they sat on a wall by the beach at Na'ama overlooking the sands, with the cross-crossing volley-balls, through which could be seen the coral reef and the deep waters of the bay.

After her experience in the Canyon of the Inscriptions, Kitty had not wanted to take any more trips. She had said so to Avi, as the bus stopped to let some of the passengers out in the main square of Eilat, where men hurried by carrying bunches of flowers to give to their wives for *Shabbat*. On the Sunday trip – Avi assured her – there would be no canyons to descend, no ladders to climb. After an early morning start to what was to be a whole day trip, they would drive along the fine highway which followed the track of the Israeli Army's 9th Brigade in the race to capture Sharm-El-Sheikh from the Egyptians in 1956. "The Mediterranean you can leave," Avi said. "The Sinai you must see. If you don't look for only thirty seconds you miss something extraordinary…" Kitty imagined she could see tears in his eyes. "It's your last chance."

Kitty knew that he referred the returning of the seemingly worthless, underpopulated, undercultivated peninsula – which came close to claiming the distinction of being the most besieged territory in the world – to Egypt for a few weeks, in exchange for what Sydney had called, at the time of the Camp David agreement, 'airy promises of peace from a shaky dictator.'

"Nothing to worry," Avi reassured her as the bus, in the capable hands of Zvi, swerved into the drive and came to a magnificent halt outside her own hotel. He helped her down the steps. "I'll see you on Sunday. Seven o'clock…" She would be awake, pursued by the grey ghosts of the night. "…*Shabbat Shalom!*"

"*Shabbat Shalom*," Kitty said, reiterating the prayer for peace on the Sabbath which seemed to have so much more meaning in Israel. Theoretically the seventh day, on which God rested from the labours of creating man and his environment, began with the darkening of the Friday evening sky, but from lunchtime onwards, everything ground to a halt. With the appearance of three stars, 24 hours later, public transport would appear once more on the roads, and the cities, wakened from their Sabbath slumber, would erupt into life. The Day with its special serenity, was only one of the things that to Kitty were special about Israel which had so many faces. The past – seen from one's car on the way to Tiberias where workmen cutting into the bank laid bare a row of Roman sarcophagi; the crunch of one's shoe on a broke shard of ancient pottery on the Beach of Caesarea; the spines and carapaces of buses and armoured cars left where they fell, as memorials, along the road to Jerusalem. The present – from barren desert a land blooming with terraced hills and delicate orchards; hedges of rosemary, green orange groves, cypresses – like dark upward pointing candles against the blue sky – and windblown olive trees, their leaves tipped with silver. The future – in the faces of the children, into whose education so much of the country's resources were channelled, bursting out of schools, indistinguishable in their coloured shirts and cotton dresses, only their features proclaiming their origins in Persia or Poland, Morocco or Hungary.

In the hotel, exhausted from the perils of her morning in the canyon, Kitty asked for her key at the reception desk, glancing as usual into the bare cubby-hole beneath her number for the message – telling her that someone wanted her – that she knew would not come, and made her way to her room.

On the dressing-table, in a narrow vase, was a single red rose with a white card. Her pulse quickening, Kitty picked it up.

'*Shabbat Shalom!*'

It was from the management.

On *Shabbat,* from sunset to sunset as her Creator had done, Kitty rested. On Sunday, she was ready at seven for the drive along the western shore of the Gulf of Eilat to Sharm-El-Sheikh – the 'Bay of the Sheikh' – which was, according to Avi, a series of reef-bound bays, between the Gulf of Suez and the Gulf of Aqaba, where the waters were infested by the Red Sea sharks and by barracuda.

Kitty was excited. Despite the rigours of the excursion to the Canyon of the Inscriptions and the Valley of the Moon, she was getting a taste for expeditions and waited with anticipation for the bus. The Sinai was familiar to her from school and from synagogue. A land trampled by history, and embroidered with tales of her people's survival, freedom and relevation. On the mountain which bore its name – not a holy place but an intangible symbol – the Law had been entrusted to Moses and – as the rabbinic story had it – all Jewish souls, past, present and future were assembled, when God made the covenant with his Chosen People. Sarah had asked, chosen for what? And Kitty had told her, it wasn't such a wonderful thing to have been chosen to 'hold fast to the covenant' and that often it could be extremely hard. As Tevye had said in *Fiddler on the Roof*: 'I know we're the Chosen People but can't you sometimes choose someone else?' Into the Sinai the Hebrews had made their painful way, as they fled from Egyptian bondage, to end up as Jews amid the figs and the grapes and the pomegranates, the 'milk and honey' of the Promised Land. The Sinai, its sand and its rock, conjured up for Kitty both the wanderings of her ancestors – the manifestation of the Burning Bush – and the martyrdom of Baruch Ben Zion as he defended the Mitla Pass. With her hold-all and the new sun hat which she had bought in the boutique, she waited with the rest of the group, outside the hotel, for the motorised caravan, with Azi at its helm, which would transport her through the desert.

Avi had greeted them like old friends. An experienced sightseer now, Kitty had bestowed herself and her possessions in a window seat. As before they had made the rounds of the other hotels. Kitty watched as the passengers, many of whom she had not seen before, lined up in their morning sweaters to board the bus. Maurice Morgenthau, in his zippered jacket, seemed not to see her as he edged his way between the seats to the rear, although she had tentatively made room next to her for her hero, her saviour from the Canyon of the Inscriptions.

The Sinai, Avi explained, when with a full complement they bounded along its shore for Watir Brook and Neviot, was named by the Mesopotamians after the moon god, Sin. Ethnologically it was Semitic, but geographically it belonged to Egypt who once more was claiming it back. On the way, he told them, they were to look out for those living remnants of history, the Bedouin, who with their camels and their tents, their Bronze Age way of life, were as integral a part of the peninsula as the mauve mountains and the flinty plains. As the bus, manipulated by the chain-smoking Zvi, his shirt white against the sepia of his neck, twisted and turned around the granite passes, crossed wadi deltas and dunes which spilled into the gulf, Kitty gasped at the new vistas with which she was greeted at every turn. While Avi explained about the race of cavemen which, according to Israeli architects, had existed two hundred thousand years ago in this much disputed area, she thought how sensible she had been to come away, even without Addie, that there were sights to see, world to conquer which did not intrude themselves into her humdrum and everyday life at home. To travel, she thought, put one in perspective. Her small world was bound by mental and physical boundaries, from which she knew she must struggle to release herself: by the legacy she had been left by Sydney, of devotion to his family. The euphoria she felt, was not, she suspected, solely the effect of the crystalline desert air which blew in through the open windows of the bus, with their little curtains, which later she would pull against the sun. It was generated by a sudden awareness, a revelation as clear as that which had appeared to Moses on Mount Sinai, that from the chrysalis of her hidebound psyche was emerging a new Kitty Shelton.

With an extended drive ahead of them to the south, they did not spend long at the coastal settlement of Neviot – Bubbling

Springs – which lay between the shallow bay of Nuweiba Tarabin, with its driftwood shacks, and Nuweiba Muzeina where palms waited regally for their summer dates. Avi called it 'Hippyville'. Beneath the trihedral tents on the beach, rootless young from the middle-class homes of Europe, the United States and Scandinavia, with their tattered vests and their guitars, stared stonily, anachronistically out to sea. A girl, with a tattooed arm and hennaed hair, reminded Kitty of Rachel. In earnest conversation with her, an Arab squatted on his haunches. Avi said he was most probably peddling dope, and in his flowing robes he made a striking contrast to the girl's near nudity.

A fat Bedouin, who introduced himself as Suleiman, invited Kitty into his *arisha* for coffee. When she refused to enter the tent with its carpeted floor, in which middle-eastern music crackled from a transistor radio and flies swarmed around a cooking pot, he offered her a coconut, a necklace made of olive wood, a ride on his moth-eaten camel. Trying to decline politely, she did not notice his companions who had come to surround her with offers of trinkets, or to stand beside her while she had her photograph taken. She looked round helplessly at the sandy robes, the dark eyes beneath the black and white *kaffiyehs* and wasn't sure how she had become separated from the group, which had made its way to the cafeteria. She felt Maurice Morgenthau's hand on her arm, his voice in her ear, as he came to rescue her from the importunate circle.

Inside the cafeteria her knight in shining armour disappeared once more. Kitty had coffee with two Germans and could catch the drift of their conversation because of the smattering of Yiddish she had learned from her father whose parents had been born on the Vistula.

When she came out, the albino from New Mexico, whose name was Maisie, was having her picture taken on a camel, while her red-faced husband haggled over the price of the favour.

This was not the Sinai Kitty hoped to see, and she wasn't sorry when Avi put two fingers between his teeth and whistled his party to the bus.

Refreshed, warm sweaters now stowed on the overhead racks from which sleeves dangled in a rainbow of colours, they set out again for the Sharira Pass, where stark walls loomed up on either side of them, plunging the bus into shade, following the natural course of the old Wadi (named Samaghi, for the sap of the acacia tree). As they bounded along, twisting and turning, clouds intermittently covered the fiery sun, changing the craggy landscape, through which they sped, from yellow to rose like a geographical chameleon. Descending to the shore again at Dahab – the golden – a Bedouin at his mid-day prayers, against a backdrop of mountain and of sea, his sandals by his side, put his face to the ground. While Avi told them about the Greek Orthodox monastery at the base of Mount Sinai where the monks, in reverence to the God whom they served, laid out their dead in rows and carefully preserved their bones, Kitty took out her happiness and examined it. It was the first time for eighteen months she had felt light of heart. Her contentment made her feel uneasy, as if Sydney had taken with him her right to be joyful. She wanted the bus to go on for ever through the mountain passes, through the blue waters, through the forbidding cliffs and the desert sands. She did not want to go home, where it was snowing and only Addie Jacobs waited for her, to her children who had lives of their own.

At Na'ama they stopped for lunch; the amenities were better, Avi said, than those they would find a few kilometres down the road at Sharm-El-Sheikh. With the rest of the party Kitty joined the slowly moving queue for the ubiquitous turkey schnitzel with its accompanying mashed potato which seemed incongruous with the outside temperature which had now climbed to thirty-five degrees. She put a bread roll and a large bottle of mineral water on her tray and carried it to a bare, plastic topped table where Maurice Morgenthau sat alone.

"No lunch?" Kitty said, surprised.

"I never stand in line for food."

"Eat this," Kitty said, putting her tray down before him and going back to join the end of the queue.

He seemed lonely, like a lost lamb, she thought, as she shuffled along the counter for the second time with her damp tray. She knew all about loneliness, it was her constant companion.

He neither thanked her for his tray nor seemed particularly pleased. Just gave her the money and addressed himself to the food. His table manners were not good. Sydney's had been impeccable. She discovered that Maurice was a physician who lived in New York. He was mostly retired now and devoted himself to painting which, he told Kitty, gave direction to his life.

When she'd finished her lunch, Kitty excused herself. She wanted to go to the Ladies'. She had left her bread roll on her tray. Maurice Morgenthau picked it up and put it in the pocket of his jacket.

When she came out of the Ladies' Room he was standing on the path. She wasn't sure if he was waiting for her. He fell in step with her, silently, and they walked towards the beach where Avi had told them they could spend an hour before returning to the bus for the short drive down to Sharm-El-Sheikh and Ras Muhammed.

They sat on the low wall in the sun – there was no shade – while Kitty chattered about her family to the strange, silent man. She told him about her son-in-law Alec, in the same profession, and about her grandchildren; she told him about Rachel and Patrick who did not want a big wedding. There were beads of perspiration on Maurice's face which looked as if it had been chiselled out of Sinai rock. Kitty suggested that he remove the zippered jacket but he appeared not to have heard. She told him about Sydney, although he had not asked. Thoughts and memories of him, their happy days, came tumbling from her lips.

"Do you have a family?" she asked.

" 'The stars through the window pane are my children'," he said.

Kitty wondered if he were quite right in the head.

When Avi's whistle summoned them from their post-prandial leisure to the bus, Maurice Morgenthau – Morning Dew – walked towards it as if she did not exist.

Ten

It is surprising how a word, a look, a letter can change one's perception of the world, bring it tumultuously about one's ears. Freda's came crashing about her when she read the message on the mauve notepaper which arrived with Kitty's postcard. After the first impact the note did not seem to convey anything, the letters of the alphabet, facing in all directions, refused to form themselves into meaningful words. '...your husband Harry...' He was upstairs, in bed beneath the blue waffle-nylon eiderdown, waiting for his early morning tea. Sometimes he brought it up. They took it in turns. He was a good husband. Harry. 'Your husband Harry'. Some said too good. It was a family joke. He treated Freda as if she were precious. She was. Or so she'd thought. They got on well. Not like Beatty and Leon, who had always confronted each other from opposite corners of the marital boxing ring – although Leon now was almost out of the count – nor Juda and Leonora, whose fragile marriage, as everyone knew, was stuck together by the delicate glue for appearances which it suited them both to keep up. It wasn't like Kitty's, who had been content all her life to play queen to Sydney's king. Not like that at all. For Freda and Harry loved each other like twin souls, thought alike and, according to some, had over the years, like dogs and their owners, grown to look alike. They never tired of each other. Despite their childless state they had no need of other people. Their leisure time was spent on the golf course in the summer. They took golfing holidays to Scotland or to Spain. In the winter they played backgammon together or watched television, while Freda knitted socks and woolly hats for them both.

Kitty said it was a question of temperament and marvelled at how equable both of them were. '...is the father of my child'. 'Grow fruitful and multiply', the scriptures enjoined. Freda and Harry were unable to oblige. The early years of their marriage, the possible years, had been beset with alarms and excursions, all of them to no purpose. Later there had been doctors and hospitals and test upon test. The long road of exhaustive investigations, and their unpalatable outcome, had served only to bring Freda and Harry closer together, to be mother and father and family to each other by way of compensation for their infecundity. They managed to survive the catastrophe that had blighted both their lives – and which now was never spoken of – each in his own way. Harry devoted two evenings a week, and sometimes many hours at the weekends, to the synagogue youth club where he was father to many, and Freda had her imaginary family which never aged and which she could summon up at will. It had been enough. Or so she had thought. Until the mauve letter. In the existence of which, although she could feel the coarse notepaper between her fingers, Freda could not make herself believe. She did a quick re-run of her day, which, although she would never forget it, had hardly begun. She had woken while beyond the blue flowered curtains, the garden and the golf course in its frosty corset, the sky was still dark. She loved that first waking moment, the sleepy warmth and contentment of it, secure in her bed and Harry's arms, where she always spent her night. They opened their eyes together. They always did. As if the harmony which they enjoyed in the day continued, of its own momentum, through the night.

"Your turn to get the tea," Freda said.

"No yours!"

It was their morning joke which re-affirmed their love for each other and indicated that all was right with their world.

Reluctantly, as always on the winter mornings although the house was not cold, Freda had got out of bed and Harry, cherishing the limbo moments between the waking and the tea, had shut his eyes. Freda's dressing-gown was blue. It matched the sprigged sheets and the quilt and was her favourite colour. Beatty went for dark red, the colour of the curtains in her sitting-room; her spinster sister Mirrie, yellow, in which she had decorated both the rooms of her homely flat; and Kitty for shades of gold, antique in the carpet and shaded velvet in what had once been Sydney's chair.

In the bathroom Freda had washed at the blue basin, examining her face in the mirror above it for wrinkles, and to see if it was a good day for her looks. Not that it worried her. Freda was not vain. Her confrontation with her mirrored self was more of an assessment, really, a daily inventory such as she carried out on the bottles in the fridge to see if it was necessary to leave a note for the milkman. She had put a quick brush through her hair and gone down to fill the kettle. So far, so good. Better even. The family, who came unbidden almost now, the children whose voices rebounded from the blue and white tiles and whose crumbs littered the mosaic vinyl floor, had given her no trouble. While she put the cups and saucers on the tray, warmed the teapot, spooned in the tea, the water had boiled. It was at that moment that the post had come. She remembered it exactly because the clatter of the letter-box had coincided with the click of the switch on the kettle as it popped automatically out. Such minor details would be remembered. Kitty's postcard, which had transported Freda for a few moments to the sunshine of Israel – she had played golf with Harry at Caesarea – then the mauve roughness of the unfamiliar envelope she had so innocently, so ingenuously opened. The nine words, like a bulldozer, had scooped up the happy years of her life with Harry and deposited them, like rubble, on the tip of her sterility.

When the strength which had left her returned to her limbs, she had gone back into the kitchen and taken up the tea. As usual. Everything must be as usual. It was important. That much Freda knew. She had trodden the stairs, holding up the blue dressing-gown with one hand, put the tray down in the darkened bedroom. Switched on the lamp, at which Harry had opened his eyes, as he always did, and smiled at her, the first smile of the day.

"Was that the postman?"

Freda carried his cup with its two sugars carefully, as if her life depended upon her not spilling it, to the little table with Harry's watch and the small change he had taken from his pocket the night before.

"Any post?"

Freda put the cup down and reached into the pocket of her dressing-gown, her fingers identifying the coarse notepaper, making their own selection. They extracted the glossy reproduction of the newly built hotel against the ancient mountains. Freda did not look at Harry.

"From Kitty," she said. "A postcard from Eilat!"

Kitty could not pretend, even to herself, that she did not know about the cable car to which one had to entrust oneself in order to ascend the citadel that was Masada. The only alternative was the narrow curves of the twisting 'snake path', tackled by the young with their back-packs before the heat of the day. It was the last excursion. Tomorrow she would be going home. She had bought her presents. A Star of David for Debbie, and for Lisa a tee shirt 'I love Eilat': for the baby, Mathew, a leather camel with sad eyes and a tiny velvet *kippah*, embroidered with silver thread, that would cover the fine red head when on his father's knee he followed the Grace after Meals; a *challah* cloth for Carol, which she would put over the Sabbath bread; olive-wood boxes, for their cuff-links, for Alec and Josh; for Sarah, a pair of filigree ear-rings and for Rachel, a colourful Yemeni blouse. For her sisters-in-law, Freda and Mirrie and Beatty, there were ashtrays and vases of hand-painted glass; key-rings and bookmarks – in which wild flowers were preserved – for her friends at the Day Centre and the ladies with whom she played bridge. For Juda's wife, Kitty took nothing, she never did. Leonora's Hyde Park flat, with its priceless antiques, was no place for souvenirs from foreign parts with a value that was sentimental rather than commercial.

The only problem that remained was Addie Jacobs. Kitty had seen nothing that would compensate for the missed holiday, that would off-set the broken ankle. When she got back from Masada she would look once again in the hotel boutique. She did not want to buy Addie's present at the airport. Other than a stone, which she had picked up in the Negev, and another from the beach at Eilat, she had nothing for herself. She would have her memories – these days it was what she lived on – and there were plenty of them, colourful and varied. The Pillars of Solomon and of Amram; the 'world of silence' with its rainbow fishes, its fine sand and lacy rock patterns, that she had viewed from the glass-bottomed boat; the Taba beach; Coral Island; the kibbutz of Yotvata, and her journey back to nature as it was in biblical times among the wildlife of Hai-Bar.

Masada was the highlight. Kitty had been looking forward to it. It was one of the trips she had always meant to take with Sydney on their visits to Israel but they had never managed it. From the moment when, as a child, she had first heard the story of the zealots and their tragic end, from the lips of her Hebrew teacher, it had intrigued her. She knew that in recent years the site had been excavated by volunteers from all over the world, that the archeological digs had unearthed miles of walls and thousands of coins dating from the time of the revolt. But it was not the finds that fascinated her. It was the stand of the few against the many, of the weak against the strong; the last fight of those who gave their lives for political, religious and spiritual freedom – choosing death rather than submission – that gave the name of the lonely and impregnable fortress in the Judean desert its magic. Kitty had been up since dawn and had got used to the early starts. She wouldn't be at all surprised if once back home she set her alarm for five o'clock, out of habit, although the highlight of her day would be neither the wonders of the deep nor the romance of a citadel, but a journey to the shoe repairers or a stint in the kitchens of the Day Centre.

It was Maurice – who for the first time sat next to her on the seat in Avi's bus – who had prepared her for the cable car (although Kitty had already been aware that she must ride in it when she booked the tour), Maurice who had brought her fear of heights and of falling into the open and had encouraged her to confront them.

He was a strange man. After the excursion to the ill-fated Canyon of the Inscriptions, and the drive down to Sharm-El-Sheikh, Kitty had looked for him among those who had boarded the bus on the other trips but he had not appeared. She had been aware of an initial feeling of disappointment, which the new sights and fresh discoveries had soon dispelled. Yesterday, after a half-day tour, she had spent the afternoon, her last at leisure, in a deckchair. Dozing, and meditating on the holiday which she had enjoyed more than she had ever hoped she would, and her family which she was looking forward to seeing, she was aware of, but did not listen to, the familiar orchestra of noises from the pool. She wondered if Josh would be at the airport to meet her, whether Sarah had put any weekend food in her flat – it would not, of course, have entered Rachel's head – whether Carol and Alec would bring her grandchildren, whom she had missed, from Godalming on Sunday afternoon to visit her.

She must have fallen asleep in the sun. She was woken by the public address system with the adenoidal consonants of its announcer. She recalled thinking how disruptive the calls were, how they disturbed the vacational calm, when her attention was suddenly aroused. At first she thought that she had been mistaken. Her mind, affected by the sun, was playing her tricks.

She opened her eyes and waited. There was nothing to be heard but the screams of the splashing children from the shallow end of the pool. She must, she thought, have been dreaming, and lay back once more in the chair. She had barely closed her eyes when there was a crackle from the amplifier and a loud and unmistakable request: "Mrs Kitty Shelton to the telephone please..."

It was she who was being summoned, beyond any possible doubt. She took the call at the bar. The pool-man handed her the receiver.

"Kitty...?"

She recognised the Central European accent beneath its New York overlay.

"This is Maurice..."

He wanted to take her for dinner to Yoske's Fish Bar in the town.

"If bone china is made from ground bones," Sarah said, "why are we allowed to eat from it?"

She was calling from the kitchen and Josh, at the end of his day, was scarcely in the door. He stood still for a moment, key in hand. It was not the question which stopped him – there were many of them these days – most of which he was unable to answer. At unexpected moments, when they were driving home from a theatre, drifting into sleep at night, sometimes when they were making love, Sarah would ask him 'who wrote the Talmud?' or 'are we allowed to leave our organs for medical research?' It was not the questions which stopped him in his tracks. It was her use of the first person plural. Already Sarah considered herself Jewish, at one with his mother and his aunts, Beatty and Freda and Mirrie, and his sisters, Rachel and Carol; already her knowledge, gleaned from Mrs Halberstadt on Wednesdays, from her own searching and her voracious reading on the subject, went deeper and was wider than theirs. When Sarah did something she did it properly, a characteristic she had inherited from her father, who by following his own precepts had risen high in the diplomatic service. It was this attribute that had sustained her in her advertising work, which earned her a salary which almost equalled Josh's. Sarah understood the ideological bric-à-brac of 'things,' as she understood people and their need for them. Her talents lay in transforming thought into visual images and latent dreams into the manifest. Given a household cleanser, a package holiday or a potato crisp, Sarah, with her alchemy, her book of spells, could make them indispensable.

At one time she had greeted Josh with the current worry about a product which was temporarily defeating her; how to market a chocolate biscuit or whether she could get away with the assertion that a washing machine had a 'pretty face'. She would spend all evening staring at a perfume bottle or pondering how to make an orange identify in the public mind with a tablet of Vitamin C. These days it was her affair with Judaism that preoccupied her. Her enthusiasm was contagious. Although the fundamental beliefs in his religious heritage, instilled by Sydney, were firm, Josh had drifted away, together with most of his contemporaries, from the practice of his religion. It had been more a case of spiritual and ritual back-sliding than a conscious decision, although sometimes – when he thought of the fate of the Jews in Germany or their present plight in Soviet Russia – he questioned the value of Jewish distinctiveness. He had not forced Sarah to become Jewish, although their children would not be unless she did. He had not asked her to. She had simply announced her decision on their delayed honeymoon in Arizona. As the sun rose over the Grand Canyon, picking out like some unseen conductor, in pink and green and ochre, the creviced contours of the rocks, Sarah turned to him.

"I would like to become Jewish," she said.

It was her wedding present to him.

She had asked for his help. Josh was no scholar as his father had been, but he had done his best, pointing her in the right direction. He introduced her to Reform Judaism, which took the attitude that modern conditions rendered the observance of many of the ancient laws impracticable, but to his surprise Sarah said that what the movement had to offer differed little from what could be found in certain forms of Christianity. She preferred the Orthodox way of life, the timeless authority of Rabbininc Judaism, harnessed at one end to the revelation of the Torah to Moses, and at the other to the arrival, one day, of the Messiah when there would be peace on earth. Josh had thought that the strictly decorous Reform services, where families prayed together, would appeal to her; but Sarah enjoyed the informal atmosphere of the Orthodox synagogue – where the Ladies sat in a special gallery – with its talking and gesticulating, its comings and goings, more reminiscent of the market place where public readings of the Torah had originally been held, than a house of God. Rabbi Magnus' synagogue, which she had attended with Kitty, made Sarah feel, she said, at home. In its confines, she was conscious of a spiritual sense of reciprocity with God and found the relaxed atmosphere conducive to spontaneous prayer.

Her workmates were intrigued by her decision. Across a table on which an aerosol can of lavender-scented polish awaited the ballyhoo which would hopefully make it indispensable in a million homes, or before the blow-up of a car destined to make the paterfamilias dissatisfied with his own, Sarah spoke of Judaism's concern with the education of the child, respect for the aged, the comforting of the sick, of the stressed need for constant improvements in human relationships to colleagues who thought it had all to do with not eating pork.

Josh was learning too: that a mans' word must be his bond (in particular in the case of a promise made to the poor), that to shame a person in public was one of the gravest offences, according to the Talmud. The dietary restrictions themselves –

although it was many years since he had observed them –
acquired new dimensions when Sarah explained that they not
only imposed restraint but taught moral freedom; that the
exercise of control over what went into the mouth promoted a
positive spiritual attitude towards life and a guard over what
came out of it. 'Who is strong? He who subdues desires.'

At the end of a demanding day bent over his dental chair,
Josh's desire was now for Sarah. He could not answer her
shouted question about the bone china. She would have to take
it to Rabbi Magnus or Mrs Halberstadt. As he closed the front
door he became aware of a strange smell which seemed to have
possessed the flat.

In the kitchen Sarah was peering into a saucepan. Josh
embraced her then followed her gaze. The aroma was coming
from a greyish, watery mass.

"What on earth's that?" He kissed Sarah's hair, her ear.

"For your mother," Sarah said. "*Gefülte* fish. She's coming
home tomorrow."

Josh looked at what should have been, according to his book,
feathery, carrot topped balls of specific dimensions, and
wondered if Sarah had forgotten some vital ingredient. He took
her in his arms and turned off the gas beneath the mess in the
saucepan.

It was not like his mother made.

Eleven

"I'm on the sea-food diet," Maurice said, while Kitty battled with her conscience and the desserts on Yoske's copious menu. "…I see food and I eat it."

He did that all right. Kitty had never seen such a prodigious appetite – in addition to his dinner he had demolished half a loaf of bread – yet Maurice was not fat. Throughout the meal she had had to pinch herself mentally to prove that he was there at all, sitting opposite her at the corner table.

His invitation had been such a surprise, so totally unexpected that she had accepted, just like that. There was no good reason why she should have refused. Except that she had never had dinner alone with a man – she did not count her nephew Norman – other than Sydney. She told herself that Maurice was lonely. He looked more lonely on the tours. Bereft. He had the air of being in the world but not of it. As if it was Maurice Morgenthau versus the rest.

She regretted her acquiescence the minute she had put the receiver down and replaced the telephone next to the basket of lemons at the end of the bar. Well, not regretted, but the invitation disturbed her, as if she would not know how to behave. She would not. The afternoon, her last by the pool, was fragmented. For what remained of it she sat upright in her chair, looking at the frenetic activity around her, but not seeing it, glad when the heat of the sun began to diminish and it was time to go to her room. In its privacy she decided that the agitation, engendered by Maurice's invitation and her response, was due to guilt. She felt guilty. That she was breaking faith with Sydney as categorically as if Maurice Morgenthau had invited her into his bed instead of to dinner at Yoske's fish bar.

After so many years of marriage to Sydney she was as ill equipped to deal with Maurice Morgenthau as she was with life in general. It required application. As usual, she transferred her anxiety to her wardrobe, standing in front of it in as much confusion as a young girl. The emotions did not age. It was something she had tried to explain to Rachel who had looked at her as if she were mad. One develop new skills, mature resolutions, which could be applied to situations, but inside, inside one's head, despite the passing of the years, one did not change. It was water off a duck's back. Rachel was no more able to understand her mother's empathy with her adolescent dilemmas than Kitty had believed in those of her own mother who had always seemed middle aged. She had one white dress. It had been Sydney's favourite. She had taken it on cruises; it had been to Israel when they had stayed one summer at Herzlia. It was a holiday dress, living the year round in a special cupboard in the spare bedroom, and looked terrible on her when she was pale. She had caught the sun. Addie would say she looked healthy. It was her last night, tomorrow she would be packing. She would put it on.

Half-past seven Maurice had said. He was in the lobby, waiting, in his zippered jacket from which he had not bothered to change. Kitty wondered whether the white dress had been a mistake. He seemed not to notice it. They took a taxi to Yoske's which was in the new tourist centre. From the vast menu, ridiculously happy not to have been sitting at her table for one in the hotel dining-room, Kitty ordered sole, although she knew it would not be the same as that from her fishmonger at home. Maurice asked for lobster. Kitty froze. Her astonishment was twofold. She had not been aware that foods specifically proscribed by the Torah were served in Israel, and she had never sat, at close quarters, to anyone eating a lobster. She wished she had not come. It had been stupid of her. She had nothing to say to this strange American, kind as he had been in helping her down into the Canyon of the Inscriptions, rescuing her from the unwanted attentions of the Bedouin on the beach at Neviot. He asked her if she wanted salad or aubergines with her fish, unaware that there was anything wrong. Everything was wrong. She was a fish out of water. Fish, ha! It served her right. For betraying Sydney. Sitting at a table – although it was only for dinner – with another man, when there had always been room for only one in her life.

Waiting for the lobster, whose arrival she dreaded as if it were she who would eat it, Kitty told Maurice of the trips she had taken without him. Maurice had been painting, he said – he had brought his water-colours with him – and, from his balcony, had captured the rocks and stones and the iridescent water that lay in the Gulf of Eilat. It was his vacation medium. Mostly he worked in oils. He got up at dawn to catch the morning light and worked through to the evening when the shadows were long. There was so much to say. In paint. The truth that was so hard to capture. The light that defied the combined talents of the colours and the brush.

Kitty listened wide eyed. No one had spoken to her before of landscapes in sonata form, of waves like fugal subjects. She knew what Maurice was talking about because of her evening class, and was about to tell him about it and that she had decided, when she had time, to take another in Hebrew language, when the lobster arrived and stopped her in her tracks. She glanced at it, as if even looking were forbidden, and thought that there was something indecent about its nakedness, something sensual and erotic about its articulated legs. She had been warming to Maurice as he talked to her – as if she had a mind of her own to be reckoned with – about his painting, about his hobby. Now, as he picked up his knife and fork, she felt alienated, as if by ingesting the gross and repulsive object on his plate, Maurice himself would become gross and repulsive. She thought of Sydney and his dedication to the laws of *kashrut* which permitted no digression, and that he was looking over her shoulder at Maurice Morgenthau as he applied himself to the contents of the two half shells. In her ears she could hear Sydney's voice when the matter was discussed at table with Rachel or with Josh, propounding the observation of Maimonides: 'The dietary laws seek to train us in the mastery of our appetites. They accustom us to restrain both the growth of desire and the disposition to consider the pleasure of eating and drinking as the end of man's existence.'

Noticing her preoccupation Maurice said:

"Something wrong with your fish?"

Kitty picked up her knife and fork. She would try not to look, not to listen to the snapping of claws and the crunching of bone that was coming from across the table.

"They do the best lobster," Maurice said tucking his napkin into the top of his zippered jacket.

"I don't eat it." Kitty's voice was small.

"You *frum*?"

Kitty nodded her head miserably.

Maurice sucked a claw. "My father was a Rabbi."

Kitty stared at him. He should have known better.

"What about Rachel and Josh and Carol and that husband of hers, Alec...they *frum*?"

Kitty stared again. He'd remembered their names. All of them. She told him about them. How Sydney, with her help and support, had reared them in the ways of their faith to observe the precepts – including the dietary laws – and guided them through the rules and regulations that governed the daily life of the observant Jew. She told him of her own home, which was run in strict accordance with the demands of *kashrut* and that she had only eaten away from it with Sydney in homes or restaurants which were kosher or in those which would serve them with omelettes or the simplest of grilled fish. She told Maurice about Carol's continuing observance – which she was passing on, by instruction and example as was required of her, to Debbie and Lisa and Mathew – and her involvement, even in Godalming, with Jewish affairs. She told him about Josh's lack of committal to, and Sarah's new found interest in, the ways of his forefathers. She explained about Rachel and how her apparent disillusionment with the religion, which was of paramount importance in her father's life, had saddened his heart. She spoke about the synagogue in Hendon where Sydney had been a regular worshipper and Rabbi Magnus' with which, in more recent years, both she and Sydney had been involved. When she stopped for breath she was surprised to find her plate had been cleared away, the lobster gone, and Maurice waiting for her decision concerning dessert. Kitty turned her attention to the menu. She had not talked so much in eighteen months. She ordered *strudel*, knowing that the calories would be as bountiful as the currants among its flaky strata, and Maurice ordered the same, with a double portion of ice-cream. When it came he spooned a vanilla scoop of it and put it on Kitty's plate. Although she was unable to explain why, even to herself, it made up in some measure for the affront, the violation almost, of the lobster. He did it with solicitude, as if she were a child. Importuning her to eat he told her about the trip to Masada – for which he had also booked – and about the cable car.

Kitty saw it first, the palace fortress with its flat, table top, standing out, lonely and impregnable, amid the mountains of the Judean Desert on the western bank of the Dead Sea. She recognised it from the picture in the guide book which, unable to sleep after her dinner at Yoske's, she had taken to bed with her. She had reread the story, too. How in the year 70 AD, after the destruction of the temple in Jerusalem, a little band of Jews had occupied the Masada fortress in order to continue the resistance against the Roman legions. It was a story of magic and inspiration. Nine hundred and sixty-seven souls, men, women and children, exchanging blow for blow with the surrounding assailants for three long years until the Roman warrior, Silva, by building a gigantic ramp which reached the fortress walls, had set fire to them. Watching the flames, the zealots knew their time had come. They destroyed all their possessions except the provisions of food, so that the enemy would see that they had voluntarily chosen death rather than submit to slavery. Families kissed for the last time – Kitty could picture them – and 'everyone lay down in close embrace'. Tears had come to Kitty's eyes. Ten men, who had been chosen by lot, then used their swords against the martyrs. When this gruesome task was completed, lots were drawn again, and one of the remaining ten put an end to the lives of his companions. When all were dead he had set fire to the palace and impaled himself on his own sword. A woman, who had hidden in a cistern, had lived to tell the tale to the historian Josephus who had faithfully transcribed it. Looking at the grandeur of the stark rock – towards which Zvi had swung the coach – rising up from the harsh shapes and bottomless ravines of the desert floor, Kitty's imagination peopled its mass with freedom fighters, with whom she identified as positively as she did with those in her own lifetime of the Warsaw Ghetto. She was one of the lucky ones. Her life, despite her personal privations, was charmed. She had not, as yet, been selected as victim in Roman siege, Russian pogrom or Final Solution. She was keenly aware of this, and reminded herself of her good fortune when suffering some small discomfort, making some minor sacrifice in the name of her religion. As they bumped along the road, approaching the eastern face of the sun-baked fortress, Kitty wondered what sort of martyr she would make, when she could not even tolerate the terrifying prospect of the cable car.

Maurice had not tried to tell her it was quite safe. She had been grateful for that. She knew very well that it operated without mishap day after day, week in, week out, carrying its passenger loads to the top of the fortress from the desert floor. He had realised that her anxiety came into the same category as her fear of flying, and that statistics did not help. He had tried to reassure her. He was a reassuring man. Not that he talked much. He sat next to her now in the coach, silently, holding on to the seat in front of him; but his very presence was supportive, his demeanour one of calm.

Over the ice cream at Yoske's, Kitty had confessed to other irrational fears, situations which she had learned to circumvent lest they disturb the even tenor of her life. Maurice had not come up with any magical solutions. He had merely listened while she talked. How she talked, as if she were drunk – on Coca-Cola! She had talked over coffee, and in the taxi, going back along the seashore, and on the beach road, along which they had strolled – to walk the ice-cream down – before returning to the hotel.

She had not talked to anyone, not even to Sydney, as she had to Maurice – perhaps because after the holiday she would not see him again – about her feelings, her innermost fears. With Sydney she had discussed the children, the family, people who were known to them, events which had happened, the substantive components of their lives. The words that she spoke to Maurice and which were borne away over the night-time ocean, beneath the black sky and the bright stars, belonged to an inner life she had never before revealed to anyone but herself. Back in her bedroom she had been astonished at her own loquacity, as if a well had been uncovered, an undisclosed spring, and its outpourings had quenched the fire of indignation sparked off by the lobster.

In the morning, in the bus, she had looked anxiously at the group outside Maurice Morgenthau's hotel to see if he was there. She had put an uncertain hand on her hold-all on the empty seat next to her, not sure whether he wanted to sit beside her or whether he would take his place, as usual, at the back of the bus, as if they had not been to Yoske's. He had taken the adjacent seat as if there were no other, as if it was his place – sat down and handed her an orange from his pocket by way of greeting.

The cable car was worse than Kitty had expected. They were counted in like sheep. Through the window she could see the hazardous zig-zag of the snake path. She could have stayed on the bus. She had not come all this way, on her own, without Addie, to sit at the base of the citadel where her co-religionists had shown such courage. She searched unavailingly for her own. At the top of the mountain, far, far away, a second car was suspended. Between them slender and seemingly ineffectual cables were stretched taut. The plight of the passengers in the upper car seemed worse. Kitty's time on the flat summit – presuming she did not die from heart failure on the way up – would be marred by anticipation of the descent. After the Valley of the Inscriptions, she should have known better. She was not going to put herself into such a situation again. But she would not have to. Tomorrow she was going home to the safety of the High Street where there were no ladders to climb, no cable cars suspended above the treacherous crags of an unfriendly valley. Tomorrow, if the plane did not crash – which was not, in Kitty's book, outside the realms of possibility – she would be back in England.

They seemed to be letting more and more people into the little cabin where the mood was light-hearted. Acceding to a request the holiday-makers shuffled towards the back of it. Kitty was hemmed in by Dutchmen and by Frenchmen and by Swedes. The lady from Nigeria was there, with her children, and the German with his camera. She looked for Maurice but he was staring out of the window eating an apple. She felt the press of bodies and the rise of the familiar panic as light-hearted reassurances were exchanged and the doors closed making escape impossible. She was not the only one who was apprehensive, but she was, she was convinced, alone in the grip of the sudden terror that seized her as the car jolted, flinging the tourists one against the other, and they were on their way. Kitty was by the window, had been jostled against it, but she could not look out. As the car climbed grindingly towards its twin, which came to meet it, she knew that below, the desert waited uncompromisingly; that it would accommodate her shattered body, and others from the crash, with as little difficulty as it had the broken bones of the Roman legions and the corpses of her fellow Jews who had made so noble a stand against them. She closed her eyes against the awesome space which surrounded the capsule as it hung, bejewelled by the sun, over the valley. When she opened them she saw the zippered jacket level with her eyes.

"Another coupla minutes," Maurice said.

They had passed the opposing car and the stares of those, packed tight, who rode in it, and were approaching the platform.

"Herod had some task."

Kitty knew that Maurice meant the conversion of the desert cliff into a fortress without the help of a cable car. Herod had built a wall on the mountain top, twelve cubits high and eight cubits wide, and on it constructed 37 towers. He had hewed cisterns out of the rock to provide water, and fortified the citadel against any enemy who might wage war on it. He had not reckoned that this fortress would be manned against his own legions by a crusading band of Jews.

Within two or three yards of the platform the cabin came to a halt with so little assurance that Kitty was fearful lest they roll all the way down into the valley again, out of control. They were jerked up a yard; then back again, swaying. The mechanism had broken.

"There's still steps to climb," Maurice said.

We're not there yet? Kitty was surprised that her thought had not been spoken. The words had jammed in her stricken throat. Another jolt. She glanced behind her into the barren valley with its excavated rectangles which had been Roman camps, and was immediately sorry.   .

"So what's the matter?" an Israeli voice enquired.

There was a nervous riposte of comments in a confusion of languages. Kitty kept her eyes on the zippered jacket. A grating sound struck at her entrails and she wondered if one felt anything before hitting the ground. The remaining yards of cable were swallowed up and they came to a categorical halt, level with the ticket collector on his reassuring platform.

Twelve

With her talent for creating order out of chaos Sandra had transformed the flat as she had transformed Norman who could scarcely recognise it. The ugly, old fashioned contours had been disguised, its chill, grim spaces centrally heated, and its unattractive floors and peeling surfaces translated into gracefulness with deep pile carpet and with paper and with paint. It was as elegant as Sandra herself, an extension of her, as was Norman. She had been away for three weeks during which the light had gone out of his life. Since Sandra had entered it, it had not been so bleak.

It was a bleak time of year. Reminders of Christmas – which Norman did not celebrate – all around him, and weather which froze his toes and his fingers and the locks of his car. There had been no Aunty Kitty to relieve the tedium of the evenings, and business, as it did annually, had ground to a virtual standstill. After the holiday it would pick up. It was the pattern in the residential property and the travel trade. No sooner had the forks come out of the plum puddings than thoughts would turn to dwellings – that were smaller or larger or nearer or farther – and holidays in the sun. It had been the longest three weeks that Norman could remember.

He made the rounds of his relatives whom he had neglected since the advent of Sandra. With her image constantly before his eyes, her voice, with its Capetown accent in his ears, he had not enjoyed his visits, Aunty Mirrie in her primrose, spinster flat had given him soup from a packet, which she had reconstituted with boiling water, and a plate of cold salt-beef, like dried cardboard, with coleslaw from a plastic container, and asked him, wheedling, to 'be a good boy' and mend her fuse.

At his Uncle Juda's Hyde Park flat he had drunk coffee from Meissen cups. His Aunty Leonora had made excuses for not asking him to dinner – although they employed a cook – as they were packing for Gstaad. He had sat in the drawing-room among the *objets d'art* while his cousin, Vanessa, who was getting married in the spring, sat entwined, on the giltwood sofa, with the effete looking Nathan, heir to banking millions, when they should clearly have been in bed. Uncle Juda, whom he had not seen for some time, had fingered the material of his new suit, appraised the Jermyn Street shirt, the accessories which Sandra had chosen: "Boom in the property, Norman?" and "Have to find you a nice young lady," his Aunty Leonora said. She was fussing over last minute arrangements for the holiday and had no intention of doing any such thing.

He had sat with his Uncle Leon, shovelling semolina pudding into the obedient mouth, while his Aunty Beatty went to the cinema, and listened to her castigation of him for allowing Leon to wet himself, when she came back. He had driven to Bushey to visit his mother's grave and had Sunday lunch with Freda and Harry. Aunty Freda had not been herself, efficient and managing. She dropped a sherry glass, smashing it, and had forgotten to make the gravy. She seemed snappy with Harry, which was unusual, and after lunch, excusing herself, had gone to lie down. "A headache," Harry said, and told Norman it was the 'change'. Norman nodded understandingly.

They had been duty visits. To pass away the time without Sandra. Her call had been a clarion from paradise, her voice the sweetest music in his ear.

"Norman…?"

He had been expecting a client about a house in Avenue
Road.

"…I'm back!"

He felt like picking up all the property particulars from his
desk, flinging them into the air, and letting them drop, like
confetti.

"How have you been?"

Lonely.

"Fine," he said. "You?"

"Great. Just great. Look I know you're busy…"

What business could there be of the slightest importance?

"They're delivering the furniture in the morning," Sandra
said. "Come tomorrow night and you can sit on a real chair."

"My Aunty Kitty's coming home. I promised to have
dinner…"

Friday was always a late and busy night at the office.

"I'd like to see the furniture," Norman said, as if chairs and
tables were the be-all of his existence. "I'll come in on my way
to Aunty Kitty's."

"My mother-in-law's coming home from Israel tomorrow,"
Sarah said. "I want to get her table ready for Friday night."

She sat in Mrs Halberstadt's cluttered sitting-room with her
notebook and pencil on her knee. She enjoyed her sessions with
Mrs Halberstadt who, in straitened circumstances, sat amongst
her riches – her books and her bronzes, her worn rugs and
embroidered cushions – in her flat in Temple Fortune. Miron
Halberstadt had been a businessman, unsuccessful because he
had belonged to an old-fashioned world which had very fixed
ideas of what was right and what was wrong. His failure had
not bothered him. The love of his life had been rabbinic
literature, evidence of which preoccupation filled, and over-
flowed from the shelves on the walls. A quarter of a century had
passed since he had died. His widow had used the time to
further her education, which had been rudely interrupted in

111

youth by Adolph Hitler, and she had been teaching Slavonic languages to Adult Education classes for many years. In addition, approved by Rabbi Magnus, amongst others, for her devotion to and her knowledge of Judaism – an enthusiasm which she shared with her late husband – she took on a small number of pupils, prospective converts, for practical religious instruction. Sarah was her favourite. Intelligent, enthusiastic, and warm, she wanted to encompass Judaism as she did Josh and her work and everything else she undertook, wholeheartedly and with love. In Mrs Halberstadt's eyes, Sarah, by wanting to give to Judaism more than she expected to extract from it, was a true convert. Looking at the girl, with her long hair and topaz eyes matching her mohair sweater, she turned her attention to Friday nights.

They had already dealt, to Mrs Halberstadt's amusement, with the disaster of Sarah's *gefülte* fish. Among her other attributes Mrs Halberstadt was an excellent cook and had earned her living at it – being the only work she was allowed to do – on her arrival in England as a refugee. In previous sessions they had discussed the importance of food – derided by those who did not understand and who saw it as a religion in itself – in the Jewish home. Food, said Mrs Halberstadt, defined the man; it was the symbol of domesticity, family and community whose values – in the world of 'fast food' and 'take-aways' – were in danger of being eroded. The shared partaking of it provided love, warmth and gratification, and security. A family dining together could shut out both the harshness of the outside world and unpleasant fantasies. The Jewish table determined the seasons. Friday night was its apotheosis.

"On Friday night," Mrs Halberstadt said, "up to eighteen minutes before sunset at the least, two candles, for the sake of *shalom bayit*, harmony in the home, and *oneg Shabbat*, Sabbath joy, are lit by the woman in the room where the meal is to be eaten..."

Kitty had not felt so happy since Sydney had died and her euphoria, her disturbing sensations of light-hearted pleasure, filled her inexplicably with guilt although she knew very well that Sydney would not have wanted her to be sad.

She had survived the cable car. The descent – suspended in the incandescent air, the pitiless sun, over the stony and implacable valley floor – had not been nice. From the top to the bottom, where they had ground to a reassuring halt, she did not think that she had drawn breath. When they'd touched the ground she'd thought – there was still the hazard of the flight home – that she just might see her family again. But it had been worth it. How it had been worth it! Standing on the table top of the mountain which was dotted with other groups, including one of the white-clad Baptists whose rendering of 'Amazing Grace' filled the air, looking down over the wild Judean desert, feeling herself at the strategically important gate of the Hasmonean kingdom, Kitty had listened while Avi had recited to his party the moving words of El'Azar's last oration as he urged the zealots to suicide: '...long ago we resolved to serve neither the Romans nor anyone else but only God...now the time has come to prove our determination by our deeds. Let our wives die before they are abused and our children before they have tasted of slavery...and after we have slain them, let us bestow that glorious benefit upon one another, mutually, and preserve ourselves in freedom...let us die unenslaved by our enemies and leave this world as free men...'

Letting her imagination – touched perhaps by the sun from which on the mountain top there was no shade – run riot, Kitty relived the heroism of her forebears. Later in the museum, she would see nuts and grains, a plait of hair and a woman's shoe miraculously preserved. Her enthusiasm had not been doused by Maurice's dry assertion later, in the coach, that Josephus had invented the fiction of the martyrs in order to please the enemy commander; Kitty preferred to believe the legend – that Masada had been the last outpost of Jewish resistance against Rome.

They had lunched at the foot of the mountain, Kitty filling a tray for Maurice and herself, and afterwards descended through the salt marshes to the lowest spot on earth – the Sea of Sedom, Sea of Zobar, the Eastern Sea, the Arava Sea, the Asphaltum Sea, Bahar Lot, the Dead Sea, as it was variously called – which had been blasted open as if by some sorcerer and which was not a sea at all. Kitty had bathed in it before, on an excursion from Jerusalem, with Sydney, floating on the surface of the mineral laden waters – for in it no form of life could either swim or drown. She knew the routine. For Maurice it was the first time. Putting on her swim-suit in the ladies' shower room, where afterwards she would rinse every particle of salt from her body, she looked in the mirror and wished, as she had intended before she came away, that she had lost some weight. There had been one consolation. In Israel, until now, she had felt neither plump nor old. It was different when you went to the Italian Riviera or the South of France.

On the gritty beach she found that half the bus-load had changed and were in the water, lying in grotesque positions – supported by the excessive buoyancy – with their toes in the hair. The other half stood – their cameras clicking, capturing the hilarity as bodies bobbed around like corks – on the shore. Kitty, self-conscious in her swim-suit, looked round for Maurice. He was a few yards into the water. Lying on it with his arms folded, in the sun. On his left forearm, blurred at the edges, as though they had been inscribed on blotting paper, were the irrefutable numerals of a concentration camp number. Kitty understood suddenly about the zippered jacket he never seemed to remove, about the cafeteria meals for which he would not stand in line, about the bread roll he had not allowed her to waste.

Later, in the coach, she thought it surprising that she had been surprised. The seven numbers had shattered her equilibrium, pierced her susceptibilities. It was the first time she had spent her days with, talked at close quarters to a survivor.

Maurice knew that she had seen the mark of Cain, the noisome reminder of his people's darkest hour. He had opened his eyes as she was staring at it. Kitty pushed her way through the heavy water towards him. She was no longer conscious of the unflattering bulges of her swimsuit.

"My Swiss Bank Account," Maurice said, hiding the figures, like blue tears, beneath the water. "In case I forget."

Kitty did not pursue the subject. They spoke of the water, sitting on it, feeling it beneath them like a chair. But Kitty remembered the attestation, it remained before her eyes, even when Maurice had showered and dressed and put on the zippered jacket.

Back in the coach, approaching the Lost Cities of Gommorah and Sodom, Zvi repeated the story of Lot's ill-fated wife, and his passengers searched good-humouredly for her outline among the tortuous salt shapes.

It was getting late. In the going down of the sun, the stark mountains of Moab were mirrored in the green and silver nothingness of the Dead Sea. If you saw the static scene – with its resplendent beauty, its iridescent reflections – reproduced on a postcard or an ashtray in the gift shop, Kitty thought, you would not believe it. In the Negev – 'the word "negev" means dry', Avi had said, it seemed so long ago, the brush of the setting sun had used pink and rose and apricot to tip the brown hills.

Kitty wanted to cry. She had cried at *Beth Hatefutsoth* with Sydney, the Museum of the Diaspora where the ill-starred fortunes of her people had been encapsulated, both in place and time, under one roof; the Jewish family, the Jewish face; sculptured groups, and historical transparencies of different countries in different centuries, illustrating the cycle of Jewish life, from birth to death, against the rhythm of the Jewish year; nineteenth-century Galicia; the thirteenth-century Rhine; Jews in North Africa, Poland, Lithuania, Bratislavia, Salonika and Fez. Models of synagogues – many desecrated and destroyed – in cities and villages and in *shtetls* which were neither, but

115

which with their own leadership, their own social unit, encompassed the whole world. 'Not by might, nor by power, but by my spirit, saith the Lord of Hosts.' The Hebrew texts had illumined the wealth and continuity of Jewish culture sustained by the Hebrew language. Through documents and audio-visual aids were portrayed the major contributions to literature and education, philosophy and art, of the people of the Book. Monotheism, relativity and psychoanalysis; it had been too much for one afternoon. From Abraham through the streets of Toledo to the creation of a National Home. Too much for one lifetime. One person. Emigration from eastern Europe; the return to Zion; a train in Czechoslovakia; the teeming decks of the immigrant ship *Exodus*. The history of her antecedents in suffering and in tears.

Maurice took a stick of gum from his pocket and gave it to her silently. They left the biblical mountains come alive on the distant shore, the dykes, the fossilised awesomeness of the salt layers evaporated from the marshes, and climbed the dusty road towards the new town of Arad.

Kitty thought she had seen everything. That Israel could hold no more surprises. One moment they were among the parched hills, the barren plains and seconds later a sophisticated 'Brighton' with paved streets and lively shops in the middle of nowhere – Arad. In its arcade Kitty bought a canvas depicting a winding street in the Old City of Jerusalem – together with the appropriate wools – for Addie, hoping it might occupy her as she waited for the healing of the broken ankle. She was paying the assistant in the crowded shop, counting out the unfamiliar shekels, when she heard Avi's whistle.

It was getting late. It was getting dark. Leaving the brightness of the electric town they plunged once more into the sudden desert. Zvi put the lights on in the coach and they snaked, like a single glow-worm over the swift black road. Avi, indefatigable – the day had been long – goaded his weary passengers into song; his native *Hava Negilla*; 'Old MacDonald had a farm' in which Kitty joined; *Allouette* for the French. Enthusiasm compensating for harmony, they sang 'Jerusalem the Golden' in four languages, supplementing the words with claps.

When they stopped at Beerhseva to let a few of the party out, it was if they were family, Zvi's family – as if they had known each other for years.

In the coach, silent now, many sleeping from exhaustion, the fervour of the impromptu concert past, Kitty thought that it had been one of the best days of her life – was it only that morning she had stood on the summit of Masada? – and did not want it to end. She was aware of Maurice next to her but did not speak, reluctant to break the spell. She was grateful to him for mitigating her loneliness, for rekindling her confidence in her own right to exist, for 'making' the last few days of her holiday. Tomorrow morning she would leave for England. On Sunday, Maurice would fly back to New York. They had exchanged addresses. She would send him a postcard of Westminster Abbey or the Tower of London, explaining how much she had appreciated his company.

As they approached the first lights of Eilat, girdled by the mountains and the sea, Maurice put his hand over hers. It was as touching – he seemed so unemotional – as it was unexpected. Beneath the reassuring warmth of his fingers Kitty remained still. The contact, skin to skin, brought back poignantly one of the harshest aspects of her widowhood; that there was no one to touch gratuitously, no human form – other than the grandchildren – whose embrace was not taboo. By this simple gesture Maurice had brought her back to life as surely as if it were she who had died, sent the blood coursing through veins which, since Sydney's death, she had imagined dry.

Thirteen

"Every seventh day a miracle comes to pass, the resurrection of the soul, of the soul of man and of the soul of all things." In instructing Sarah on the importance of Friday night in the Jewish week, Mrs Halberstadt had done her work well. To Josh it was ironic. Having freed himself from the unrelenting ritual of the eve of the Sabbath which he had observed in so far as it satisfied his father when he was alive – he was being re-initiated into the preparatory ceremonies of the day of rest by Sarah.

"Inwardness," Mrs Halberstadt had said, "important though it may be, is not enough. There must be likewise be an outward form, a pattern of conduct, a definite way." To this end Sarah had prepared for Kitty's homecoming. While they waited for Norman – who was the guest that on Friday evenings it was the *mitzvah* to invite – Josh, in the sitting-room, listened to his mother's tales of Israel, and Sarah examined the table she had set with the white cloth kept especially for the Sabbath. The candles in their silver candlesticks, two of them symbolising the unity underlying all apparent duality – man and woman, speech and silence, creation and revelation – had already been lit by Kitty. While Sarah watched, she had, with a circular motion, drawn her hands around the flames towards her face, directing the warmth and light of the seventh day unto herself. Covering her eyes she had recited the blessing – acknowledging the fact that the commandment she was carrying out was dictated directly by God – then silently added a few personal prayers, after which she kissed her daughter-in-law warmly and thanked her for all she had done.

To Sarah it had been no hardship. She was fascinated by the psychological and physical dynamics of the Jewish week, which existed only because of the Sabbath. To begin with, the days, in Hebrew, had no independent names, but were referred to by their relationship to the seventh day. Sunday was the 'first day', Monday the 'second' and so on, until the Sabbath – prepared for with the utmost care and detail – was ushered in and welcomed like a bride. Each physical preparation had its spiritual equivalent. The dwelling must be cleaned and extra delicious foods cooked; the mind must be emptied of all weekday thoughts, and 'matters of consequence' left behind. Any new clothes which had been recently bought should be worn for the first time; there should be money apportioned on Friday afternoon for charity. The table must be set as beautifully as possible; some moments should be spent in meditation, in reviewing the past week and allowing it to fall into perspective. There was an added bonus. The Sabbath, according to Mrs Halberstadt, gave everyone an additional soul whose presence as it entered the body on Friday night, to depart at the close of *Shabbat*, could be clearly felt by those who observed it. The basic theme of the twenty-four hours – perpetuated in the evening prayers and in the propitiousness (according to tradition) of sexual love – was creation; the atmosphere – good food, candlelight, songs, quiet talk, enjoyment of both the corporeal and metaphysical love of the family – sensual.

Sarah was sad that she had not known Josh's father. The Friday nights, as Josh had described them, which he had found rigid and oppressive, and to which she would certainly not have been invited by Sydney, seemed, she thought, to instigate a unique moratorium. The frenetic activity of the secular week was suspended, and a 24 hour respite enjoyed from the tyranny of the office and the telephone, the vagaries of public transport, and the contemporary nightmare of overpopulated cities and roads. Man had become the slave of the environment that he had invented, and the Jewish Sabbath seemed to make sense, in that, for one day out of the seven, he could free himself from the demands of a society – in which he had become increasingly depersonalised – to rediscover his basic humanity. The daily chores of winnowing, grinding and threshing, forbidden from sunset to sunset, may no longer have been relevant, but their modern counterparts stemmed directly from the original 39 proscribed acts. Checking the preparations she had made for Josh's mother, as instructed by Mrs Halberstadt, Sarah had an overwhelming sensation of the day's almost supernatural power.

While in her sitting-room – describing to Josh the highlights of her holiday and the unfounded terrors of her airborne journey home Kitty waited for Norman. Norman, outside the flat overlooking Hampstead Heath, waited for Sandra. It surprised him that he had managed to get through the day. He had woken to images of Sandra from a night in which she had dominated his dreams. He forgot to time his breakfast egg, boiling it hard; locked the front door leaving his car keys on the hall table and got to the end of the road before he noticed his socks – one blue, one black. The specific demands of the forthcoming day had been so much gibberish coming from the lips of Mr Monty, and to decipher the hieroglyphics on the correspondence on his desk he would need a Rosetta Stone. He had tried to write with the cap on his pen, stapled the first page of one set of property particulars to the second of another and spilled his paper clips in a silver eruption on to the dusty floor. When dealing with clients on the telephone he mouthed phrases in the hope that they were appropriate, for in truth he had not heard what they said; when they sat before his desk, seeking guidance, their forms dissolved to leave Sandra, with her translucent skin, her slate grey eyes, within tantalising reach. No day had seemed longer. Not even the Day of Atonement with its 25 hours of neither food nor drink. Each time he looked at his watch, the progress of the hands seemed minimal. There had been work after hours, as on a Friday he knew there would be: negotiations he must complete before the weekend; and details to be prepared, appointments to be arranged, for the weekly crescendo of viewing – frequently futile, regarded by some as diversion to fill the vacant hours of a Saturday morning.

When Mr Monty had finally called it a day, Norman had, he supposed, said his good nights and driven his car through the bottle-neck of Finchley Road and up the long hill towards the Heath but he could not recall getting there. He had rung the bell on the entry phone of the outer door of the flats and listened, a grin on his face, for Sandra's voice. There was no reply. Entering the block with a homecoming man he ran up to the second floor. There was a note on the door, fastened with sellotape: 'Norman I won't be long'. Glad of an opportunity to allow his thudding heart to revert to its normal rhythm, he sat down on the stairs to wait.

"I can't think what's happened to him," Kitty said, meaning Norman, as Josh took the white satin *cappel* from his pocket and covered his head preparatory to making the blessing over the wine in the small, chased silver cup which had been a wedding present to his parents from his Uncle Juda.

"Well, there's no reply from the office," Josh said, turning the red-edged pages of *The Authorised Daily Prayer Book*, immortalised in translation by the late Reverend Singer, to find the Sabbath Evening kiddush.

"I hope he hasn't had an accident," Kitty said. Since her traumatic flight to Israel and her hair-raising experiences while she was there, she had had accidents on the brain. "It's not like Norman."

"And it was evening and it was morning..." Josh said. His Hebrew was less fluent than Sydney's whose melodious voice he had not inherited. "...and on the seventh day God had finished his work which he had made; and he rested..."

It was nice to be home, Kitty thought, looking at Josh standing where, on a Friday night, Sydney had always stood, at Sarah, motionless by her chair while her husband sang the benediction, following his every word. It was good to be back among your own things. Among your own. She had enjoyed the holiday more, much more than she had expected she would. She had tried to keep her enjoyment of it in a low key when she had popped into Addie, given her the tapestry from the arcade in Arad. "Talk to anyone?" Addie had said, wanting to hear every detail of the hotel, a verbatim account of Kitty's every waking moment, while she, confined to her flat, nursed her ankle in its plaster. Kitty told her about the solicitor from Hampstead Garden Suburb who knew the Klopmans, and about the family from Solihull who had befriended her. She did not mention Maurice Morgenthau. She did not mention him on the telephone to Rachel when she had phoned – her tumbling words racing the pips – from Somerset where she was on holiday with Patrick. She had not mentioned him to Carol who was relieved that Kitty had enjoyed her holiday, and had not spoken of him either to Sarah or to Josh.

"...Blessed art thou, O Lord," Josh said, "who hallowest the Sabbath."

He drank from the cup then handed it to his mother, who said the blessing over wine before she 'sipped. When it was Sarah's turn she held the cup and looked to Josh for guidance. He said the words slowly and Sarah repeated them in the unfamiliar Hebrew.

Josh removed the embroidered cloth from the two loaves – symbolising the double portion of manna which was received in the wilderness on Sabbath Eve to provide for the Day when none fell – of the traditional plaited bread sprinkled with poppy seeds, which Sarah had bought in the Jewish bakery and set before him, and picked up the knife.

"You have to *break* it," Sarah said. "The knife is a weapon of war!"

Josh looked at her.

"Honestly. Mrs Halberstadt said so. 'And they shall beat their swords into ploughshares and their spears into pruning hooks'."

His father had always used the special silver bread knife, the word *Shabbat* engraved on its handle. One learned something new every day. Josh broke small pieces of the bread, then sprinkled them with salt: 'By the sweat of your brow shall you get bread to eat'. He did not hand the pieces directly to his mother and to Sarah but offered them from a small plate for it was not from man that one received one's bread. The *motze* ceremony over, Kitty and Josh sat down, while Sarah went into the kitchen for the soup which she had made to replace her disastrous *gefülte* fish.

All thoughts of his empty place at Aunty Kitty's table had fled from Norman who had had every intention of being there. He had waited for half an hour on the stairs outside Sandra's flat wishing he had stopped to buy an evening paper. At every foot on the staircase, every ascent of the lift which sped past the floor where he sat, his heart began to race again. When Sandra came, laden with parcels, he wondered if she was real.

"They've fixed the fridge," she said, her arms around the supermarket carriers, "I had to get something to put in it!"

After Capetown Sandra was radiant. Norman had not remembered her so beautiful, so brown. He took the keys from her strong white teeth and opened the door.

"I'm really sorry, Norman," she said as he followed her down the corridor towards the kitchen. "How have you been?"

Devastated. He was devastated now.

"Fine."

"Had a good Christmas?"

He had had a kipper with Aunty Mirrie who did not celebrate it.

He helped her stow the milk and the butter and the eggs and the bacon and the yoghurt, in various flavours, and the three varieties of cheeses into the fridge, which swallowed them up with no trouble. It was gold and vast and had an interior light and an exterior light over a gadget which dispensed iced water and ice – cubes or crushed – at the touch of a lever.

"Isn't it magnificent?" Sandra said, meaning the kitchen. And indeed it was. With its cherry-wood units, and its ceramic floor, and its squeezers and mixers and toasters and grinders and waste disposal and trash compactor, it bore no resemblance to the old-fashioned room, with a single sink, for which Norman had apologised to Sandra what seemed so very long ago.

"Come on. I'll show you the rest."

In the sitting-room the two enormous sofas were covered in white knobbly wool. Norman had to sit on them at Sandra's insistence, to admire the square black-lacquered coffee table, on which she had already put some glossy magazines in neat alignment and an arrangement of dried flowers which was repeated on the dining-table at the other end of the room.

"Like it?" Sandra asked.

"It's amazing," Norman said, looking at the cream jersey dress which caressed her body beneath the fur coat which she had been too excited by her new furniture to take off.

"I'll show you the bedrooms."

Hilton's and Milton's were identical. Small, but furnished now with everything a small boy might want. Norman thought of his own room, as a boy, with its bed, its corner washbasin and its single wardrobe.

"And this is mine!"

Sandra flung open the door of the master bedroom. The largest bed Norman had ever seen occupied almost the whole of one wall.

"Try it!" Sandra bounced on the mattress which was patterned in blue, matching the carpet.

Norman sat down next to Sandra. The familiar perfume, of which he had been deprived for the three weeks that she had been away, tickled his nostrils.

"It was wickedly expensive..." Sandra said lying back and pressing her hands into the buttoned softness. "...But oh, the bliss!"

Norman turned to look at her, cream and vulnerable, in the brown silk lining of her coat, her hair corn among the blue flowers, her fine leather boots extending over the edge of the bed. For one brief moment he thought of Aunty Kitty's where he should have been dining. Then he obeyed the bells in his head and the fire in his veins and the insistence of his bones and covered Sandra's body with his.

"Strange about Norman," Josh said.

They were preparing for bed.

"I expect he forgot," Sarah said. "Went to the cinema or something."

"Not Norman." Josh watched as Sarah put the Victorian bangle he had bought her on the dressing-table, took off her sweater, shook out the long hair which fell almost to her breasts.

"It was nice of you to go to all that trouble..." Sarah looked at him. "...for mother, for Friday night. She really appreciated it."

"I enjoyed it. Preparing for the Sabbath. All those little customs repeated over and over down the years. Handed on from generation to generation. At home there was only Christmas and you can't get much mileage out of a turkey. It makes you feel good."

"There's another custom," Josh said.

"What's that?"

"For Friday night."

He took the *cappel*, the white satin skull-cap, with which he had covered his head for the benediction before the meal and the grace after it, and threw it on to the bed.

"It's what my great-grandfather used to do in Cracow when he wanted to make love to my great-grandmother."

He looked into Sarah's laughing eyes and held out his arms for her.

Fourteen

Kitty looked out of the window at the rain falling steadily on the stationary traffic and tried to take herself back to the warm, dry air of Eilat, where she had looked down from her balcony at the pellucid water. With the last of her summer clothes, which she had put away in the wardrobe in the spare bedroom, the gates had closed on what had been a memorable fortnight, and her thoughts, which she had collected up from the Canyon of the Inscriptions (the belladonna and the tumbleweed), the mystic colours of the desert stones and the heroic battlements of Masada, took their place again in her everyday mind where they were directed towards Rachel's wedding. Addie had commented, grudgingly, on her suntan; Beatty, when she had gone to visit Leon and to take them the hand-painted ashtray, that the rest had done her good. Kitty knew that neither the rest nor the sunshine had been wholly responsible for the new dimension she had brought back with her from Israel, together with the dried up desert rose, which she put in a tiny container of water on the sitting-room mantelpiece above the Magicoal fire.

She had noticed the change in herself on the journey home, in the aeroplane. She had not been afraid. No, that was not true, She had been afraid but not with the blind fear, the panic which had taken hold of her on the journey to Tel Aviv. She had sat by the window, and she had looked out of it. She had kept her seat belt fastened but paid no attention to the fact that the other passengers walked up and down in the aisles. The seat next to her was empty but in it – taking strength from his calmness, as she had on the ladder in the Canyon of the Inscriptions and in the cable car – she had imagined the enigmatic Maurice Morgenthau. Maurice had given her strength. He had endowed her with a confidence for which, accustomed to relying on Sydney, she had previously never felt the need, and which she had since put to good use in the manner of Rachel's wedding dress.

Hettie Klopman had hardly waited for her to unpack. The opening salvos on the telephone had concerned the postcard, for which she thanked Kitty calling her 'dear', although they had only met once, commenting how nice it must have been in Eilat, although Herbert never went anywhere but the Hilton where the manager knew him and where they always had a suite on the Jaffa side of the hotel.

"Herbert wants to take Rachel to Paris to see the new collections," Hettie said. "To choose her wedding dress. When is she free?"

It had taken Kitty by surprise. Paris had so many more exciting ideas, Hettie said, and being in the fashion business Herbert had the entrée to all the best houses. He wanted Rachel to have something special – Nina Ricci or Dior – something with a long train which would be held by Patrick's three girl cousins from Leeds. Kitty had felt the ground shift beneath her as the river of Hettie Klopman's loquacity flowed on over flowers and colour schemes and how everything must match or be complementary – she hated to see *chuppahs* which hadn't been properly thought out, all bits and bobs – and would Kitty come over some time to discuss menus with the caterer, there'd be so much to do later on that it was better to get ahead, and she and Herbert were going on a Caribbean cruise in March, so it would be wise to deal with as much as possible straight away.

Kitty guessed that the menus and the flowers – for which it was certainly premature – were to camouflage the edict of the wedding dress for which Hettie, primed she guessed by Patrick, had expected opposition, but Kitty was not deflected. She had jumped from a boulder into the Canyon of the Inscriptions, climbed a perpendicular ladder to get out of it, hung in a cable car suspended high above the Judean desert, she was not going to be cowed by Hettie Klopman, to let her walk all over her.

She told Hettie about Cupid of Hendon and Rika Snowman who had made Carol's wedding dress, and that she had already been approached about Rachel's. Kitty would not hurt her friend's feelings for the world. Hettie Klopman had been non-committal. She was only the adjutant. As soon as he came home from his office Herbert was on the phone. "Give us the *nachas,* Kitty," he said. "We haven't got a daughter of our own..." Kitty did not yield.

She thanked Herbert politely for his generous gesture but stuck to her guns and Rika Snowman where she was going now with Rachel for whom she was waiting and from whom she had had no support. The dress in which she was to be married was a matter of indifference to Rachel who would happily have worn her jeans. She considered it as much a waste of money as everything else to do with the wedding, which threatened to engulf her, and in any case could spare only one day before she went back to college for her final term before the exams. Kitty had spoken to Hettie since, but the atmosphere had been less cordial. She had invited her future *mechutanista* to accompany them to Cupid of Hendon but Hettie had a previous engagement. It was no way to go on Kitty thought as, mesmerised by the slanting rain, she waited for Rachel who, with ingenious excuses of disasters which had befallen her, was invariably late.

Norman stood on the black and white floor of the Mayfair flower shop waiting to be served. Through an open doorway he could see three girls in checked overalls – whom he presumed were assistants – transfixed by animated conversation and what he assumed was their coffee break. One leaned, smoking, against a wall, another was putting the finishing touches to a wreath, and the third sat on a desk, swinging her legs, as she blew into a steaming mug round which she had clasped both hands. Norman didn't mind waiting. He didn't mind anything. He had pains in his liver, his lungs and his midriff which were palpably the manifestations of love. He loved Sandra to whom as the most insignificant token of his passionate and consuming devotion he was going to send a magnificent bouquet of flowers. Aunt Kitty had told him where to get them when he had telephoned to apologise for not turning up on the Friday night when she had come back from her holiday. The best flower shop in London, Norman had said. He had not told Aunty Kitty why.

Standing patiently among the rigid gladioli, mauve and pink and yellow, among the shaggy, overblown football heads of chrysanthemums – a superior version of those he had regularly bought from the man outside the station for his mother, when she was alive, for New Year – among the spray carnations and the tiger lilies, the daffodils, and the snowdrops which had been forced, he allowed himself, as he did in his idle moments and some which were not, by way of a small treat, to go back to that Friday night which, although it was already becoming confused with other magical nights of the past ten days, he would always remember.

"Try it," Sandra had said, sitting down on the bed. The inflexion in her voice, the words, whose invitation he could not be sure if he had read correctly, were still in his ears and would remain there. He had sunk on to the blue patterned mattress beside her, and before he knew it, almost despite himself, as if another Norman were in charge, he had taken her, fur coat and all, into his arms. She had not objected. How foolish he had been, how short-sighted, to think that she would. Nothing in his thoughts, however muddled, had prepared him for her response. She had been warm, giving, loving, everywhere. Compared with his brief experiences on the back seat of his car with Della, it was as if he had never known a woman before. He had not. At first, the love they had made had been short and urgent. Later it had been long and slow. It had to do with mouths and limbs and secret places to which Sandra invited him, and his discovery that her skin went on forever and was flawless as a sun-tanned body stocking, and with caressing words he did not know he knew, and with waiting and with patience, and with ardour and with eagerness, and with passion and with cries and cataclysms and with the desire to weep with happiness and with content. Afterwards he had fallen asleep and Sandra had covered him with her fur coat.

When he awoke she was in the sitting room at the record-player. His feet made no sound on the pale carpet which was shedding its tufts. At the touch of a knob the raucous voice of Piaf crashed like a road drill into every corner of the room, filling it, into every crevice of Norman's body. '*Non, rien de rien, non, je ne regrette rien…*' Sandra turned towards him. '*Ni le bien, qu'on m'a fait…*' They flowed, amoeba-like, together. '*…ni le mal, tout ça m'est bien égal…*' Her hair was beneath his chin, soft golden, '*Non, rien de rien…*', he put his lips to it, '*…non, je ne regrette rien…*' Their bodies swayed as one, keeping time to the music, '*Car ma vie, car mes joies, aujourd'hui, ça commence avec toi…*' Norman wanted the night to go on for ever, for it never to stop. Later they had both grown tired and it was the first time – although now too late – that Norman had thought of Aunty Kitty. Although she had asked him for dinner since, he had not accepted. He had been too busy with Sandra, making the most of their Elysian nights in the flat, in which Norman helped her with the finishing touches – Sandra had bought scarlet sheets for the king-sized bed – before Hilton and Milton came back to their new home.

"Can I help you, sir?" A voice broke into his dreams.

"Some flowers." He wanted them to wrap up the whole shop.

"What did you have in mind?"

Sandra's body. He would never tire of it.

The girl in her checked overall waited.

Norman looked around at the lengths and shapes, smelled the fusion of perfumes from the palette of colours which surrounded him.

"Did you want them delivered?"

Norman nodded.

"Local?"

"No." He gave Sandra's address.

"We charge five pounds for delivery and two-fifty for gift wrapping – that's if you want them in a box with ribbon and cellophane – and then there's your VAT on top of that."

Norman stared at the girl. He seemed to have spent almost ten pounds without having bought anything. He was not accustomed to flower shops. He pointed to some white roses. Sandra, he thought, would like white roses to echo the furniture in her sitting-room.

"A large bunch of those!"

"Those ones are three pounds..." the girl said.

"That'll be fine." Norman reached for his wallet.

She drew a single stem from the bucket. "...each!"

"I got stuck in the lift!" Rachel said.

Kitty had given her up as a bad job and started to make an apple cake for Norman who at last was coming for dinner. If anything happened it happened to Rachel who seemed to have been born a victim. She missed trains and appointments (I didn't realise it was Tuesday yesterday), discovered split seams and microscopic holes in any garments which she bought, necessitating their return to the shop, and seemed to be the prime target for any pickpocket (my chequebook *and* my cheque card), flasher and molester who happened to be around. She lost keys (there was a hole in my pocket) and lecture notes (I must have left them on the train and they weren't even mine), and to lend her the car was to invite attention from every bumper denter (it wasn't *my* fault!) paint scratcher and aerial bender on the road. In the borrowed council flat she was supposed to be keeping a low profile as it should not have been sub-let. Already, mistaking the floor, and expecting Patrick to answer, she had rung the bell, peremptorily, of the identical flat above, provoking the wrath of an irate night-shift worker roused from his sleep, and when unloading her gear had parked Kitty's car in the place sacred to the Chairman – who turned out to be an extremely officious woman – of the Residents' Association, who wanted to know exactly what Rachel was doing in the building at all.

In the purple padded coat which came almost to her ankles which were encased in shocking-pink leg warmers, with the green and crimson scarf she had knitted threatening to strangle her, the whole topped by the burning bush of her outlandish hair, she looked, Kitty thought, as if she had just arrived, not from Mornington Crescent, but from some fringe town in the Himalayas or the Yukon.

"I was expecting you at ten," Kitty said, arranging slices of apple neatly in her tin.

"It wasn't my fault," Rachel said. "That lift's always breaking down. Luckily there were some children around who heard the alarm. It took them three quarters of an hour to find the caretaker. They thought it was a great joke." She looked at her watch. "I'm meeting this girl at the library at twelve."

"Rachel," Kitty said. "How can you expect to choose a dress for the most important day of your life in half-an-hour?"

"How long does it take?' Rachel said, opening the fridge. "You'll have to hang on a bit because I haven't had any breakfast."

"Where are you going for your honeymoon?" Rika Snowman asked Rachel who sat in her padded coat on the gilt sofa between herself and Kitty as they leafed through back numbers of bridal magazines.

"Haven't thought about it."

"She's too busy with exams." Kitty excused her.

"There's time." Rika turned back a couple of pages. "This is the lace I was telling you about, but not this neckline – you need more bosom for that – more of a mandarin..." She encircled her own neck. "...and a little stand-up collar, we could edge it with tiny white flowers..."

Rachel stared at the headless bride sketched on the glossy page.

"Got anywhere to live yet?" Rika asked. "You should see Bernice's..." Her own daughter had married a chartered surveyor in the summer, and set up home in Kenton. "...it's like a little palace. They've got a through lounge-room with a picture window, a downstairs toilet, a nice little garden, not too big, but large enough for children – please God – to play, and a beautiful kitchen with everything in it – they were very lucky, the people they bought it from emigrated to Canada – dishwasher, washing machine, tumble dryer. The bedrooms are small but you can't have everything. No garage, but a carport, which is all you need, and five minutes from the station for Howard..."

"I think Rachel's in a hurry, Rika," Kitty said, jabbing a finger at a bride in a dress whose hem dipped in eight handker-chief points. She couldn't picture Rachel with a tumble dryer, and a downstairs toilet, and a carport in Kenton, with Patrick going off neatly every morning to the station.

"They're always in a hurry," Rika said equably. "I'll show you some materials so that Rachel can get an idea, then we can take a few measurements and see how we go. Have you thought about bridesmaids?"

"Debbie and Lisa," Kitty said, "Carol's two little ones."

Hettie Klopman wanted Patrick's three girl cousins from Leeds to attend her, whose ages, according to Rachel, ranged from thirteen to sixteen and who were by no means dainty. Rachel had said 'no way!' and Kitty had left her to deal with her future mother-in-law.

"There's a lovely new organdie nobody's even seen yet, for bridesmaids," Rika said, searching on a table among swatches of material, "with a little print – like a Liberty print almost – and it comes in a very pale mauve or a very pale yellow or a very pale…"

Rachel was looking at her watch.

"Let's get Rachel settled," Kitty said.

"All right, darling." Rika took a heavy baton of white material from against the wall and unwound a length.

"This is the lace. I got it last year and was keeping it for someone special. You can't even get it any more. They can't do it for the money. Feel the give in it…" She draped it across the bosom of Rachel's purple padded coat. "Take your clothes off sweetheart and I'll show you some others. We've got a beautiful moiré, not a white, more of a parchment, and a watered silk – but that might be more than you want to go to, Siek's gone crazy – she might not like the lace. I don't want to force her. She's got to wear it, haven't you, darling? We want you to be happy with it."

Rachel, refusing the privacy of a cubicle, removed her clothes. Beneath the purple coat was a cardigan of Patrick's which came down to her knees. She pulled it over her head to reveal another of her own which Kitty had knitted for her while she was still at school, and which should now, by rights, have been in a jumble sale.

"Okay?" Rachel said.

"We can't take measures like that," Rika said. "It's got to fit like a skin," she smoothed a hand over her own hips. "It falls to the body, laces does, that's the beauty of it…"

Rachel pulled off the cardigan and the tee shirt and the granny vest she was wearing as one, and stood bare-breasted, in her scarlet tights and shocking pink leg warmers, before the mirror in the salon.

"Isn't she tiny?" Rika said, spanning her narrow waist with her tape measure. Her eyes were moist. "She'll make a beautiful bride, Kitty, like a living doll!"

Fifteen

The letter, in its blue and red battlemented flimsy airmail envelope, addressed in a spidery hand which had not been learned in the United States, was waiting on the mat for Kitty when she got home, having dropped Rachel at the library. She had not expected it. She had sent Maurice Morgenthau a postcard showing Big Ben and the Houses of Parliament and had anticipated an aerial view of Manhattan or a close-up of the Statue of Liberty in return. She put her apple cake into the oven, made herself some coffee – of which she was in need after her morning with Rachel – and sat down to open the letter which cheered her up even before she read it.

Few people wrote to her. There was a cousin in Greenock whose husband had found difficulty in holding a job, even before the days of mass unemployment, to whom she used to send the children's outgrown clothing when they were young and with whom she tried not to lose touch. There were notices of forthcoming events and broadsheets containing news from the various societies to which she belonged. Apart from that Kitty's mail consisted of bills, from which when Sydney was alive he had protected her, and appeals for donations from the Central British Fund for Jewish Relief, and from the Home for Aged Jews – for which she sent the Head Housekeeper five pounds for nine loaves of bread, or ten pounds for fifty-five pints of milk – and from the Jewish Blind Society which Sydney had supported and which she considered it her duty to continue to support. Her immediate family, and Sydney's extended one, all lived within telephoning distance. A personal letter was a rare treat. She drew the pages from the long envelope and unfolded them:

Dear Kitty

How goes it with you? The snow here is three feet deep in places and the temperature nine degrees below. I look out my window and try to take myself back to Sharm-el-Sheikh or Masada – remember the heat on top there? No wonder they had water at strategic points, what must it have been like to excavate! I tried but could no longer feel the sun, the vacation, whose last days' meeting you made memorable. The people down below on the street, in boots and coats, leaning against the wind – the present – is the only reality. You can't go back. I've never tried, except in my painting which possesses me wholly, and through which I am driven by an inner necessity to express longings and anxieties, in which are symbols of death and destruction which cannot be visualized, let alone understood, by those who have not been where I have been, and seen what I have seen. Maybe I should have gone back. To examine that past you recalled with your loving eyes when you looked at the number on my arm that evening in the Dead Sea – I rewarded your concern with cynicism – a flip remark of which I am not proud.

Maybe if I had gone back to re-examine the past, if I had spoken about it to someone, to anyone, I wouldn't be such a lonely, disagreeable old man. In mitigation I say that it was too painful. I wasn't the only one to stagger out of Europe almost 40 years ago with a bleeding heart – but I was to myself. You can't just lump people together. Blacks. Jews. Prisoners. *Survivors.* As soon as you start doing this you isolate individuals from the human race.

It's no more valid than supposing that everyone who lives on the same floor of the same apartment building is the same and should behave and react the same, have the same loves, hates, fears and dreams and take the same size in socks. When I think of you Kitty on the coach or in Yoske's – about the lobster I have a theory it's more important what comes out the mouth than what goes into it – I think of your family, your children, and grandchildren, and envy you each one of them with a consuming envy. Of my entire *mishpacha* – brothers, sisters, parents, grandparents, uncles, aunts – I was the only one left after the war. One finger from a whole hand. There was no one to love, no one to live for.

People matter, things don't. (There's something sad about the materialism, the showing off of possessions in American life.) Automobiles, fancy clothes don't interest me. Offer me a chicken or a rose, I'll take the rose. Why didn't I marry, I hear you ask – you were too polite at Yoske's – to begin with I could never have children. When I think of them in relation to myself it's to see them – condemned never to grow old – go into the 'showers': 'Mummy, I've been good. It's dark in there!' or, old before their time, trying to stretch their little necks towards the rod whose arbitrary one point twenty metre height divided those tall enough to reach it from those who would be gassed. An SS guard with his baton put an end to any dreams I may have had of progeny of my own. There have been women – fireflies – who have illuminated my life for brief periods, then left me alone to wrestle endlessly with questions which I could not voice and which were unanswerable.

You were so generous with your family, sharing them with me and getting nothing in return except that I was a physician and a painter, and the odd stick of gum. I am diffident, Kitty, about a *curriculum vitae* that starts at

Majdanek and ends in Buchenwald, whose middle name, Auschwitz, has been discovered by Hollywood, immortalized in second-rate films – colossal monuments to bad taste – which would make the Creation sound banal and inadequate fiction, reduced to glib words and reductive phrases, and now has a coach park, a cafeteria and a souvenir shop. (You have seen for yourself the pedlars from Acre and Nahariya selling peanuts and popsicles outside the Memorial Museum.)

Although I said not a word to you Kitty, I find it easy to talk to you – perhaps because there are 3,000 miles between us – may I? Are you interested in the ramblings of a pale ghost? The real Maurice Morgenthau died in 1940. I will not, I hope, distress you because the truth is untellable. Personal experience – childbirth or the act of love – cannot be conveyed. And if I could knock my head against the wall of silence, anything I could relate about those years which left the biggest blot Rorschach has ever seen on the copybook of evolution and on my life, would be like a grain of sand on Long Beach – absolutely nothing to what really happened, and which you would need a pathological imagination to appreciate. No, I would just like to write you from time to time, to redeem some bits and pieces of Maurice Morgenthau in the hope of resurrecting him. Soon there will be no one left who looked into the sun of Gross Rosen and Dachau, Flossenberg and Belzac, no walking dead who eat and sleep and work and play – like puppets when the strings are pulled – but who belong in the mass graves of Kharkov, Lublin and Kovno, in the crematoria of Treblinka or the ghettos of Theresienstadt. Soon the most Machiavellian, relentlessly perpetrated act of genocide mankind has ever known – to use the term 'holocaust', 'complete destruction by fire', is already to mitigate – will be consigned neatly to the history books, and with a great sigh of relief will be heard from the conscience of the world. I will understand if you've heard enough of the meanderings of an old man and do not reply to your coach companion, Maurice Morgenthau.

P.S. How is Addie? Is her ankle healed? MM.

The envelope fell from Kitty's lap on to the floor. There was something else in it. A pencil sketch on a piece of thin card – Kitty, jumping from the rock into the Canyon of the Inscriptions. The expression on her face – which Maurice had caught exactly – was one of terror. She did not know whether to laugh at it or whether to weep at the pathos of the letter.

The timer, telling Kitty that her apple cake was cooked, and the telephone rang at the same time. They broke into her thoughts which were of Addie (where she was going for lunch – although she had popped in and out in the ten days she had been home from Israel there had, incredibly, not been time for a good talk) and of her sister-in-law Freda, from whom she had had a mysterious phone call, and of Norman who was coming for dinner, and of Maurice Morgenthau and the reflections the two pages of his script had stirred up within her, and of Sydney who was rarely out of her mind. It surprised her that now they no longer had Sydney, his family seemed to regard Kitty as its head, to be deferred to and consulted. By rights the distinction should have gone to Sydney's younger brother Juda whose interests, as the family realised, did not extend further than – if indeed as far as – his own home.

Unlike Sydney, Juda was a selfish man whose horizon was strictly limited to his own needs. He would spare neither himself nor his resources for the betterment of the 'Jules Stanley Gallery' where the walls were lined with rare drawings and fine paintings, or in the furtherment of his not inconsiderable investments, but he was not the least bit interested in the day to day problems of his sisters, Freda, Beatty and Mirrie – nor, except in the most superficial way, in those of his immediate family. The forthcoming marriage of his only daughter, Vanessa, would cost Juda a substantial sum of money which his wife Leonora considered, in her relentless social climb, well spent, but no sleepless nights. When problems to do with the wedding arose, as they had in the past week, Leonora had aired them in the surprised ear of Kitty who had never found her sister-in-law particularly friendly. The Queen's dressmaker was making the wedding dress for Vanessa, who would be wearing a tiara lent by Leonora's *mechutanim* who were tenuously attached to the aristocracy – and be attended by four page-boys. Manners, rather than curiosity, prompted Leonora to ask what Kitty herself was planning, and the information that Rika Snowman would be making the wedding dress for Rachel who would be followed down the aisle by Debbie and Lisa, elicited a barely audible acknowledgement.

When Kitty enquired where Nathan's *Aufruf* was to be, Leonora had grown distant. She didn't think they'd be having anything like *that* she said, as though Kitty had suggested a public lynching, rather than the calling up of the bridegroom to the Reading of the Law in synagogue on the Sabbath before the wedding, which was generally followed by a lunch. Kitty was not surprised. Vanessa's Nathan, from what one heard – the engagement, advisedly Kitty thought, had been in Barbados where Nathan's parents had a house – was more at home on the grouse moors or the hunting field than in a synagogue where the wedding, were it not for Juda – who although there was little evidence of it in his daily life was superstitiously attached to his origins – would not have taken place.

Kitty let the timer ring – a few minutes more was not going to hurt the apple cake – and answered the phone. Beatty's anxious voice superseded the pips.

"Kitty?"

"What's the matter?" Kitty said.

"It's Leon. The doctor didn't like the look of him. He can't pass water. They've taken him in." Beatty's normally strident voice was shaky.

"Where is he?"

"St Mary's. He wants to do some tests."

It was Kitty's bridge afternoon.

"I'll come over," she said. "What ward is he in?"

"Mary Magdalene. That's all he needs. There's a *yossel* over the bed!"

"I'll bring an apple cake."

She'd open a tin of fruit for Norman.

"You're a *gutte neshumah*," Beatty said.

Getting the cake out of the oven, the gas jets burning her face as she stooped, Kitty thought suddenly of Maurice Morgenthau, for whom ovens had a different connotation than for apple cakes, and it was not a faceless column who shuffled unwittingly towards the furnaces but herself and Carol and Rachel and Josh and Beatty and Leon although he was sick and Addie despite her plaster cast which was coming off tomorrow and Dolly, Norman's late mother with her bad back and Leonora whose wealth would not save them and that the Gestapo had come into *her* flat smashing the bird's eye maple furniture and the glass-fronted bookcase in the hall which held the Festival Prayer Books and hit Sydney across the face knocking out the teeth he had always cared for so meticulously with dental floss and marched them off along the Finchley Road where Rabbi Magnus was down on his knees scrubbing the paving stones before an amused truck of SS men and into the waiting cattle trucks packed so tightly there was no room even to sit down. She shut the oven door on her unbidden thoughts – complete destruction by fire, Maurice had said – and tested the apple cake with a skewer before going over to have lunch with Addie who was grilling some mackerel.

Kitty didn't like hospitals. Who did? she thought, as she walked down the green linoed corridor along which third world maids clattered cups on to trays and spruce sisters smiled into telephones, and boys and girls no older than Rachel – with white coats and stethoscopes – intermingled with porters pushing chairs and trolleys, and physiotherapists hurried importantly, and visitors, with flowers and shopping bags, looked uneasily for wards, and out-patients came tentatively in, and in-patients went thankfully out. Sydney had died at home. That was one blessing. At least he hadn't spent his last days harnessed to machines in strange and frightening surroundings, cared for by bright faced nurses and impotent doctors.

Beatty sat by the bed with a plate of grapes which she had peeled and which she was trying to insert into Leon's closed mouth in the men's surgical ward.

"He hasn't touched a thing," she said. "They've put a tube in." She indicated the catheter which snaked from beneath the bedclothes into a bag in which there was an inch of blood-stained urine. "The lunch was hamburger. I told them he was kosher – they were very nice I must say – and they've put him down for kosher meals tomorrow – Sister did offer him a salad but I told her he never touches salad – rabbit food he calls it, so I thought I'd try a few grapes…"

"He doesn't look very hungry." Kitty put the tin with the apple cake she had made on the locker on which Beatty had already put a big bowl of fruit and a jar of chicken soup and some horse-radish and beetroot sauce. She looked at Leon with his waxen face, and sunken cheeks, who seemed to have aged ten years since she had last seen him. "What did the doctor say?"

"He didn't say much. Something about his kidneys. They take you for a fool." She leaned towards Kitty. "That bed there," she said, looking down the ward, "next to the one with the curtains closed. I nodded to the wife and she gave me a smile. I think he must be one of us."

Kitty followed her gaze to where a woman in a Persian lamb coat sat beside a balding man with glasses and a black moustache.

"I'll go over and talk to her later..." Beatty said, secure in the knowledge that *kol yisrael chaverim*, all Jews were brothers, "when I've given Leon these." She arranged the grapes on the plate as if by making them attractive she could will Leon to open his lips.

"He must eat. They brought him in an ambulance. He doesn't know me."

Leon opened his eyes and looked through Kitty.

"Hello Leon," she said, taking his thin hand.

"Uncle Leon's in hospital," Kitty said. "He doesn't look at all well to me but Aunty Beatty doesn't want to know." She looked across the table at Norman whom she hadn't seen since her holiday. He looked exhausted, she thought, in his hand tailored suit and his dove grey tie. She'd had a shock when she'd seen him, dark shadows beneath his eyes.

"Are you all right, Norman?" He had hardly touched the casserole she had made for him and had already put his knife and fork down.

"Fine."

"You're looking tired. Not overdoing it are you?"

Norman looked at his Aunt who was collecting up the plates. He got up to help her.

"Sit down. I'll do it. How's Sandra?"

"Fine."

Kitty stood by the door. "I made an apple cake but I took it to the hospital for Leon – I expect Beatty will eat it – I've got a tin of peaches in the fridge."

Overdoing it. You might say that, Norman thought when Kitty had left the room, but it wasn't work. It was the love he had made with Sandra every night at her flat, and which he was not going to share with anyone, not even with his Aunt. The days had been torture. He had gone about them in a stupor, moving mechanically to complete tasks which had become meaningless. Contracts and mortgages. Surveys and Exchanges. Freeholds and fees. Sandra. Last night they had had a farewell dinner to celebrate the end of their freedom. Today Hilton and Milton, accompanied by Sandra's sister-in-law, were coming back from South Africa. Sandra had gone to meet them.

She had set up the dinner as she set up everything. Norman had never been to such a place. It was a club so discreet that there was no name on the door. A butler had let them in as if to a private house. Arnold Caplan was a member. They knew Sandra and greeted her, taking her fur coat from her solicitously before the log fire in the hall. Upstairs in an elegant drawing-room, people whom his Aunty Beatty would have referred to as 'moneyed' sat around casually over Black Labels in their up-market clothes. This was a restaurant? Norman asked Sandra. A dining club. She had never looked lovelier. A shirt of slate-coloured silk complemented her eyes which rarely left his face. A waiter brought menus. On Norman's there were no prices. "You're my guest," Sandra explained. "I love you." They ordered asparagus, which was out of season and lamb – whose degree of rareness Sandra discussed with a seriousness Norman had thought applied only to beef – and at a given signal, moved to a plush sofa in the darkened dining-room where they sat side by side against a wall. Their appetites were as attuned as their bodies. The asparagus, with its accompanying sauce, was eaten without words. Norman did not remember eating the lamb. Sandra asked for a slice of chocolate cake – a speciality of the chef – with two forks, with an assurance Norman would not dare to assume even in the Wimpy in Golder's Green, and commanded its inundation with cream from a silver jug, with an aplomb which, even with his new found assertiveness, Norman knew he would never achieve. They had coffee with cape gooseberries thickly encrusted with icing sugar, and although Sandra had protested, he had looked over her shoulder when she signed the bill, to find that it came to almost as much as he earned, sometimes, in a week. He tried not to let it cast a shadow. To ignore the affirmation that he was not as others – others Sandra and her escorts to whom money was a commodity to be lightheartedly disbursed – round the room. He had been living in a world of make-believe at which he had not protested when initiated into it by Sandra. He re-entered it, not protesting now, when she stood up to take him back for their last night at her flat.

"Sorry about the apple cake…" Kitty said.

They had squandered little of the night in sleep.

"I know you like peaches."

In the morning Sandra had said: "I must go to Harrods. They have both grown out of their socks."

"Norman!" Aunty Kitty was holding out his plate on which there were two yellow domes.

He had felt resentful. Of Hilton and Milton and their need for socks. Displaced.

"I'll make one next week," Kitty said.

Norman stared at her.

"An apple cake. Which night will you come?"

Sixteen

Freda watched Harry like a cat a mouse. She was making herself ill. She had lost weight. Harry had sent her to the doctor who had confirmed his suspicions that her bizarre behaviour could be directly ascribed to her 'time of life', to the 'change'. She did not confide in the doctor, who was their friend and who played golf with Harry, did not tell him what was troubling her. He had given her pills which she did not take, advised Harry to keep an eye on her. They were keeping an eye on each other. Into the large house which they had filled with their harmony, their contentment in the simple pleasure of each other's presence, a chill had crept, a shade, shattering the warmth which had nothing to do with the central heating which emanated from the gas boiler and which was pumped into the house through vents in every room, but with love. Like an extra cardigan Freda wore her suspicion.

There had been another mauve letter. She kept it in her drawer. Beneath her underwear. 'Harry Goldstien is my son's father'. A boy. Harry had always wanted a son. He'd said so in the early days when it had been a subject for discussion. A son to play cricket with in the large garden and later golf, in which Harry would instruct him; a son who would accompany him to synagogue where he would become *barmitzvah* and who would follow him into the silver business, which had been Harry's father's, old man Goldstein's, a son... With another woman who was scarcely literate and whose notepaper was mauve. Freda watched Harry's every step. When he went out in the morning the lie of his tie, the crease of his trousers as he set off for the station, the degree of attentiveness with which he kissed her goodbye in the mornings, and with which he greeted her at night. Lately his solicitousness had increased, and it seemed to Freda more to confirm his guilt, his clandestine liaison with the writer of the mauve letters, than to be brought about by the doctor's injunction for vigilance.

She wondered why she had been so foolish for so long. How she could have been. Harry often worked late. Clients, he said, wanting to sell silver or to buy. It wasn't unknown for him to go out at night to their homes, to value their crumb scoops, their Birmingham tea services and their Sheffield cake baskets. Now Freda wanted to know *precisely* where he had been. He had to describe to her the soup ladles and the caddy spoons, the sugar basins and the sauce boats. He could have been making them up. He could have been making up the two nights a week he spent at the youth club, coaching the youngsters in table tennis, organising debates. Freda went to spy on him, called for him at the synagogue in the car, ostensibly to save him the walk home which he enjoyed. "Harry!" she'd heard someone call, recognising her, "Your wife's outside." "Is anything wrong?" Harry had said, worried, as he'd got into the car. Freda shook her head.

Everything was wrong. She had nightmares at night, and day dreams by day, which displaced the family she had created by the immaculate conception of her imagination. In her kitchen now she saw Harry's son whose eyes and smile owed nothing to her genes. In bed she turned her back on Harry inhibited by the fact that he had made love to another woman and by the thought of the child he had fathered. Harry accepted her apparent loss of interest in him as confirmation of her menopause as it had been explained to him. The more concern he showed for Freda the more she shrank from him. The more he pleaded that she confide her wretchedness to him, the more she cried inside. Where she had waited eagerly for his nightly key in the lock she now dreaded his treacherous step over the threshold she kept so brightly polished. She searched his briefcase and his pockets for a sign of his perfidy. She followed him to town, to his shop, peering through the window with its salvers and its cream jugs to make sure he was there. On the day he was not – she had stood in the street until her back ached – she had rushed round to Kitty not knowing where else to turn. Had stood on her sister-in-law's mat with an airmail letter, which Kitty had picked up and put on the hall table beneath a book to go back to the library.

At Kitty's kitchen table, over the coffee Kitty had made, and the marble cake which Kitty had put in front of her and which she did not touch, Freda told of Harry's betrayal, and of the bombshell of the mauve letter, which had arrived to shatter her life together with Kitty's postcard from Eilat. "Harry?" Kitty said. *Harry*, who would not say boo to a goose! She could not believe it. Freda could not believe it either. "Why don't you ask him?" Kitty said. She knew the answer. Freda's life, bound up in Harry, in whom she had invested her entire stock of dreams, the sum total of her love, might have been disintegrating, but she was neither strong enough, nor willing, to face the final *coup de grâce*.

"I'm going mad," Freda said, lighting a cigarette, and crying on to the marble cake. "I don't know what to do."

Kitty put her arm round her sister-in-law and tried to think what Sydney would have said, what he would have advised. Recalling Sydney and her own widowhood she thought how lucky Freda was to have Harry alive, and by her side, despite the mauve letters, and that a good marriage was worth all the tea in China, and that there were transgressions – although she was not completely sure that Sydney would have agreed – that must sometimes be overlooked.

"Men are funny sometimes..." Kitty said. She knew that there were men, religious men, in Rabbi Magnus' congregation who had transgressed – sometimes it was public knowledge – and been accepted by their families again.

She was saved from further comment by Addie, who had a key, and who came limping – although her plaster cast had been taken off – into the flat. She looked at Freda's tear-stained face.

"Not interrupting anything am I?" She didn't wait for an answer but sat down at the table and eyed the cake. "I wouldn't mind a piece, Kitty. The plumber's come – I'd almost given up – and the banging goes right through my head."

By the time Addie had gone, having regaled them with the vagaries of her pipes, and the fact that she had had no hot water for three days, Freda had composed herself.

"You can at least ask Harry where he was this morning," Kitty said. "Set your mind at rest."

"You won't tell anyone?" Freda said. She was powdering her face, covering the stains of her tears, at the mirror in the hall.

Kitty looked at the corner of the airmail letter which poked out from beneath the books and which she would read when Freda had gone.

"Who would I tell?" These days she was the keeper of her own conscience.

"The family," Freda said, tying the belt of her fur-lined raincoat, meaning Mirrie and Beatty. She did not want them to know of her humiliation, her disgrace.

Dear Kitty,

The bridal gown sounds fine and you were right to give it to your friend. Paris was a great idea but it would have been out of your hands, anyway, who needs it? When your letter came it was like sunshine brightening up my day. My studio is across the hall from my apartment. I came out of it ill-humoured – nothing had gone right – and went down to the mail-box. I rarely bother. No one writes me.

When I saw your letter the whole world opened. I didn't read it immediately, not till I'd washed up, as if you'd come in person to visit me. You say you aren't much of a letter writer. Fancy sentences don't make a letter like it's not the canvas and a few dollars worth of colours that make a picture. I could really see your Sabbath table with the *challahs* and the silver candlesticks – Sarah sounds a grand girl – and Rachel going with you to the bridal store like a polar bear! It's the same here on the sidewalks, like a parade of trappers, kids dressed up as Eskimos and Afghans, Alaskan squaws and Transylvanian peasants. I guess they're trying to say something, to protect themselves, with indescribable layers of clothing, from their view of the world. Can you blame them?

I said I would tell you something about myself. Kitty are you listening? I thought they would listen when we came out of the camps, that the whole world would be waiting, with open arms, into which those of us who made it would run, to annul the injustice, expunge the crimes, to which we would testify. I came to England first and opened my mouth to relate events that would make Dante's *Inferno* look like a Broadway comedy. To tell of acts perpetrated upon human beings – whose only crime was that they were Jews or gypsies – so awesome that there were no words that would not diminish them, when I was stopped with a pat on the shoulder – as if my war had been spent in a peaceful town in Silesia – and the news that it had been tough in England too – five inches of water in the bath and dried eggs. America was no different. There are 210,000,000 people living in this country. Who's interested in the Jews? People get upset about Nigeria or Guatemala. They want to build a new Cuba and get very upset about the blacks or the Puerto Ricans, but the Jews... We love you, they said, but we don't want to hear. I shut my mouth and have not opened it again.

I felt *ashamed* of my experiences, as if it was some kind of *disgrace* about which I must keep quiet. Others did not. They are much in demand now for whistle-stop tours, to answer the questions of the second generation, the students of history – what do you think about? (expecting the answer 'immortality' instead of 'soup'!); to explain that those responsible for massacring men and women, for tearing little children by their hair from their mothers' arms, for firing their guns at living targets without hesitation, and without guilt, were *not* hooligans (a special breed of monster drawn from a gutter society of social misfits) but men who held degrees in medicine and philosophy and the fine arts, who were bank managers, store keepers and real estate brokers, loved music and their children and went home, when they'd perpetrated their day's evil to their wives.

If I wanted to keep silent, I hear you ask, why did I not remove the affidavit from my arm as others did? Without it, Kitty, how would I know, that although the nightmare which had robbed me of my past was over, I had not been dreaming? America has been good to me. I came to the United States with three dollars in my pocket. The Hebrew Immigrant Aid Society gave me ten dollars – I spent it on candy and on cokes which I had never tasted. They gave me clothes and helped me through school, but to lead a well adjusted life you have to have common memories with the people who are your friends. I live among Americans, and the bridge between their backgrounds and mine cannot be crossed, so I stay an outsider and commune with the easel in my studio. Last year I had an exhibition. The critics liked my pictures but no one wanted to hang them on their walls – they found them too uncomfortable. I work all day until the light goes – an unending vomit of experience of which I wonder will I ever be purged. Don't answer a miserable old man, you

don't have to, but I shall look in the mail-box in the hope
that you are still listening to your correspondent, Maurice
Morgenthau.

PS. Glad Addie is out of plaster. Tell her to take care. MM.

Addie could take care of herself. Kitty did not pass the message
on. She did not show Addie the drawing Maurice had enclosed
of her own distraught face looking out over the valley through
the window of the cable car, nor convey the thoughts his letter
had evoked, that her terrors – of which with his sketches he
made gentle frun – were as nothing compared with the terrors
he had faced, and that when measured against the plight of the
Jews in Germany and Czechoslovakia, Hungary and Poland,
which Maurice had remarkably survived, even Freda's problems
were negligible.

"We want it to be the best wedding anyone's ever been to,"
Hettie Klopman said.
   They sat in Hettie's sitting-room, Kitty and Hettie and Mrs
Klopman and Unterman, who wore his *cappel* in the house,
discussing 'ambiance'.
   Hettie had got over the clash of wills concerning Rachel's
wedding dress, although Kitty had been aware of an
undercurrent of vexation – as if she were the fly in the ointment
of the 'Klopman' wedding – when Hettie had invited her to
discuss arrangements with the caterer. When she had arrived,
Kitty, by way of a peace offering, had described to Hettie and old
Mrs Klopman the dress which Rika Snowman had suggested.
   "Don't you think lace is a little bit…overdone?" Hettie had
said. "You see it in the windows of all the department stores."
   "There's lace and lace…" Kitty said.
   "There'll be a lot of fashion people there," Hettie said, and by
her tone Kitty knew that the subject of the wedding dress would
be an irritation which was not going to go away. Because of it

she had agreed to compromise – "do whatever you like," Rachel had finally said – on the question of the bridesmaids. Debbie and Lisa, appropriately dressed, were to walk behind Rachel up the aisle to be followed at a discreet distance in *evening*, but not bridal wear, by Patrick's three cousins from Leeds.

"Evening?" Kitty had said.

Sydney had not approved of evening weddings.

"Dinner and Ball," Hettie had said.

"There'll be people coming from Dublin," Mrs Klopman said.

"What about Florida? And Israel? Must make it worth their while," Hettie said. "And what we really wanted," she addressed Kitty, "before Unterman comes, is to discuss colours, for under the *chuppah* – we must have a theme – so we don't all clash. Mine has to be finalised before we go away."

"All?" Kitty said. It was the custom of the parents of the bride and the parents of the groom to stand beside them beneath the marriage canopy.

"I suit lavender," Mrs Klopman said. "And I'll have to have a chair."

"And my mother's blonde. So anything blue-ey…"

"Under the *chuppah*?" Kitty said weakly.

She and Sydney had always shuddered at the weddings at which grandparents and other relatives, whose place was not beneath the marriage canopy, threatened to destroy its simple dignity by overcrowding. In place of Sydney, Juda, who would shortly be giving away his own daughter, would give away Rachel. Kitty had already asked him. There were no grandparents – although Kitty thought with regret what *nachas* her own parents, who had had only known Rachel as a baby, would have derived from the day – on the Shelton side. The *chuppah*, supported by its four poles which traditionally referred to the chamber reserved for the bride on her wedding day, was going to look decidedly lopsided.

"I thought a print," Kitty said. "Something summery."

"For the *evening*," Hettie had said, as if Kitty had suggested appearing in a bathing suit. "Herbert thought paper taffeta for me, with shoestring straps – I'll be like a walnut after the cruise – with a little jacket I can take off, for the *shul*."

"I don't like straps…" Kitty said.

She saw Hettie's face darken.

"For myself, I mean," she added hastily.

"I thought of something yellowy, for you," Hettie said, "then the whole thing will meld."

"Meld?" Kitty said.

"Mine will be turquoise…" Hettie opened her handbag. "I brought a piece to show you. I've got an aquamarine the same colour…"

"I was thinking of turquoise," Kitty said.

"Well, we can't have the same! That would look silly."

"I can't wear yellow," Kitty said, "not with my skin."

"Not yellow," Hettie said. "More gold-ey…"

"Not even gold."

Kitty saw Hetty exchange glances with Mrs Klopman.

"My material's been ordered," Hettie said firmly. "Herbert's having it dyed. Turquoise…"

Kitty said nothing.

"…I'm wearing an osprey to match!"

Seventeen

Norman, like a caged bear, waited for Sandra whom he needed like the air he breathed. She had been busy; with Hilton and Milton and their new school; arranging teachers and times for their lessons on the cello and the violin. Busy with her sister-in-law, Arnold's sister, who had brought them over from South Africa and who was staying with Sandra in the new flat. Now that the boys were home Norman could not spend the night there. Sandra would not let him. She thought it wise that Hilton and Milton – not recovered from the trauma of her divorce from Arnold – were spared his presence in their mother's bed. Having delivered her sister-in-law to the airport, and arranged a sitter for her sons, she was coming straight to Norman. In his mother's house. He never thought of it as his.

In anticipation of Sandra's coming he had cleaned it from top to toe. Hoovered and dusted and shaken rugs, becoming increasingly aware of its shabbiness, seeing it through Sandra's eyes. He had put the kettle on the New World cooker – three times now – turning it off when it whistled, had taken the gold-rimmed china from the break-front cabinet, arranged biscuits on a doily, as he had seen his mother do.

It was raining. Each time Norman heard the hiss of a car on the wet road outside, he went to the window hoping to see Sandra's coupé in the light of the street lamps. When he did not he sat down on the sofa, covering the discolouration on the tobacco brown, uncut moquette – where his mother's invalid food had slipped from her hand – with a cushion and wishing it were white knobbly wool and that the room was like Sandra's, light and bright. He was wearing one of his new suits and had wished too late, as he made his bed with the coarse wartime sheets with the utility label, which his mother had bought with her coupons, that he had thought to replace them.

"She must take you as you are," Kitty had once said over dinner, when he had discussed with her some way in which he was striving to improve himself for Sandra. And indeed she did. It was Norman who was dissatisfied with himself. Sandra had helped him, more than she would ever know, to stand up for his rights, assert himself in situations where previously he would have given way, but she had put no finger on the emptiness of his inner being which even Norman himself could not touch. In his own eyes, although he was already using his return ticket, he was still a small boy at his mother's skirts, clinging on to them, unable to function on his own. He put on his act, his other self, like a coat of armour as Sandra had instructed him, but felt, at bottom, that Mr Monty at the office was the grown up – for all Norman's new found assurance – and he the child, and that the world was the arbiter against which Norman was endowed with no real will of his own. He did not hear Sandra ring the bell. She did not ring it. She tapped on the window – Sandra like – and he thought it was the barren tendrils of the wisteria blown by the wind. Then she called, through the letter-box: "Norman!"

She rushed into the narrow hall, into its dark corridor with the oval oak mirror, like a scarlet streak in her wool cape, and into his arms.

Something was wrong. Had gone wrong. Norman lay on his back, with his arms behind his head and Sandra beside him, and stared at the ceiling, with its unsightly mark where he had once waged war against a summer mosquito, and tried to go back over the last two hours in an effort to discover where the chemistry, which had previously precipitated such sparklers and rockets, such heights and depths, such mutual pleasure and tender understanding, had failed.

Sandra had refused both his tea and his biscuits so painstakingly set out, and had produced a bottle of champagne which Norman had opened to celebrate their reunion. In her scarlet dress she illuminated the sitting-room. In her glow, the down-at-heel sofa, the dismal paint, the tired curtains, receded.

"I've missed you, Norman." The red of her lips with her intimate knowledge of him echoed exactly the pleats which moved with her body.

"Is this your mother?" Sandra picked up the tortoiseshell frame from the nest of tables, to look at Dolly – protesting at the Brighton sun – against the shingle and the pier in happier days. "Was she ill for a long time?"

She had never been well. Not since his father had died and the chronicle of her manifold complaints had been effaced by her final indisposition. He could see his mother now – in the chair in which Sandra had settled – small, complaining.

"Come upstairs," Norman held out his hands to Sandra. It had been a long time. In his bedroom where the bed was too small – he had never moved into his mother's, not liking to – the springs vociferous, they had sought each other out. For Norman the quest had been unavailing.

"Too much champagne," Sandra said into his shoulder.

But it was not the champagne. It was his mother standing at the wooden bed-end, pulling the faded curtains, opening the door – 'Time to get up Norman!' – knocking on the dividing wall.

"It's this house," Norman said. He looked at Sandra, like a jewel on his pillow.

"It's a nice house," Sandra said.

Driving to the Day Centre, Kitty thought neither about the lunch, baked *Klops* – anything made with mincemeat always went down well – which she was going to prepare for the old people, nor about the problems of the family, nor of Maurice's letters, each of which revealed to her a little more of the uncommunicative man, but about Rachel's wedding, with which, despite herself, she was like Hettie Klopman becoming increasingly preoccupied.

The session with Unterman at Hettie's had been prolonged. The earnestness of the discussion, the attention to detail, was, Kitty thought, more appropriate to some national spectacle – a coronation or the Lord Mayor's Show – than to the few hours in the King Solomon Suite where the 400 guests – mainly on the Klopman side – would celebrate the marriage of Rachel to Patrick.

The allocation of the invitations had been made clear from the start. The observation, that this allocation was more or less in line with the financial contribution Kitty insisted upon making, as Sydney had wished, was never actually voiced; Hettie's opinion concerning the format of invitations it was her privilege, as mother of the bride, to send out, was. Kitty proposed a simple copperplate, identical to Carol's except that this time, without Sydney, it would be '*Mrs* Kitty Shelton' who requested the pleasure of 'your company at the marriage of *her* daughter to Dr Patrick Klopman…'

By the silence that followed Hettie's reading of it Kitty knew that there was something wrong. Nothing was right. The black lettering on the plain white card was considered inadequate. A *gold* card, Hettie thought, with a turquoise satin bow as precursor of the general colour scheme – the *theme* of the wedding – with raised gilt lettering, and a deckle edge, and a printed, stamped, reply card. Then there was the wording. Many of the Klopman guests, particularly those from abroad, would never have heard of Kitty. Jointly with Kitty, Hettie and Herbert must indubitably request the pleasure… And what about Patrick's address together with Rachel's at the foot of the missive? Why should the bridegroom be forgotten? Kitty was non-committal. She would ask... No she would not ask Sydney. She would discuss it with Rachel who although she was the *raison d'être* of all the controversy would look at her as if she were mad.

She *could* discuss it with Juda whose discreet invitations for Vanessa's wedding were already out, but what would be the use? Since it was early days Kitty decided to let the matter rest. Unterman, whose diplomacy was worthy of the United Nations, and who knew on which side his bread was buttered, to whom Hettie had appealed, said either invitation would be acceptable, and after all, what really mattered was the quality of the function itself. Which brought them on to décor which was what this early confrontation was about.

The turquoise and gold colour scheme having been decided upon (by Hettie), the next question was its interpretation. Unterman waxed lyrical and tossed off in turn, for their considerations, a Venetian Palazzo, a Moorish tent, and the Royal Palace of the Queen of Sheba at which point Kitty, who would not have been surprised had he suggested coloured lights and spiral staircases or doves flying out of gilded cages, made a mental resolution to stick to her guns over the invitations lest her family and friends had doubts about her sanity. The turquoise and gold theme was to be homogenous. From the gold ribbons on the bridal car (Herbert's Rolls with its personalised number plates) in which Rachel would arrive at the synagogue, to the flowers and napery, china and booklets – containing the seven blessings and grace after meals – place cards and book matches, which would be inscribed with Rachel's and Patrick's names. The wedding was to be Hettie's big moment. Her chance to shine.

That much was obvious to Kitty as Hettie came up with ideas – personal, and what she considered unique, touches – which she bounced upon Unterman with an enthusiasm which, as the time dragged on and the caterer started looking discreetly at his watch, did not wane. Hettie was not, Kitty thought, regardless of her bright exterior, a happy woman. Despite her indulgent husband, her worldly wealth, she seemed somehow dissatisfied, and the handicapped son could not have been much help. If her moment of glory was to be Patrick's wedding, Kitty would not deny it to her. She only sought to temper its excesses and to prevent herself being trampled upon in the stampede for the turquoise and the gold.

The dinner, in this opening encounter with Unterman, a past master of epicurean banquets, had not been discussed. Unterman was bidden only to apply his mind to the question, and to devise for the next meeting an array and variety of dishes which were as delicate in their composition as they were original in concept. There were to be none of his filled pineapple halves or melon boats masted by a cherry and a slice of orange on a stick, Hettie said, followed – because it was summer – by the inevitable strawberries and cream.

Kitty was intrigued to see what Unterman would pull out of his hat, out of his briefcase which had been filled with glossy photographs of the various interiors he had at one time or another created for the King Solomon Suite, and menus of past triumphs. Stopping at a zebra crossing for a woman with a pushchair, she switched her mind from increasingly persistent thoughts of Rachel and her wedding, and concentrated upon the reality of the Day Centre and the *Klops* in which images of turquoise and gold seraglios had little place.

The Jewish Day Centre cared on a non-residential basis for the old and the lonely whose plight, in a world which boasted advanced communications and space travel, had paradoxically been accentuated. Sequestered in cars, isolated before television sets, suspended in high-rise flats, the basic need of human beings for contact and companionship had been overlooked. For six hours, twice a week, those lucky enough to have reached the top of the waiting list for a place at the Centre could associate

with their peer group, paint, sculpt, exercise, dance, listen to
music or to visiting speakers, or simply exchange reminiscences
of lives which had once been satisfying, of families to whose
periphery they had now been removed.

The old people were cared for by an indispensable and
selfless army of volunteers, whose devotion to the Day Centre
provided, in many cases, appropriate therapy for their own
repressed needs.

Kitty parked her car in the side street behind the mini-bus
which under the aegis of the cheerful driver and one of the
volunteers was discharging its load. It was not quick. Arthritis
and cataracts and spongy lungs and hardened arteries made
merciless inroads which were painfully evident, as the senior
citizens with their sticks and their walking frames, took hands
and arms and negotiated the steps of the bus and the steps of the
building and felt the icy hiatus of the street pierce their clothes
and their skin – which was no longer elastic – to seek out their
tired, their aching bones. There was not one of them who had
not a story to tell of happier days, of partners who had pre-
deceased them, of better times. There was a tendency to lump
them together – what was it Maurice said about lumping people
together? – as some of the younger helpers tended to do, to
think of them as 'old people', a separate breed, to invalidate
them as persons, when they had in their time been husbands
and fathers and sons and lovers and professional and
businessmen and artists and musicians in which roles they had
received, in varying degrees, the respect of their families and of
the world. In the lounges of the Day Centre they reassured
themselves. With tremorous hands they exhibited cherished
photographs, Kodacoloured reminders that life had held
pleasures other than the rivers of tea with the home-made cakes
dispensed by the ladies, the warbled rendering of 'Those were
the Days', and a seat in front of the small screen; that it had not
always been pinned hips, panaceas and pension books. It is you

and I, Kitty thought, and life, which cruelly and very often, had a twist in her tail.

Many of those to whom the Day Centre was a lifeline thrown out twice a week had known other days. You heard them talk. '…two rooms like little boxes when I'd been used to space…' 'I was always in the garden, now I have to make do with a window-sill…' '…I gave it all to my daughter…what do I want with silver…?' '…my son invited me to live with them but the last thing I wanted was to be a burden…' If these were burdens, Kitty thought, what of the next generation, the single parents, the feminists with their fight for independence – as if every human being were not by the very nature of his existence dependent – where would they be with their slogans, their battle cries raised in their selfish prime? Where, when their faculties diminished and their bodies failed them, would they turn for solace? Who would there be to comfort them but an impersonal and overtaxed State.

Kitty took off her coat in the Volunteers' Room, and with it shed thoughts of Hettie Klopman and the wedding, and of Norman and Freda, and even those of Sydney and of Maurice and his letters, and went out into the hall where the old people were arriving and being given assistance with their various outer garments. A hand stopped her on the way to the kitchens.

"I didn't show you the photograph of my great-grandchildren…"

Kitty had already admired them. Twice, She did not remind Mrs Mendel, who could remember the court in the East End of London, where 89 years ago she had been born, but not the events of yesterday.

"Can you spare me a minute?" Mr Spitzer said. He was originally from Poland and had been coming to the Day Centre for many years and spent most of his time locked in verbal battle with his arch enemy Solly Kischka who had been born in Lithuania. A coronary infarct over Kitty's barley soup had sent

Solly to hospital, since when Mr Spitzer, deprived of his sparring partner, had been like a button off a coat.

"What news of Kischka?"

"He's making progress," Kitty said, "I expect he'll have to take it easy."

"A *Litvak*!..." Mr Spitzer – who would miss his companion on the outings to the West End and to Westcliff – said fiercely, "When did he ever do anything else?"

It was one of the hazards of the Day Centre. New friends and proxy families replaced those of a lifetime who had died or were no longer interested. Romance had been known to blossom. The severing of these terminal attachments was hard to bear.

"Why don't you send him a card?" Kitty suggested. "Ask Mavis." The mechanics of cards and messages and stamps and post boxes required assistance.

"I only *enquired*," Mr Spitzer said.

There were other restraining hands. "How's Addie?" "Did you see my son on television?" "How's the wedding?" "I left my stick here, I've asked everybody..." "Hello Kitty." "What's for lunch?"

In the kitchens the waste-pipe had frozen, Julie Pearl's daughter had run off with a pop singer and the meat hadn't arrived for the *Klops*. At noon the old people would sit down for their dinner, the highlight of their day. The waste-pipe, Julie Pearl's daughter and the butcher notwithstanding, Kitty thought, come hell or high water, they would not be disappointed.

Eighteen

Dear Kitty,

Your letters are like music – a spiritual food for which there is no substitute and without which life would be a mistake. (Nietzche not MM!) It's good that your classes have started again. That exaggerator Berlioz (both in his music and his lifestyle), with his incredible ear, and the tight-assed (excuse me) Ravel, were interesting studies, but I'm happy your term begins with Beethoven. The F minor is not my favourite but is both exciting (esp. last movement), and prophetic of the later quartets it took him fourteen years to get around to. I will listen to it and think of my fastidious Kitty on Monday nights in the Performance Studio, where the odours of the previous dance class still linger!

You ask me how it is I am lonely and if I am happy? I have been lonely since Dr Mengele put my mother (she was forty-six years old) and my father in a cattle truck (I thought how nice for them they wouldn't have to walk!) and took my lame kid brother from the bunk where we slept together (I have a permanent cold shoulder in the spot where he lay) for his experiments in genetics. I am lonely when I see families with brothers and sisters and parents and grandparents (sometimes *two* sets!), a ring of uncles and aunts and hordes of cousins. I am lonely in that

I have no one to love, no one to live for. This is not the same, Kitty, as being *alone* – I can live with my records and my books, I don't need people around – which for an artist has two advantages. The first in being with himself; the second is *not* being with others. As for happiness, human beings do not need to be happy, nor can they be. Like other Jews I have a strong will to live (Got knows where we get it from, can it *only* be a reaction to persecution?), to paint my pictures (not because I think they are of value, an artist unless he is an imbecile never knows – Virgil on his deathbed wanted the Aeneid buried!), to testify, to bear witness to what is no longer.

Don't think I mean to change the world. Men do not change nor do they learn anything (read any day's newspapers) and no one has the right to speak for the dead or make them speak, as every day for some second's fraction they speak to me; a can on the sidewalk brings back discarded canisters of cyclone B, flower beds (the Nazis loved nature and orderliness) and birch trees the entrance to Auschwitz (men and women from every European country passed under that tree). For me 'Canada' is not a country but camp-jargon for the barracks, where they stored the loot stolen from our numbers – calculated in men's suits, children's shoes, in spectacles and shaving brushes and artificial limbs – and 'Mexico' the woman's section. I have to blink hard to restore the proper meanings to 'haircut' and to 'bath', and even now look for flotsam – buttons and bits of paper – in the bottom of my soup bowl.

You were right to give way about the invitations if it makes Hettie happy – what difference do a few words make – and to stick to your guns over your dress – never mind the feather she had dyed! So there'll be two turquoise dresses. Rachel will still get married. Vanessa's wedding sounds very grand. It'll be a rehearsal for you.

Glad you're going to Carol and Alec for Purim. Your grandchildren sound adorable – send me a photo Kitty, and one of yourself. Purim is one of the happiest holidays of the Jewish year. Will you go to synagogue to hear the *Megillah*? I remember, in Frankfurt, going with my mother and my brother and my three sisters, and stamping our feet and making lots of noise whenever the word Haman was spoken, so that you could not hear his name. The wicked Haman is still remembered. I wonder how long will Hitler be – and Goering and Goebbels and Streicher and Mengele...you see I *am* obsessed. But seriously, the destruction of the temples (Ninth of *Av*), the Fast commemorating the breach made by the Romans in the wall of Jerusalem (Fast of *Tammuz*), Nebuchadnezzar's siege... Where is the Fast for my Uncle Oskar who was an engineer at the Vienna Technical Institute, for my grandfather who conducted opera in Berlin (Otto Klemperer, your Thomas Beecham, Monet and Rodin were his friends), for my uncle (my mother's brother) Dr Felix Stein, for my Aunts, Leah and Lottie, for my pious father Dov, for my darling mother (she was beautiful Kitty), for the children on the street of the suburb where we lived... WHERE IS THEIR DAY? Don't write me any more Kitty. It's not good for you. I'll look at your photograph (don't forget to send it) and remember – Ofira and Masada, happy times. Look after yourself. Maurice

PS. In the Heiligenstadt testament Beethoven writes: 'Sometimes I have been driven by my desire to seek the company of other human beings, but what humiliation when someone, standing beside me, heard a flute from afar off when I *heard nothing*, or when someone heard a shepherd singing and again I *heard nothing*! Such experiences have brought me close to despair...'

PPS. Wasn't it Thoreau who said: 'Most people lead lives of quiet desperation?'

PPPS. Did you know that the Encyclopedia Judaica lists a hundred special Purims ranging from a Purim of Algiers to a Purim of Vidin (Bulgaria).

PPPPS. I am not such a lobster-eating *dumkopf* as you thought. MM.

"If we'd had a son," Freda said, "a boy. What would you have called him?"

Harry was getting dressed. The snows had melted from the golf course and the naked greens outside the window waited patiently for the approaching spring. Freda was trying to trap him. She was always trying to trap him, to find out to what manner of woman he had given his seed, where he was secreting the fruit of his loins. There had been other mauve letters. There was getting to be quite a pile of them in her underwear drawer. They were becoming vindicative. Harry, they said, would be named. Freda had tried to trace the writer from the postmark but it was never the same. Hammersmith, Ealing, one from Barkingside after which Freda had been sure. It had come after she had gone to Bond Street, to the shop, to look for Harry to check that he was there.

"I came up to town this morning," she'd said. "I called at the shop. Where were you?" "A client," he'd said, "in Redbridge." "You didn't tell me you were going out." They told each other everything. Freda had thought they did. "A silver valuation. It came up unexpectedly." "What silver?" "Silver." "*What* silver?" Freda persisted. Harry had looked at her. Searching for his alibi. "Tea service, entrée dishes, one rather nice casket, as a matter of fact, Omar Ramsden…" "Show me!" Freda had said. "Show you what?" "The valuation." "You must be joking," Harry said. "No." Harry played for time. "Why on earth should you want to

see the valuation for some old lady's silver. It's nothing special."
"I just do." "Freda, I'm worried about you." Changing the
subject. "Where is it?" "What?" "The valuation." "In the shop,
Miriam is typing it. I'll bring it home." Crafty. "I'll come to town
with you. I want to look for shoes." "Please yourself."

And she had gone with him to town, accompanied Harry
along a waking Bond Street whose face was being washed and
windows dressed, to his life. Freda had waited, crying silent
tears, while he unlocked the door and turned off the burglar
alarm, stood by the counter patterned by the diamond winter
sun which came through the grille, watched as he searched
through papers in the office at the back of the shop.

"Freda, this is madness," Harry called. "What's got into
you?" "The valuation," Freda demanded. "Perhaps Miriam's
taken it home with her. She does sometimes." Freda looked in
the show-case at the grape scissors and the wine labels which
paid for their oil central heating, and their summer holidays,
and their subscription to the golf club. "Here it is!"

Freda had been trembling. On Harry's stiff notepaper with its
logo of the British Antique Dealers' Association, in Harry's
meticulous hand. 'Mrs Eva Solomon, Applegarth Drive.
Valuation for Insurance. Victorian Silver Pin-Tray 1887...
Silver mounted cut glass claret jug... 'Lighthouse' sugar caster...
Silver casket with rock crystal ornamentation...' "What is it
Freda?" Harry had said amid the wasters and the basting
spoons, amid the hip-flasks and the fruit knives which, with
their mother-of-pearl handles, reposed in their blue velvet nests.
And Freda could not say. Not for the life of her. Could not voice
the thoughts which had taken her over and which were
reinforced at regular intervals by the mauve letters. Harry had
put his arms round her, then taken his medallions and his sugar
tongs from the safe and sent her off to look for her shoes.

Now, from her bed, the morning song of the birds not
cheering her, Freda watched Harry brush imagined fluff from
the new suit he had had made by a tailor in Conduit Street,

whose cloth she had selected from a swatch he had brought home, select a tie with care. She could see what the writer of the mauve letters saw in him. An ageing but still handsome lover. A caring and uncomplicated man.

On one occasion Harry had brought up one of the mauve letters himself with her morning tea. Laid it on the bed. "Aren't you going to open it?" Freda had feigned sleep. "Eileen," she lied, her mouth dry, mentioning the daily help. "...She's on holiday." "In Battersea!" "With her sister. Spending a few days..." Harry was looking into the mirror. New suit. New tie. She had bought it for *Chanukkah*. On a Thursday.

"Where are you going?" Freda said, not properly awake. She had taken a sleeping pill. Harry smiled at her. Crossed to the bed. Rumpled her hair. Fobbed off. Like a child. Oh God. A child.

"Where?" Her voice flirted with hysteria.

"Vanessa's wedding," Harry said.

"You'd think it was royalty!" Beatty said in the unmoving reception lines in Claridges. "I'll pass out from the heat in a minute, and I don't like the look of Freda – she's like a stick..."

"Vanessa looked lovely." Kitty tried to change the subject, nurturing Freda's secret.

"...She needs an X-ray. I've never seen her so thin."

"She's seen the doctor."

"Doctors!" Beatty shuffled forward an inch. The line was four deep, emerged from the furs and the overcoats in the cloakroom. "You have to *tell* them. They want to move Leon to a geriatric ward. *Geriatric*. I said over my dead body..."

"I expect they need the bed," Josh said from his mother's elbow.

"I'd rather look after him at home..."

"You couldn't..." Mirrie said, she was as small as her sister Beatty was large. As easy going as Beatty was demanding.

"They'll walk all over you if you let them," Beatty said. She peered round the side of the queue." It'll be finished by the time we get in." Her feet were spilling over her patent leather shoes. "It was the same with the kosher meals. Stone cold. Every day. I had to speak to Sister. I said, listen dear, I know you're very busy – they work like nobody's business – but even if a person's ill he doesn't have to eat cold food…"

The line stretched along the tapestry carpets beneath the chandeliers. Standing in it, beneath the torrent of Beatty's verbiage, the waterfall of her words, Kitty thought that Maurice would not have stood in it and that, in their wedding finery they were in line not to shake hands with Juda and Leonora and Vanessa in her tiara, but had been 'selected'…she found herself thinking like Maurice, identifying with the terrible truths of his letters.

Addie had brought the last one in with its drawing of Kitty supine on the waters of the Dead Sea, intercepting the postman. "So who do you know in America?" She had turned it over inquisitively, examined the envelope, the initials MM and the New York address – done everything but opened it. "A cousin. Of Sydney's." A duet of lies. Kitty had read it when Addie had gone, climbing with Maurice's parents on to the cattle truck, passing, with her suitcase, under the birch tree. It required a leap. Of the imagination. She had not known anti-Semitism. Once in a department store she had been trying on hats when she'd overheard an assistant, holding a mirror for a tweed-suited matron up from the countries, "Not that one Madam, it's a Jewish hat. They buy them for the Festivals." She'd wondered should she call the buyer. Complain. She had done nothing. An innocent remark. In Germany, in the thirties, the Nazis had innocently decreed that the Jews were beyond the pale of citizenship, that they were really not human beings at all.

Kitty found herself waiting for Maurice's letters, drawing sustenance from them. She had gone to the library – where generally she filled out cards requesting undemanding novels, recommended by her bridge friends, or the Sunday reviews – and asked a girl behind a double-decker of ticketed books to direct her to the works of Thoreau.

Haltingly, a few pages at a time, at night, she had begun to follow Henry David Thoreau's existence in the woods of Massachusetts, his determination to reduce life to its lowest terms and find its essence, as she searched for the essence of her strange correspondent. Having shed her clothes and her cares concerning the small dilemmas of her daily life, and of the Day Centre, and Addie's grumbles – her ankle was still troubling her – and Rachel's wedding, for which Kitty had started to compile a guest list – including, then striking out again, friends and relatives who over the years had drifted away, or with whom she had lost – she transported herself to Concord from which the hooting owls, with 'their wailing hymns or threnodies' serenaded the lamp-lit bedroom and the pink satin quilt which flatly protected the emphatic emptiness of Sydney's bed. Kitty had not removed it. Josh had wanted her to. Sometimes she closed her eyes and spoke to Sydney as if he were there. Lately, when she waited for his answers, it had not been easy to hear his voice. It bothered her that she had difficulty at times in conjuring up his face. She'd put a hand on the coverlet wanting to cling on, to prevent the memory of her soulmate, her husband, and the father of her children, from disappearing altogether. She did not want Sydney to vanish. Not before the wedding. Issy Miskin had recalled him when Kitty had asked him about the champagne in his cellar. "He knew he wouldn't live to see Rachel married," Issy Miskin in his *cappel* said. "But Sydney will be there." Kitty knew what he meant. Sydney would be under the *chuppah*, in her heart – as he would be in Rachel's – as he would be for ever, but she did not much care for the fact that his voice was receding.

"Lord and Lady Brownlow!" the tail-coated toastmaster who could himself have graced the House of Lords called. "Miss Clarissa Brownlow."

"She's not going to like it when they call out Solomons," Mirrie said, meaning her sister-in-law Leonora. Leonora had been born Levy, her father an aspiring barrister – later to take silk and become a circuit Judge – who had put her through Roedean and afterwards a Swiss finishing school, which expunged, like a carwash, all but the most stubborn traces of her origins. As a child reared in an observant home, Leonora had attended synagogue regularly, and a Hebrew teacher had been entrusted with her religious instruction. Now she purported not to know. When her brother had died one August, when many people were away, she had asked Sydney to be sure to bring Josh to morning prayers, as she didn't think there would be enough men to make up "whatever that thing was called beginning with 'm'." Ever since, when *minyan*, the quorum of ten, was mentioned, it was 'that thing beginning with "m".' A family joke. As was Leonora with her airs and graces which Kitty thought, in pre-war Germany, in Hitler's and Maurice's Germany, would not have saved her, would not have earned her one extra ounce of camp bread.

"The Right Honourable Mr Terence Ormerod and Mrs Ormerod."

"My feet are killing me," Beatty said, shuffling towards the hubbub from the smoke-filled room ahead. "I'll be glad to sit down." She spoke her name to the dignified figure in his morning suit.

"Mrs Beatty Wise!" he called, and when she was safely launched inclined his elfin head towards Mirrie.

"Miss Mirrie Solomons!"

"You'll come with us," Josh said.

He was considerate, Kitty thought, both he and Sarah. Kitty was getting used to being an oddment. It was not like Mirrie, who had always been on her own, or Beatty who still had Leon although he was in hospital. For so many years it had been Mr and Mrs. They had imagined they would grow old together, she and Sydney, spoken of golden weddings. So often she wanted to go back now along the railroad of their life amending here, putting right here.

"Mr and Mrs Joshua Shelton and Mrs Kitty Shelton!"

Leonora, in pale grey crêpe extended a limp, gloved hand, as though it were too heavy for her to lift. Leaning forward into the stratosphere of 'Opium', Kitty kissed her sister-in-law.

"Vanessa looks gorgeous!"

"Please God by Rachel!" Juda by his wife's side said, before Leonora quelled him with her glance.

Nineteen

Driving down to Godalming Kitty had to smile at Beatty's face. When they had finally been processed by the wedding party – Vanessa's handshake had been even limper than her mother's and Kitty hadn't cared for her dress even encrusted as it was with a million pearls – and shunted forwards into the reception room, there wasn't a chair to be had. A thousand people seemed to have been compressed into a space for half that number, and, face to face, shoulder to shoulder, to be enjoying the privation. When a waiter finally reached them with a silver salver of champagne, Beatty had sent him away for orange squash.

"Not that I'll ever see him again," she said resignedly. "Did you notice what they're handing round? Dates. Dates! They keep you standing out there for more than half-an-hour, take away the chairs, and give you a date. I don't suppose it's cheap either!"

Beatty was greatly concerned with her comfort and her stomach. In happier days, before the recession in the fur trade and Leon's illness, she'd entertain on Sunday nights asking relatives and neighbours for what she called a 'bite of supper' in her semi-detached house, where her sons Austin and Charles would have carried the three-piece suite into the garage, and lined the walls of the knocked-through sitting-room with hired gilt chairs. Pre-supper drinks of advocaat and cherry brandy would be accompanied by balls of Beatty's *gefülte* fish, and chopped herring on water crackers, handed by the daily help, in carpet slippers, who went round with napkins and small plates.

Beatty's dining-table would be groaning beneath the weight of her stuffed carp in its pale jelly, her expertly fried haddock fillets, her halibut in sweet-and-sour sauce. Afterwards there would be Beatty's stewed fruit and her trifle, her plum tart or her cherry, according to the season. Back on the hired chairs, the men on one side of the room, and the women on the other, would talk of synagogues and politics, children and schools until the help, flagging, came back with the tea trolley, and you refused her *kipferl* or her almond cake, her yeast ring – 'light as a feather' – or her butter biscuits, at the risk of mortally offending Beatty.

She had neither Sydney's intellect – although Beatty was by no means stupid – nor his refinement, but she shared her late brother's concern for other people and stood out, in an increasingly egocentric world, as a human being. If a neighbour was ill, lonely or in the midst of a family crisis, Beatty was there. She could be relied upon to fetch and to carry, to succour and to nourish, characteristics of the Shelton family, which manifestations in Sydney's brother Juda, had been summarily nipped in the bud by Leonora, who was the epitome of selfishness.

Vanessa's wedding had provided a timely dummy-run for Rachel's now incredibly only fifteen weeks away. After Passover, for which Kitty had been invited by Juda and Leonora as she had been the previous year – when the Klopmans would be back from their cruise – it would be time to get down in earnest to table plans and brides' lists, although goodness knew when Rachel and Patrick would ever have a proper home. They were talking about going round the world or some such nonsense before they settled down.

Passover would not be the same. Had not been since Sydney's death. The warm, family *seders*, when the Hebrew songs of liberation had flowed like honey over the traditional table – with its *matzo* and its Shank Bone and its Bitter Herbs – had been replaced by Juda's rendering of the service in which the questions were asked in English, because of the inadequate Hebrew knowledge of the guests, the debate was non-existent, and the main object of the exercise was clearly to reach the celebratory meal. The yearly communal reading of the *Hagadah*, the Passover story, which had degenerated almost into another of Leonora's dinner parties – they did not even bother with the post-prandial portion of the service – was one of Juda's vestigial links with his up-bringing, the *seder* and the two white candles at Friday night's dinner with *kiddush* before and grace following the meal after which he and Leonora very often went out. Juda put in a brief appearance at the synagogue on Yom Kippur but he did not close his art gallery on that day. It was not the same. Nothing was the same, as Kitty herself was finding out.

With Sydney as her mentor it had not been difficult to lead a fully Jewish life following the dicta which governed every aspect of daily life. In principle she still adhered to the old ways, but she was slipping. Had slipped. Alone, she switched on and watched the television on Friday nights, resorted to the calorific comfort of milk chocolate before the statutory time had elapsed after her meat dinner, and paid the milkman on the Sabbath on which day she had also driven her car. True, the latter had been in response to a summons by Beatty – an emergency almost– but even with Kitty's new, more, liberal attitude to life it had not felt right. She had been getting ready to go to synagogue, which she attended at least every other week, more out of habit than conviction.

She had been putting on her hat when Beatty phoned.

"They think he's going!" Beatty, distraught, said after the pips. "Pneumonia on his chest. His breathing's terrible!"

"Leon?" Kitty said.

"Of course Leon. They've given him antibiotics but he hasn't got the strength."

"I'll come," Kitty said.

"I wish poor Sydney was here," Beatty said by way of thanks.
Kitty had taken off her hat, her *shul* hat, and gone down to
the car which was parked outside the flats. She felt like a
criminal. As if she were stealing, robbing, murdering, instead of
violating the fourth commandment. She had been putting the
key into the ignition, when Louis Hyman, from the ground
floor, in his trilby on his way to the synagogue, had looked at her
in amazement, then looked again, as if his eyes were not to be
trusted. Kitty had wanted to tell him about Leon, that her
brother-in-law was dying, to explain, but by the time she had
opened the window, her downstairs neighbour had walked self-
righteously away. She had trouble starting the engine, for which
she blamed God's anger with her infringement of the seven
day's proscriptions, rather than the icy weather. The Saturday
morning traffic was slow moving. Preoccupied with matters of
the spirit Kitty had not encountered it before, could not credit
that so many people were out, heavy with bags and children,
doing their shopping when normally she was quietly at home or
in *shul*. She watched the road, reluctant to turn her head to the
bustling pavements, in case, in her shame, she encountered the
gaze of anyone who knew her or whom she knew. It was as if
Sydney were watching her mortification, her fall from grace,
although she was aware that one of the permitted reasons for
infringing the Sabbath was to save a life or to visit the sick who
would otherwise be alone. Kitty was not sure whether the visit
to the dying Leon fitted precisely into either of these categories.

The road to the hospital, which was not far from where
Beatty lived, passed three synagogues. Stopping at crossings, for
huddled worshippers in their Sabbath clothes, Kitty felt their
condemnation and averted her eyes. 'I don't usually do this,' she
wanted to explain, 'but I'm on my way to the hospital...' She
could not get it into her head that no one either knew her nor
cared. It was as if hers were the only car on the stocks of the
road, vulnerable to the derision, to the rotten eggs.

Leon's skin had been the white of the pillow, two circles of scarlet were rouged by the fever on his cheeks. Beatty, not letting go of hid hand, willed him fiercely to live. Kitty had sat with her all day, adding her prayers to Beatty's, although in view of the nature of Leon's illness, and the fact that he no longer seemed aware of what was going on around him, she thought it would be a blessing if his tenuous hold on life were relinquished. As darkness fell in squares through the windows of the ward and the lamp was switched on by the curtained bed, the breathing grew quieter and Leon rallied, as if he drew sustenance from its light, and the Singhalese doctor – "he's very kind" Beatty had said, surprised – with his stethoscope had proclaimed Leon's pyrrhic victory over his secondary disease. "It will happen again," he told Beatty. "It can't be helped. Do you want us to give him the antibiotics?" Beatty had looked at the doctor as if he were mad. "He's my husband," she said and her voice indicated that Leon was also her sun, her moon, and her stars, for all that their life together had been a battle ground, and that she would fight to keep him in the world – in which he no longer acknowledged her – with the last drop of her blood.

Kitty had driven home among the paired stragglers emerging from the evening service where, with plaited candle and jingling spice box and with wine, they had blessed a God who discriminated between light and darkness, between the seventh day and the six working days, between the holy and profane, had asked for their sins to be pardoned – that their offspring and their possessions be multiplied as the sand and the stars in the night – and wished each other 'a good week'. Back in her flat Kitty was surprised to find that everything was as she had left it, that there had been no apparent punishment for her transgression, that the heavens hadn't fallen.

There were other changes. The afternoon of her life was turning out to be different from the morning. Through her evening class, her music, she had been attending concerts. She had confessed neither to the old man, eighty if he was a day, in

179

his cloth cap and his green anorak – what he did not know about music seemed hardly worth knowing – by whom she usually sat, nor to the bearded, impoverished, Ph.D student on her other side, that it was for the first time. Sydney had had little time for secular music, with his Talmud study and his prayers. They went to the theatre sometimes on Saturday nights – a comedy, Sydney liked to be entertained – or to charity performances of musicals where they would meet their friends. Kitty had been neither to the Festival nor the Albert Hall for which the teacher of the class, a dynamic young man with patched jeans and a long, pudding-basin haircut, had obtained reduced price tickets, and certainly never to a Sunday Concert in the Conway Hall of whose existence she had not even known. On a hard cold chair with her classmates, she had sat in her coat and listened to a Mozart concert, enthusiastically executed by an unbelievably young and passionate string quartet, and in the interval read, on the notice-board in the draughty foyer, of Humanist Holidays which were a far cry from Herzlia, visits to Broadstairs to see the Dickens Museum – which reminded her of family holidays when the children were young – and the activities of the South Place Ethical Society.

The class 'Listening to Music' had also taken her, for the first time, into the saloon bar of a pub. Most of her fellow students who did not have trains to catch, gathered there every week, after the class. They always invited Kitty politely, but politely – because she did not drink – she declined. Recently inspired, she felt by Maurice, to broaden her horizon, she had timorously accepted the invitation and followed the two Italian girls, one inky dark, one corn fair, and the bulging lady with her bulging shopping bags seeming every week to overflow, and the neat civil servant with his rimless glasses and his brown shoes who was the wit of the class – "I'm coming to sit next to the ladies if I may" – and the other, with the corduroy jacket, who was always the first to put up his hand, along the shadowed streets and into the orange glow of The Three Musketeers. She didn't know what she had expected. A bordello. A den of vice. Certainly not the cosy room with two or three evening drinkers and a tired little girl behind the bar.

They had pooled their money on the beer mat and the men had fetched their drinks, mostly Guinness and draught lager, and brought them to the table – they had moved three together – where Kitty, feeling wanton, abandoned, had sipped a vodka and orange. She had enjoyed it. She could not contribute to the conversation concerning Finland – they had spent the evening with Sibelius – but she had blossomed in the warmth of the realisation that in the saloon bar she was not Sydney's widow, nor Rachel's mother, nor the Klopman's *mechutanista* nor Beatty's sister-in-law, nor Norman's aunt. Not even Mrs Shelton, but Kitty. First names, she had noticed, were *de rigeur*. It became a weekly ritual, the vodka and orange. Sometimes she had two. Now, when Rachel told her she was meeting 'this girl', 'this guy', in the pub, Kitty no longer tutted with disapproval.

In the melée of Vanessa's reception – "It's a blessing..." Beatty, crushed and perspiring, said, "...it only lasts an hour!" separated by the crowds, Kitty had hardly spoken to Rachel whose bizarre appearance had made ripples in the family mill-pond. Rachel had arrived, with Patrick in a blue serge forties suit and short back and sides, in a square-shouldered new-look dress complete with forward tipping black-veiled hat and scarlet lipstick. Kitty had telephoned her later – when Josh had taken her home from the reception and she'd collapsed, exhausted, slipping her shoes from her aching feet.

"If you've telephoned to tell me off..." Rachel, always on the defensive, said, "I bought it in Portobello Market..."

"I thought you looked lovely, darling," Kitty, to whom Rachel's appearance at the wedding had come as a bit of a shock, said.

"What did you ring up for?"

"I wanted to know," Kitty said, "about Nietzsche."

Rachel, whose subject was philosophy, paired with psychology, had been taken aback. Kitty could tell from the momentary silence at the other end of the phone.

"Nietzsche!"

"Nietzsche," Kitty said firmly.

"I'll bring you a book," Rachel told her, when she'd recovered.

A life of the Protestant pastor, the grandfather of German philosophy, now lay alongside the Thoreau by Kitty's bed. Rachel had tried to extract from her the reason for her strange request, but Kitty had kept to herself the new dimension which had come into her life with the letters from Maurice. Rachel had shrugged – she had other things to think about, not least herself.

Now, on her way to Carol's, of whom she did not see nearly enough, Kitty thought of her grandchildren. She missed them. Debbie, Lisa and the baby Mathew, whose growth she had not been able to monitor as she had done when they lived nearby. On the back seat of the car was a tin of *hamantashen* – three-cornered cakes – which she had baked for the children's Purim, to remind them of the wicked Haman's traditional three-cornered hat. Carol had made fancy dresses for the girls, the secret nature of which they had suppressed, in muffled giggles, on the telephone. The masquerading was an old custom. In Eastern Europe, where Kitty's ancestors had lived, the community gathered together to watch a Purimspiel where clowns and ventriloquists and acrobats performed. In Israel today, the festival was celebrated with a big parade, *Adloyada*, with colourful floats and marching bands. Kitty thought of Maurice, with his hundred special Purims, and wished he could see her grandchildren, Debbie and Lisa, who waited excitedly on the doorstep, a diminutive Queen Esther tripping over her dress, cheeks rouged beneath her crown, and a masked Haman with his black crayonned moustache, as she turned into the drive of Peartree Cottage.

Twenty

Seeing Carol brought home to Kitty how much she had missed her elder daughter. At first Kitty had been angry with Alec, but as time went by, observing Carol's happiness with her family in Godalming the resentment had grown less. Kitty could talk to Carol. She was not like Rachel, wayward, headstrong, seeming to occupy another planet whose *mores* had to do neither with the religious observances, nor the behaviour patterns, in which she had been reared. Mother and daughter, they sat at Carol's kitchen table, looking out on to the lawn where the children, anoraks over their fancy dress, had been sent to play. Kitty confided to Carol the arthritis in her neck which had been troubling her lately, the problems at the Day Centre, the fraught arrangements for Rachel's wedding. Carol surprised her mother by telling her – bubbling over with news – that she had had a poem accepted by a woman's magazine. It was about a city park and a country meadow, comparing them. In the park, on the benches, tired mothers sat with prams, transistors played, and office workers ate their sandwiches, while in the meadow, within the confines of the hedgerows, barefoot children picked the daisies. Mixed with her pride – Kitty had no idea that Carol could write poetry – was the fleeting disappointment that, as with Rachel's wedding, Sydney had not lived to see her achievement. Carol in print. With her name beneath the poem. He had sown, but reaped only a small corner of his field.

When Alec came home from his surgery, greeting his mother-in-law fondly, they had a festive dinner – Debbie and Lisa showing off for their grandmother – and afterwards in the sitting-room with its log fire, the curtains drawn, played Purim bingo – with squares of cardboard, on which the children had drawn a star of David, the Israeli flag, a spinning top – 'Pin the Crown on Esther' and 'Pass Haman's Hat'. In the bosom of her daughter's family, Kitty sighed a little for the passing of the years and of Sydney, seeing in Carol with her children the embodiment of all that he had wished for in terms of continuity, the fulfillment of his prayers. In the morning she took Mathew into bed with her, feeling the warmth of the small wriggling body, and made room for Debbie and Lisa, showing them squares of the organdie print Rika Snowman had suggested for their bridesmaids' dresses, one pink, one blue. When Mathew, jealous, held out his pudgy hand for the material, she gave him the sample of yellow.

Together they walked in the dormant country, the children skipping by their sides like lambs, and Alec and Carol, proud possessors of another secret they had kept until Kitty's visit, showing her their new house. It was Queen Anne, and far too large Kitty thought – three floors and two staircases – and in the village.

"Have you bought it?" Kitty said as they stood in what was once the drawing-room but was now to be the main bedroom after the structural alterations which Alec proposed.

Carl nodded.

Kitty looked at her daughter. When Sydney had been alive his advice had been sought not only by his children, but by the entire family. When a special purchase, a major step was proposed – in the case of Rachel and Carol and Josh when they were young, even a new coat – Sydney had expected to be consulted.

"We've exchanged contracts," Carol said, "but there's one snag."

Kitty thought that, in the old, draughty house she would not have given a thank-you for, and which was right on the main road, there were several, but she held her tongue.

"There's a lot of work to be done on it and we've got a buyer for Peartree Cottage…"

"We thought…"

"We wondered…"

They wanted Kitty to have the children, Debbie and Lisa and Mathew, after Rachel's wedding, with Carol going up and down to supervise the work on the new home.

"Will you take us to the zoo, Grandma?" Debbie hopped on one leg."

"And to *Cinderella on Ice*…?"

"There's no ice in the summer, silly!" Debbie said.

"Of course I'll have them." Kitty would look forward to it to mitigate the silence in the flat.

"The builders want three months," Carol said. "I'm afraid it would be until they go back to school."

After the Queen Anne house, Peartree Cottage looked welcoming, as if it belonged to Carol and Alec and the children, and they to it. Kitty remembered with what horror she had regarded it, when they had first moved to Godalming. She was not good at changes. She liked things to be the same, for them to go on.

"It's *very* grand!" she said to Carol of the new house.

"We were afraid you mightn't like it," Carol said, relieved, the dust of happiness in her eyes.

Alone, at night, with her Thoreau, beneath the eaves, Carol had come to sit on her bed. She took her mother's hand.

"Guess what?"

"More surprises?" Kitty dropped her eyes to Carol's waistline, whose secret she had already divined.

Carol nodded.

"When?"

"For *Rosh Hashana*."

The New Year was only five months away. Carol had not confided in her.

"You don't show!"

"I can't do my skirts up!"

"You'll have your hands full!"

"Mathew wants it to be a kitten."

Even the children had been told.

Kitty pulled Carol close to her and kissed her dark head, her pleasure in the fact that she was to have another grandchild making up for the small hurt of her exclusion.

It was why, Carol said, they had to hurry with the house. The rest of the weekend passed in the warm glow of the expected baby. When it was time for Kitty to go they had seen her off – the children blowing kisses through the window – and Alec had waved her out into the narrow road. Leaving them, so patently happy in their leaning cottage, in the cocoon of their life, she was glad that she had not revealed her own secret to Carol. Her correspondence with Maurice belonged to the new Kitty, as did Thoreau and 'Listening to Music'; and she had no wish to share him, she had discovered, as she did the other ninety-nine percent of herself, with Addie Jacobs, with Sydney's family or with her children. When she got home from the country there was a letter waiting for her. She had hoped there would be.

Dear Kitty, dear Kitty –

Why do you persist? I tell myself you won't bother any more, that each letter is the last, then can't wait to go down to the mail-box. When it's empty a gloom descends over my day. When I see your handwriting and those English stamps (I love your Queen) there is a whole new dimension to it. My spirit lightens, my mood lifts, my heart sings. I am a man given to great *élans* and deep discouragements – no more or less I guess than any artist – so what do you want with me? I am not like Sydney. Little by little, as I read your letters, I am building up a

picture of him. What a fine and upright man. What a loss.
Poor Kitty. If whom the gods love die young, this miserable
old sinner will go on to eternity. I could never have been a
good Jew, as Sydney was, even though I was raised to it. I
kicked against the outward observances in my youth. One
Sabbath I told my father I was sick and while the others
were in synagogue (they burned it to the ground in the
'*Kristallnacht*' pogrom of 1938), I took the trolley down-
town and bought a *bratwürst* (sausage!). After that it was
easy. I obeyed my father, who was tryannically strict,
traditional, and rigid (although he often kissed and hugged
us), as did most children in that other life, but *within*,
what a ferment, what an uproar. My body was enslaved
but not my spirit. I guess it was the creativity, which had
not then emerged, but which is the antithesis of the habit
which was imposed on me.

One of my earliest memories of Frankfurt – I must have
been about ten or twelve at the time – was a whole troop
of brownshirts marching down the street singing a song
about Jews and how their heads would roll. I didn't
understand but it frightened me. Later they trained dogs to
run after us – 'get the Jew' – and there were park benches
for 'Aryans only', pubs, theatres, cinemas and stores
where 'Jews and pigs' were strictly forbidden – dogs were
permitted! The signs bothered me but I learned to live
with them (we all did), to *expect* kids to be waiting outside
the synagogue with rocks to throw at us, to *accept* that
anti-semitism was a part of everyday life. My Uncle
Manny, who was a quilt-maker, had his business taken
from him, they confiscated my Uncle Karl's driving
licence, ruining him (he travelled in pharmaceuticals). We
had special passports with a yellow 'J' and the name
'Israel' (Sarah for the women) added to our own. The
woman in the corner store, who had always been friendly,
suddenly started hurling abuse at us – she made my sister

cry. My mother lost her maid because she was not allowed to work for us. Jewish teachers and professors were expelled from their jobs, including my Uncle Felix who was given 'immediate leave of absence', and a few months later was dismissed from the university. It crept up on us. "It isn't going to last" my saintly father said. "Hitler will disappear."

People often ask why the Jews of Germany, knowing of the existence of Dachau (in 1934!) having read *Mein Kampf*, were so foolish as to stay on. Why didn't we all just leave? If you told Josh or Alec or your brother-in-law, Juda, or his wife – Leonora isn't it? – who scarcely acknowledges her Jewishness (Goering said "I'll decide who's Jewish!") that something *might* happen in England, would they be so quick to move to a strange country where they don't speak the language, and to which they could take neither money nor possessions, and would not be able to practice their professions or make a living? Anti-semitism is a disease. Its only fundamental cause, it has been said, is that the Jew exists. He will *always* exist. If we run away Mount Sinai runs after us. Anti-Semitism will not be eradicated any more than greed, which, contrary to the beliefs of our denigrators, is a human – Carnegie, Rockefeller, Frick, Mellon, Harriman, Huntington, Whitney – and not a racial prediliction. Because of my Uncle Felix whom I admired, and whose practical and colourful world I was more able to relate to than the sombre, and deeply spiritual one of my father, I had always wanted to study medicine. I think it saved my life. (Even with hindsight it is difficult to say what actions at that time were proper or improper, what decisions would save lives and what destroy them.) In the camp I told them I was a doctor, although I was nowhere near qualified as I had not been allowed to continue with my studies and they put me to work in one of the barracks where the transports disgorged their human cargo (*five hundred thousand* Hungarians in one month alone). I had enough to eat for a while and got some of my strength back. I tried to tell the newcomers what was happening (the crematoria were working overtime) but they *would not listen.* I could not make them believe any more than I had believed what I was told when I first came to the camp, any more than the world believed (your Eden knew what was going on), any more than *we* believe that husbands, brothers, fathers and sons are being tortured right now in Brazil and China, in Turkey and Iran. Where are the farmers falling over themselves to leave Rhodesia, (pardon me, Zimbabwe), the white South Africans? Yet the graffiti are there! Ugh, Kitty. Rather than change the world we go into therapy to make it bearable or put on sneakers and run. Tell me about the wedding. It's getting close. You're not going to believe this Kitty but I've only ever been to one (my office nurse, and that in a church), it's what you get when you don't have a family.

Weddings are important. Rabbi Jose bar Halafta was once asked 'How long did it take the Holy One, blessed be He, to create the world?' The answer was 'six days'. 'And from then until now what has he been doing?' 'The Holy One, blessed be He, is occupied making marriages.' Do I believe this? Kitty I don't know. Sometimes I think he saved your cynical correspondent and sometimes how *can* He exist if innocent children had their heads smashed against a wall? There are some things that can be explained away (particularly by the behaviourists) but you cannot put down to hunger, sex, rage or fear the curious reactions one experiences when listening to Mozart (I have a seat for *Don Giovanni* next week at the Met.), looking at the ocean, or reading John Donne's 'Holy Sonnets' for the first time. Tell me what happens with Unterman and about the wedding list. I should like to send

Rachel a small gift – I feel I already know her. I know nothing about your Benjamin Britten (although I saw *Peter Grimes* which was commissioned by Koussevitzky), *you* will have to tell *me*. I look forward to it and your next letter. Bless you. MM.

PS. I am re-reading Thoreau with you and taking a fresh look at nature and society. 'My life has been the poem I could have writ, but I could not both live and utter it.'

PPS. Like yours truly Nietzsche never married, never had children. We both had 'aunts', who lived with us, his August a and Rosalie (really his step-sisters), mine Lottie and Lena. There the analogy ends. MM.

A sketch of Maurice, cap on his head, at his easel was attached to the back page.

When she'd read the letter and unpacked the small case she had taken to Carol's Kitty picked up the phone to ring Norman who she felt had been avoiding her.

Norman, in bedroom slippers, gardening trousers and one of the mis-shapen pullovers knitted by his mother, could scarcely bring himself to answer the telephone. He roused himself sufficiently to do so, in case it was Sandra whose call he was expecting. 'Yes', he told his Aunty Kitty, 'yes', he was quite well. He wasn't sure if this week he could manage dinner – even shepherds' pie, his favourite, which was the carrot Kitty dangled. No, there was nothing the matter! It was not true, Norman thought as he replaced the telephone on the table in the hall, looking at his dishevelled appearance in the oval oak mirror as he did so. Something was the matter.

Something had crept in, like a thief in the night, between himself and Sandra, to undermine their alliance, the close harmony of their relationship, which had come like a shooting star into Norman's life. That all was not well had been achingly clear to Norman from the moment they had transferred the protestations of their love from Sandra's flat to his bachelor bed, since when the matter had gone from bad to worse. Sandra refused to acknowledge the impasse, which gave her, in Norman's book, a place among the angels. The more discouraged Norman became the more she praised him, the more depressed he declared himself to be, the more reassuring was Sandra. He tried to attribute his slipping commissions to the general recession which, naturally, was having repercussions in the property business; Sandra would not let him. He was going through a bad patch, she said – she had faith in him – things would improve. He had left the suits he had so headily selected with Sandra hanging in his wardrobe, and gone back to his old clothes although Sandra had bought him a cashmere sweater – still in its cellophane in his drawer – and three new ties. Norman declared his life was over; Sandra – holding him close – said it was no such thing. He had made a resolution. If his own world was going to pieces he would not allow himself to shatter Sandra's. He would give it one more chance. If tonight he found himself unable to love Sandra, if on this occasion, as on the other occasions lately, he failed, he would write a letter refusing to see her again; begging her to leave his life as decisively as she had come into it, and direct herself to her sons, Hilton and Milton and to their future. He was slightly drunk. He had been drinking lately. Just a little. Then a little more. Until the hateful image of himself was drowned, the pain of his debâcle less acute. He was pouring another drink, from the bottle on the floor beside him, into the glass in which he had given his mother her nightly medicine –the only one to hand - when Sandra, using the code they had adopted, tapped at the window.

She brought a lustre, a fragrant halo, into the dim-lit hall. Kissed Norman beneath the dead, black, light bulb he had not bothered to replace.

"Hi!"

He took her coat, from whose soft arms she got more consolation than from his own, and followed her into the sitting-room.

"Milton's ecstatic," Sandra said, "He's playing the solo in the end of term concert. César Franck. In front of the whole school."

Norman could not work up any enthusiasm for Milton's musical prowess. He felt as disinterested in the week's activities of her two sons as he was in Sandra's breasts, whose outline was explicit beneath her angora sweater, and the symmetry – which once he had found divine – of her legs. She sat on the sofa and chattered, curled herself at his feet in place of the whisky bottle, undid buttons and zips, then led him upstairs to bed. He fumbled with the china doorknob of his room.

"Not in there," Sandra whispered.

Norman looked at her, the whisky robbing her face of its outline. She opened the door of the other room, his mother's bedroom, where the double bed had lain untrammelled since her death.

"Sandra!"

Sandra pulled at him but Norman would not come. He stood horrified on the worn axminster of the landing while she sat on the bed, Dolly's bed – where she had breathed her last – and with deliberation removed her clothes.

"Sandra!" Norman, with a crystal clarity, could see his mother in the bed, lying there as he had found her, icy cold, then Sandra, her nipples erect, her arms extended.

"It's all right, Norman."

Norman flung himself, sobbing, on to the bedside rug, and buried his face in Sandra's lap.

Twenty-one

Kitty could not pinpoint exactly when the idea first came to her. It had crept leisurely, *piano, adagio*, into the recesses of her mind. At the dining-room table, the dishes from her solitary dinner not cleared away (she carried her meal into the dining-room even when she was alone, Sydney would have liked her to, to keep up his standards), she faced the pad of notepaper, her pen in hand. Her leisure moments during the past week had been spent finalising her guest list, trying to fashion it within the limits imposed upon her by the Klopman confluence. By asking only those closest to her on the Ladies' Guild and confining the helpers from the Day Centre to the one or two women whom she knew best, she had arrived, within a few either way, at her permitted number.

There was no reason, she thought, looking out of the window – the evenings were getting lighter, the days longer – why she should not invite Maurice to Rachel's wedding. He was her friend. If only on air-mail paper. Maurice, she felt somehow (even at a distance of three thousand miles), knew her better than her children, was more familiar with her than her family, understood her better than had Sydney. He would not come. He was too shy. In Israel, other than at Yoske's, he had scarcely spoken. Why should he cross an ocean to be present at the marriage of two people he did not even know? He wanted to send Rachel a present, true – he was a kind soul – but that

193

didn't mean he was prepared to go to the expense of coming to England to attend a function at which, apart from herself, he would know no one, to allow himself to be cast upon an alien sea of unfamiliar faces. A present was something different.

Kitty had found a sample bride's list in a magazine, which she was going to show to Rachel, for whom she was now waiting. Together when Rachel could spare the time, they would select the items at one of the stores, although Rachel and Patrick had not at the moment any intention of setting up home. They had in fact asked Kitty if they could stay with her – the council flat had to be given up – after Carol's children had gone, until December, when they planned to start on their global trip, South America, Australasia, The Far East. Hettie and Herbert, for a wedding present, were buying them a house but they would not hear of it until their return. Any gifts, Patrick said, which they might receive, would have to be kept in the Klopman attic. The list, in alphabetical order, for Rachel's approval, was on the table beside Kitty. With Maurice's request in mind, she looked at it. 'Aprons'. She could not see Rachel in one. Her daughter's cooking, as far as Kitty knew, was confined to the rock cakes she had learned to make at school and the brown rice and lentils, on which they seemed to subsist, which was generally cooked by Patrick. 'Carpet sweeper'. Kitty's mind boggled. 'Grapefruit spoons'! 'Ironing board'. Rachel seemed to manage without an iron. Perhaps, after all, she would not show the list to Rachel. 'Vacuum Cleaner'. 'Vacuum Flask'. Nothing there for Maurice. Wine Rack. 'Wok'. She had an idea. She would ask Maurice to send Rachel a painting. Rachel would like that. She liked anything 'real', anything which had been created – rather than manufactured – lovingly by the sweat of one's brow, by hand.

Dear Maurice,
Thank you for your short note. It set my mind at rest because I wondered what had happened when I did not

hear from you. I have grown used to expecting your letters
– I'm like a child, waiting for the postman, they mean such
a lot to me – and hearing about your life. I'm only sorry it
had been so tragic. Sorry too that you've been ill. Shingles
is very painful and drags on. I know because my sister-in-
law Mirrie had it, a few years ago, and it was very
unpleasant. What about your shopping? Did you ask your
neighbour? People are usually only too pleased. I know
you don't eat much but you have to keep your strength up,
especially when you are ill. You must look after yourself.
Talking of food, you wanted to hear about the dinner
menu for the wedding. Dinner! It's going to be more like
a medieval banquet. Hetty would not let Unterman go
until he had agreed to the most original (and expensive)
meal he has ever served...

Kitty thought of the session, the interview with Unterman
which had left him damp and pale, hardened as he was, as if he
had survived an obstacle course. Which he had. Hettie, tanned
from her cruise with a brown which was almost black, had
given him no quarter. He had arrived with typed menus,
consecutively numbered according to price – having to do with
Cornets of Smoked Salmon, with Asparagus and Lamb Chops in
Pastry, Roast Poussins, Cherry Pom-Pom, and *Profiteroles* –
which Hetty would not contemplate. *Canetons à la Bigarade,* she
suggested having scoured her recipe books, *Capilotade de Poulet
Paysanne*. To Unterman's credit, Kitty thought, he had not
flinched. Yes, he could sauté his chickens with garlic and with
parsley and with chervil; yes, with bitter oranges and lemons,
with clarified butter (except that it would have to be *Tomor*
margarine) and with sugar, could he anoint his duck. Kitty
could see that he was not keen. That he was reluctant – despite
the fact that money was apparently no object – to throw the
Unterman catering staff, with the dishes they were accustomed
to preparing, into disarray. Manfully, he agreed to serve a kosher

195

Gâteau de Foies de Volailles à la Bressane, four hundred *Sole Dorée du Guesclin* (omitting the Dublin Bay prawns); to produce at the apposite moment, a *Soufflé aux Fraises*, or for those preferring a cold dessert, a *Mont Blanc Glacé* (with synthetic cream), and to subdivide the meal with a *Sorbet* of *Citrons Verts*. He assured Hettie that during the reception hour preceding the dinner there would be none of his run-of-the-mill 'canapees' (eight to a person), miniature Welsh Rarebits or hot mushroom *vol-au-vents*, pronounced too commonplace by Hettie. Instead there were to be *Mousse de Saumon Fumé au Cresson* – served with hot matzos – stuffed vine leaves, miniature spinach puffs, hot Danish tartlets filled with smoked roe. There were to be flowers, fresh fruit, printed menus and place cards (following the colour scheme) on all tables, a *challa* for the blessing over bread, satin skull-caps (not paper) for the men, and small, ribbon-tied boxes of Belgian chocolates for every lady guest. There was to be a banking of flowers in front of the top table, and a wedding cake (for which Unterman produced coloured photographs, supported by gold and turquoise pillars of icing, consisting of four tiers.

When the statutory time had elapsed following the meal, evening tea was to be served with miniature sandwiches, diminutive reception pastries, and a generous helping of raspberries with cream. Unterman was to provide a full bar (spirits and liqueurs, sherries and aperitifs, together with lagers, beers, fruit juices and soft drinks) and a *Möet et Chandon* which would of course be available throughout the evening. Volunteering that which Sydney had laid down in Issy Miskin's cellar, Kitty was aware that it would be a veritable drop in the champagne ocean. Hettie did not protest.

'I have to admire her,' Kitty wrote of her *mechutanista*. 'There's not a thing she has not organised, nothing she has left out. (We're going next week to see the choir-master about the music.) She has given me a huge table plan (supplied by Unterman) and as the replies come in I have to think where to put everybody. The Klopman guests are to be interspersed with ours. (Better, I agree with Hettie, than seating the two families separately.) Speaking of guests, I wonder Maurice, I know it's expensive just for a wedding, you don't have to, but I thought you might like... May I send you an invitation...?'

Kitty looked at what she had written. It *was* a cheek. Why should Maurice want to come to Rachel's wedding just because they corresponded, because they had spent a few hours in each other's company in Eilat? She was about to strike out the sentence, to scratch it out so that it was obliterated, when Rachel rang the bell.

"You look terrible," Kitty said, at the sight of her youngest daughter's white face.

"I *feel* terrible. We had a Chinese take-away."

"What did you eat?"

"Unmentionables," Rachel said.

"I told you to come to dinner with me. I fried some liver..."

"Don't!" Rachel groaned, peering at the table. "Who are you writing to?"

"May I bring Sandra?" Norman asked his Aunt Kitty on his next visit. He knew that to bring her to Rachel's wedding meant running the gauntlet of the family, of subjecting Sandra to Kitty's appraisal, to the critical eyes of his Uncle Juda, to Beatty's tongue.

"Delighted," Kitty said, and she was, as she saw Norman blossom, Norman reborn, Norman come alive.

Norman himself felt like a Goliath, as if the world were his to deploy, and that everything was within his power. There had been a bad time when he had felt himself regressing, descending once more into the pit of his old, untutored ways. Sandra had rescued him. At the moment of his going down for the third time in the sea of his despair, Sandra had taken him, unworthy has he had felt himself to be, firmly by the hand. The turning point had come on the night that she had lured him to make love to her in his mother's bedroom – his bedroom now, he had taken it over – where she had with the body she so unstintingly yielded, slain the demons which had threatened to devour him. It had been neither quick nor easy, but Sandra was not pressed for time nor would she be deflected.

Norman had raised his head from Sandra's lap as she sat on his mother's bed, looking up into her face, golden framed in its diaphanous hair.

"Not in here!" Norman was aghast.

"In here!"

Norman could see Dolly, in the dressing-gown she had worn during her last illness, standing, reprovingly at the end of the bed.

Sandra, her flesh polished, cool to the touch, seemed unaware of the disparaging presence.

Norman's girl friends had, when Dolly was alive, been pronounced 'common', 'plain', 'no better than they should be' (Della). He did not want Dolly to see Sandra.

"Come into *my* room!" He tried to pull her.

Sandra lay down on Dolly's bed – where he had found her, morning-cold – in his mother's hollow.

"Norman I can't go on like this."

He heard the ultimatum in her voice. Their love, in this house, in his mother's house, had been troubled. Troubled, Norman looked at her. Her breasts, despite Hilton and Milton, were firm, when she walked they trembled, and were fruit heavy when he held them in his hands. Her belly undulated from its button, its down shimmering in the light that was operated by a string from above his mother's bed. Her legs were not long, but athletic, useful, their toenails painted red. Norman recognised his Armageddon. That it had come. And that he must not lose Sandra as he had lost Della, sacrificing her upon the altar of his filial loyalty. He removed his clothes, slowly, putting them on the chair where as a baby Dolly had nursed him – how proud she had been of keeping that chair – and where at night she had lain the underwear which had embraced and supported her.

The bed – in protest Norman thought at the unaccustomed weight – creaked as he lay down next to Sandra. Cowardly, he reached for the light, but Sandra was there before him.

"No." Her voice, in its velvet glove, was iron. Norman put out a hand and was surprised, when it made contact with Sandra's flesh, that its fingertips were not singed. His touch was tentative. The voice in his ears, 'Norman!' – hurt, shocked, surprised, grieved – insistent. To silence it he buried his head in Sandra's perfumed hair.

"Norman." Tender, loving, it was another voice. "It's all right Norman." It charmed him with its reassurance, superimposing itself upon the other.

"It's not that I don't love you…" Norman's fingers grew braver, his hands stronger. "I love you." He wanted to prove it to her and their bodies drew close, making passionate silhouettes, coming together and parting, a magic show on the rose-trellised walls. They were a symphony; a single voice. Over the months they had learned the notes together, perfected them. Lately, Sandra's performance had grown in strength, while Norman's had faded away almost to extinction. Now his *andante* matched her *rallentando*, his melody her plain-song. The bedroom receded, as did their forms, whose inner core produced agitations and disturbances, impressions and sensations, depths and understandings, comprehended only by those who in their wanderings had found a mate for their souls. Ridge responded to hollow, places to pressure, secrets were given up. Then downstairs – caught by the wind which blew through the letter-box into the privacy of the hall – a door slammed.

'Norman! Is that you?'

His mother's voice, clear, unmistakable, sent Norman, from his space mission, back to earth. He raised his head from Sandra's body.

"It was only a door," Sandra said.

'Norman, what on earth are you doing?'

His mother's mouth was open, scandalised. He wondered, sometimes, how she had conceived him. He grew limp before her gaze, the room, which had been warmed by the sun of his passion, cold. Sandra was waiting. He could feel the suspension. Waiting for Norman. Disentangling his limbs from hers, he got up and moved to where Dolly was standing, followed her to the bed, on which she lay down to escape from him. With a grim determination Norman gathered Sandra up with arms so strong, so firm, she cried out as their grasp caressed her body then ravaged it, besieged it like a conqueror, made with it a solemn covenant on which he could not renege. With his heart he avowed, with his manhood he swore, with his passion he underwrote his love for her which was paramount and which he would not relinquish. Later, apologetically, in a spun web of silence, he reiterated it more gently, tears blinding his view of her, christening their happiness, baptising it. Weightless, they lay entwined in the womb of their world, until it was time for Sandra to leave. When she had gone Norman moved his possessions into his mother's room.

Twenty-two

Shavuoth, 'Feast of Weeks' (seven weeks from the time of the barley harvest at Passover), 'The Day of the First Ripe Fruits' (when the Israelite was to bring a thanksgiving offering to God for the produce of his fields), 'The Season of the Giving of the Torah' (relating to the revelation of God to the assembly of Israel at Mount Sinai and the declaration of the Ten Commandments) and the *yahrzeit* for Sydney fell on the same day. It was hard to credit that he had been dead for two years. Last night, on the anniversary of his death, Kitty had lit the 24-hour memorial candle – 'the spirit of man is the candle of the Lord' – which still flickered in its glass beside her late husband's photograph on her mantelpiece. Today, in synagogue, with Sarah by her side, she would spend the morning in prayer and meditation. Tomorrow, the second day of the Festival, Josh would recite the *Kaddish* for his father. 'May the Lord comfort and sustain you among the other mourners for Zion and Jerusalem.' Thus had the pious spoken to her during the seven days of mourning immediately following Sydney's death, when Kitty had sat on the low hard chair with her friends and family around her. She had been both comforted and sustained.

She had persisted. Without Sydney. She had not thought it possible that she could, that she would discover within herself untapped sources of strength, reserves of whose existence she had not dreamed. Two years. Sometimes she felt ashamed to find, more recently in particular, that for days on end she did not think of him, that there were nights when he did not enter her dreams. She tried to cling on, but recognized that it was salutary to let him go, to let him rest in the hinterland of her memory where his place was undisputed.

Poor Sydney. How he had suffered. How – before her impotent eyes – he had changed from a strong and loving husband, a caring and upright human being, to an ailing shadow of a man, whose ultimate release from the shambles of his life was blessed. How he had loved his Festivals. With what devotion he had observed them. The legacy of his religious commitment, together with her own more tempered attitudes, led to Kitty's continued participation in the celebratory services of the synagogue which, in addition to the regular Sabbaths, appeared at variegated intervals in the calendar of the Jewish year. There was another reason for her faithfulness, her adherence to the ritual which without Sydney's firmness of purpose might well have become more tenuous. Sarah. It was appropriate that on this festival of Pentecost, this Feast of Weeks – when the Book of Ruth with its moving story of the Moabite girl whose conversion to Judaism due to her marriage, was read in synagogue – Sarah was by her side. In her white beret, her hair flowing over the shoulders of her white dress, she was engrossed in the service.

In instructing her daughter-in-law in the ways of her household, Kitty, a practical adjunct to Mrs Halberstadt, felt that she was the instrument of Sydney and spoke with his voice. Because of Sarah's determination to become Jewish, Kitty was never alone on Sabbaths and on Festivals. It was a blessing for which she was grateful. Josh was ambivalent about his synagogue attendances and Rachel did not put in an appearance at all. Kitty's friends in the Ladies' Gallery had long ago accepted the presence of Sarah, and Kitty herself, for long periods of time, forgot that Sarah, like Ruth, was a stranger in the land.

Today, the synagogue – the early summer sun enriching the colours of the stained glass – was made beautiful with flowers. Kitty had helped to decorate it, as a reminder of Mount Sinai, which was covered with vegetation in honour of the great event of the Revelation. The synagogue decorations for Rachel's wedding had already been decided upon – white and green – and the preparations had now entered a calm. Standing up simultaneously with Sarah, before the treasure house of the Ark was opened and the Ten Commandments recited, Kitty was glad that the bones of contention concerning the preparations – including her own and Hettie's dress – had for the most part been removed, the differences ironed out. Although in the beginning Kitty had seen Herbert Klopman as an over-bearing man, unused to being thwarted, she had learned that his bellicose exterior camouflaged a well-placed heart whose tentacles had reached out to her last night on the eve of *Shavuoth*. Hettie had telephoned her early in the week, but it was not, unusually, about the wedding.

"Rachel tells me you have *yahrzeit* for your husband," Hetty said. "Would you like us to come over?"

Touched by the suggestion, Kitty had invited her *mechutanim* to dinner, to eat the traditional dairy foods associated with *Shavuoth*. Josh had sat at the head of the table in Sydney's place – where first he had been taken ill – and Sarah next to Sydney's sister Mirrie, opposite the Klopmans. Kitty had invited Norman, who was busy with Sandra, and Beatty, who was spending the evening – as she did every evening – at the hospital with Leon, and Freda – who refused to go anywhere lately, seemingly almost to have become a recluse – and Harry, and Rachel, who was in the final throes of her exams and was reluctant to spare the time, and Patrick, who was on duty at the hospital. She was grateful to Herbert and Hettie who had arrived with the biggest basket of fruit she had ever seen, glad even of the distraction of Herbert's stories, which prevented her from dwelling on the summer's day when Sydney – with no farewell – had collapsed and died, and from being morbid. Kitty did not resent Herbert's humour, misinterpreting it as uncaring, had laughed even, over the *Shavuoth* cheesecake for which she was renowned, at his story – *à propros* of weddings – of the woman who rushed excitedly into her neighbour and said: 'Zelda, Zelda, guess what? I'm having an affair!'

'*Mazelov!*' was the response, 'who's catering?'

After the dinner, at which Josh had recited the Grace after Meals with a demeanour which, Kitty thought, looking at her only son through half-closed eyes, could have been Sydney's, they adjourned to the sitting-room where Herbert's stories – he was now in full flood – kept Sydney's shade at bay. He told them the one about the young Irish priest who went into a Dublin shop whose sign read: 'Cohen and O'Grady', to be greeted by an old man with a beard and a skull-cap. The priest smiled. 'I just wanted to come in and tell you how wonderful it is to see that your people and mine have become such good friends – even partners. That's a surprise!' 'I've got a bigger surprise,' said the old man. 'I'm O'Grady!' and recited Abraham Ibn Ezra's apt description of the *shlimazl's* lot: 'If I sold lamps, the sun, In spite, Would shine at night.'

Despite Herbert's well-meaning attempts to keep her from her memories, Kitty was not sorry when he took Hettie home and she was left alone – she would not let Sarah and Mirrie stay behind to help with the dishes. She stood on the hearth, facing the guttering candle's leaping shadow, and tried, like Aladdin from his lamp, to summon Sydney. She found it not incongruous that when he did not appear she sat down in the light that flickered beside the rose of Jericho – now opened wide – that she had transported from the desert, to re-read Maurice's letter.

Dear Kitty
Better yes, but weak as a kitten. Your letter was my best medicine. Of course, of course I'll come to Rachel's

wedding – I have already put a tuxedo in hand, midnight blue – I haven't had one since I graduated from medical school and found myself in the middle of New York, starting a practice with no money, no connections and up to my ears in debt. The day smallpox arrived in the United States – everybody had to be vaccinated – was the first time my office filled with patients. From that – was someone looking after me, Kitty? – the practice grew, and little by little – I couldn't afford a car for the first four years – I paid off my debts, even the payments on the cardiograph!

I cannot give Rachel a painting. Don't misunderstand me, Kitty – I would give her all my paintings – but I don't paint a jug, a sunflower, I paint the truth, my truth, in which everything is gray – gray barracks, gray sky, and the gray mass of miserable humanity – which has no place at a wedding nor any *simcha*. (I saw a woman wrap a shivering child in a gray blanket. The guard told her not to worry, it would be very warm where she was going!) I started painting in Frankfurt when I was no longer allowed to continue with my medical studies. My Aunt Lottie, (she was a teacher at the Städel School) taught me everything she knew – pencil, crayon, watercolor, Indian ink and pastels as well as oils – she had plenty of spare time! Painting to me is living. The pleasure I derive from it is more powerful even than that from music. I paint from the depths of my personality which was affected by, not created by, my experiences. The canvas and the oils are my therapists, they keep me in daily analysis which will never end. I didn't paint in the camps, except in the hospital where I drew medical diagrams and charts. Others did, on scraps of paper with stubs of pencil for which they exchanged their bread. The Nazi's found themselves with some of the world's finest artists as their prisoners and could not resist using them for their own purpose (German soldiers, SS men and policemen liked to have their portraits painted), consigning them to the museum, where they painted on glass (as slowly as they dared), or made small wood sculptures, until they were transferred to work in the crematorium, to be beaten (broken jaws and feet) or to cleaning Nazi quarters and streets.

I died there, Kitty. I could not do a thing. Who can paint a *million* gassed children, the scourging of Europe, six million ghosts? Who can commit to paper the fears and agonies of being deported, shot, burned to death, or thrown alive into a pit? Are there not extreme situations beyond the reach of art? Should art not be aware of its own limitations and keep a certain distance from the unspeakable? Only now, after forty years, can I face the fact that every piece of testimony, every recollection by the victims (both those who survived and those who did not) is precious, that there are values which supersede aesthetic ones, that the more you lost, the greater the obligation to remember, and that *silence is the real crime of humanity*. Only now can I raise the question, (although there are no answers) so that people should know. Know what? The canvases are stacked deep around my studio walls. 'Wagons' – loaded with stones and pulled uphill, where men are the horses; 'Roll Call' – one thousand racially inferior products standing *nineteen hours* in the cold; 'Little Orphans' – abandoned on the face of the earth. I would like to be remembered Kitty, not as a physician (although I had many grateful patients) nor as an artist, but as a man sounding an alarm. (They ring night and day in the city but no one heeds them.)

Enough of MM. How gratifying it must be to feel needed (by Carol and Rachel). I can picture Carol's Queen Anne house (in New York there is nothing old) and her delight (how proud you must be) at getting into print.

Mazel Tov on her pregnancy (another grandchild!) Something to look forward to. The wedding feast sounds splendid (I won't have the tuxedo too close fitting and will try to lose a few pounds) and the details of it always cheer me up no matter how black my mood. I too now have something to which I can look forward. (I have your photo on my high-boy but it's not the same.) I have made my reservations (Pan Am) and have started whistling while I paint. I just noticed it. I didn't think happiness was on the agenda of the life of your affectionate correspondent, MM.

PS. I would like to give Rachel a silver wine *becher* although I guess Patrick will not be making *kiddush* right now on Friday nights! People change.

PPS. About the choir music. Why don't you have 'O Isis und Osiris' from *Die Zauberflöte*? (It *is* a prayer.)

Standing next to her mother-in-law, for whom she felt a deep attachment, Sarah watched as the *Sefer* Torah – the five books inscribed on parchment in one unbroken scroll – with its breast-plate of silver topped by its pomegranate of tinkling bells, was taken with great ceremony out of the Ark. The further she progressed in her sessions with Mrs Halberstadt, the more intriguing she found the instruction in Judaism, whose object was to encourage man to perform ethical and moral deeds based upon a recognition of his link with God. Her stumbling progress with the Hebrew characters was rapidly improving, her knowledge of Jewish history widening. She had learned to accept the ritualistic requirements which governed the daily life of the Jew, from the moment he awakened in the morning until he came to rest at night, rather as techniques – or visual aids – to reach goals, and not as an end in themselves. Every action throughout the day – ablutions, prayers, the type of food he was allowed to eat – was linked in one way or another to Judaism, which had a special prayer for all eventualities in life, from birth to death. Sarah found this comforting, as she did the principle that every individual must assume personal responsibility for his actions. She accepted that no one had died to save her, that salvation would not come through faith in a mystery, that no holy trinity of spirits would protect her, but that she was on her own before God.

It had not been easy. From her first application to the *Beth Din*, where the reception had been chilly, all manner of difficulties had been put in the way of her determination to embrace her husband's faith. Rabbi Magnus, once a close friend of Josh's father, had explained to her, in simple terms, the reason for this seeming indifference. Judaism, like parents, must accept its natural children, healthy or crippled, upright or delinquent. But in adopting a child it is free to choose, entitled to take all reasonable precautions, to ensure that he will be a source of pride and joy to them. Sarah was not deflected by the intransigence of those on high. She had always been determined. Her staying power had kept her from being diverted from her school work in her peripatetic childhood, and she would not be diverted now.

Sometimes she felt that the observance of the ritual gave her life the stability which, before meeting Josh, it had lacked. Certainly it did not irk her as it did Josh. She was willing to make the leap of faith necessary to conduct herself in accordance with the rabbinic rules, which she saw as cohesive and satisfying, rather than as a force making for denial. She liked the goodwill, even the humour, with which the precepts – in the case of Kitty and her family and Mrs Halberstadt – were carried out, and she had started to live her life in accordance with them. The *Shema*, asserting her belief in a single God, which she recited daily, did not reach back into her childhood as it did into Josh's – it was the first sentence he had learned in Hebrew, his night prayers as a child – but it was comforting to feel that the very words had been repeated by Jews in diverse circumstances throughout the ages. If she could not be identified as a Jew by birth, she would, like Ruth before her, be accepted by her adherence to a way of life which was handed down unchanging, from generation to generation, to the statutes which they were now about to read. Of the three instructions incumbent upon the Jewish woman, Sarah was already observing two. On The Eve of the Sabbath she lit candles, symbolising the continuity of Jewish family life; she sanctified her Sabbath table with the traditional loaves of plaited, egg-glazed bread. The *mikveh*, the formal act of conversion carried out by ritual immersion, would come later, when Sarah had convinced the Court of the Chief Rabbi of her sincerity in wishing to adopt the Jewish faith. It would be, Sarah thought, as the first of the edicts was intoned by the Cantor... 'The Lord is God, the Lord is One'...just in time, for she was to have a child. A fact that she would divulge to her mother-in-law, as soon as the Ten Commandments had been read. If her progress with Mrs Halberstadt kept up at the present rate, he would not be brought up to feel at home in neither the religion of his mother nor that of his father. With a bit of luck – contingent as it was upon her reaching the required standards – Sarah's child would be Jewish and, together with Josh, she would raise him beneath the satisfying umbrella of his creed. With Kitty, Sarah recited the injunctions, the first five concerning Man's relationship with God, the latter governing his behaviour towards his fellow. As the final phrases rose from the steps of the Ark to the light, which burned continuously – as had that of the Temple – above it, to the leaves and the giant hydrangeas, which adorned the holy place, Sarah, unable to keep her news to herself any longer, nudged Kitty:

"I'm going to have a baby."

Kitty, considering the tenth commandment concerning, *prima facie*, the fact that she must not covet her neighbour's ass, thought she had not heard correctly.

"You're what?" she whispered.

"A baby. I'm pregnant."

Tears came to Kitty's eyes. Carol and Sarah. Two more grandchildren. God was good. She covered Sarah's hand with her own, squeezing it, and her happiness was complete when, from the corner of her eye, at the back of the Ladies' Gallery, she saw Rachel, who had crept into the synagogue, Kitty presumed – where she looked ill at ease – to say a prayer for her father.

Twenty-three

Dear Kitty,

It fits (the tuxedo), and reminds me how lax I have become about my person. There is no one to dress for except MM and he does not care, does not look into the mirror, for fear of encountering mocking eyes, six million pointing fingers. This will be my last letter (about myself). The time to weep is over, (was over long ago), and we must talk of Rachel and her wedding and my trip to England.

There is not much more to tell you about MM. I have long ago stopped trying to reconcile the new Maurice Morgenthau with the old, to match the slim and *even then* optimistic medical student, who rode the box car three days, without light or air or food, with the pot-bellied (I've been doing push-ups) cynic in his flat cap. The pieces do not fit. We do not come out the same after any experience. Mine have left a shell around me which, until I met you, has been my protection against my emotional involvement with another person. I have many acquaintances but few friends (I show them respect but do not bare my soul). Many of them are non-Jewish and there is always a wall of glass between us. Perhaps I would not have been so alone if I could have gone to a synagogue (I did try once but they asked me if I had a ticket. A *synagogue* Kitty, not a concert

211

hall!) or a church. But I could not pray. My father prayed.
I heard the *Shema* recited by men with pistols in their
necks. Praying is something I cannot do, any more than I
can believe in a power which would be pleased if I ate this
or did not eat that. I have been left with an ability to
differentiate between what is important and what is
unimportant, which sets me apart; to value life and
freedom, to discard trivia, to learn tolerance, to despise
hate and violence. Sometimes, you know, I look round my
apartment for a sign (do you realize Kitty that there is not
one photograph of my family, it is not only that they are
not but it is as if they had never been), some *mezuzah* of
the soul, some testament of ashes that I could touch on
going out or coming in. 'What is your duty? Goethe said.
'What each day requires...' So, every day I add to my
deposition, a tear here, a brush stroke there, in the eternal
hope that one single moment properly understood can
shed light on the whole. I paint the dead but look forward,
since meeting you, to life.

I don't want you to worry, Kitty, that when I come to
England I will be sad. I am not going to embarrass you or
your guests. I have said my *kaddish* (the *el mohleh
rachamims* would extend into eternity and there are not
enough candles). I just wanted you to know, to share with
you my past, as you shared Sydney, trusting me (as I trust
you) with his dear memory. I thank you, darling, but I will
not come to England for the *Aufruf* – which for MM has
other connotations which waken me, even now, from my
sleep – but shall think of you, with your family around
you, at the lunch afterwards. I shall arrive in time for the
wedding (there is no need to make a reservation for me,
my hotel room comes in a package with the air fare). Don't
be afraid. I won't speak any more about the past and spoil
your happiness with my neuroses (Freud said it was no
sin to be a neurotic!). With my tuxedo I will put on joy

and gladness and come to you a typical New Yorker, an American tourist from Avi's bus. Have you told Rachel about me? I look forward to meeting her. And you Kitty. I can hardly wait. MM.

PS. Did you know that the tradition for the *Aufruf* is so old, that the Talmud tells how King Solomon built a gate in the Temple, where residents of Jerusalem would sit on *Shabbat*, to perform kindnesses to bridegrooms who came there. After the Temple was destroyed the custom arose of honoring the groom in synagogue – some congregations throw candy and raisins for a sweet life.

PPS. The fitting for the wedding dress should go well. I can see Rachel standing before the mirror. Will you have her portrait painted?

PPPS. I am over the shingles now and am in good health. *'Ich bin gesund.'* It was what the early prisoners had to write to pass the censor, when they were starved, beaten and maltreated. By the time the letters arrived they were often dead. No more I promise. I will remain silent and let my pictures speak. MM.

"You've left Austin and Brenda's children off the invitation," Beatty said. "Was it a mistake?"

Kitty sighed. She had done her best, lying awake at nights with names and faces circulating in her head in an effort not to offend, not to upset anyone. In an ideal world she would have liked to invite everyone to Rachel's wedding, every friend, every acquaintance, every member of the WIZO group, the Day Centre, the Ladies' Guild, with whom she had worked. The Ladies' Guild had presented difficulties. In the interests of her limited numbers Kitty had decided not to include them, *en masse*, but she and Sydney had been asked to the weddings of

213

both Joy Kaye's, and Rika Snowman's children. Could she invite them on this basis, without upsetting the other members of the Guild? She could not. Nita Cooper and Barbara Brill were distinctly put out. Not that they had said anything, but she had sensed it when they had assembled in the synagogue hall to prepare their weekly Sabbath *kiddush*. Joy Kaye and Rika Snowman had rallied round her, talking of the wedding; the other ladies had arranged herring on plates, cut honey cake into squares. Nothing had been said, but there was an air of reproach. 'You're bound to offend somebody' – Kitty could year Sydney's voice in her head – and he was right.

Among those she had offended there would have, of course, to be Beatty. No, it wasn't a mistake, Kitty said, the parameters of the guest list had stopped at Rachel's *first* cousins. "A couple of little children!" Beatty said, missing the point. "How much do a couple of little children eat?" Kitty had tried to explain, but Beatty took the omission as a personal affront, an assault upon the persons of her grandchildren, and would not be mollified. Her curiosity, however, overcame her pique, and when she wasn't going to and from the hospital, with little foil-covered dishes of calves-foot jelly and of junked she had made for Leon, to receive which he opened his mouth like an obedient child, Beatty made the journey to Kitty's to inspect the wedding presents, pricing them up as they arrived. Kitty had cleared her dining-room for them and already it was well filled with crescent salad dishes, chopping boards and coffee grinders, and heat-resistant table-mats with Florence views. "You'd think they could do better than that," Beatty would say, picking up a pair of towels and inspecting the card that came with them. "They got them in the sale, you can tell because the label's been marked," or "Pity they couldn't manage more than a travelling clock considering what Sydney – *olovasholem* – did for them." Decanters, which she could hardly lift, and solid silver bread baskets ('who wants a silver bread basket?') were identified immediately by Beatty as having come from 'the other side'. She was generally right.

Kitty had never seen such generous presents, china and silver, crystal and glass. Together with Rachel, who had finished her exams, she entered them all in the book she had ruled with headed columns, suggested by the practical Patrick: the name of the guest, with his address, the nature of the gift, and a final space to be ticked when an acknowledgment had been sent. While Patrick was at the hospital Rachel sat at the kitchen table chewing her pen. '...Thank you for your unusual ramekins...' 'Patrick and I were thrilled to receive your Fondue Set...' "I hate Fondue!" "Never mind," Kitty said. "If people go to the trouble..." She knew she was on to a losing wicket, that Rachel, amenable as she was being, engulfed in a sea of jam spoons and steak knives, Martini jugs and flower vases, which belonged to an alien lifestyle, was becoming increasingly disenchanted.

"We don't *have* to go through all this!" she'd said to Kitty one night, from the floor where she was sitting with Patrick, surrounded by brown paper and tissue paper and cardboard boxes and polystyrene snowflakes and by string. "All Patrick has to do, according to the Talmud, is to give me an article of value and a written document and we have to cohabit..." "You do that all right," Kitty said, "...in the presence of witnesses, and that's it. It doesn't say a thing about butter dishes and deep-fat fryers..." "You'll be glad, later on," Kitty said, winding string round her fingers (Sydney had never thrown away string), with more conviction than she felt, "Don't muddle up the cards!"

It was a time of stress for all of them. Hettie was panicking about the catering (what if it was a hot night, would the *Caneton à la Bigarade* prove too heavy?), Kitty about her table plan (where could she put Beatty so that she would create the least waves?), Herbert about the synagogue and the cars (would Kitty supply him immediately with a list of those guests on the Shelton side who did not have transport), Rachel about what she had let herself in for, and Patrick about his speech. Between

Kitty's flat and Hettie's house the telephone lines burned: Hettie's parents would be arriving from Florida, would Kitty invite them for the *Aufruf*? It would be nice, Hettie suggested, if old Mrs Klopman could *participate* in the Marriage Ceremony, could she give Rachel her second cup of wine?; corsages for the bridal party; buttonholes for the ushers (led by Norman); presents for the bridesmaids, which Hettie would choose and Patrick would present; frilly knickers and socks for Debbie and Lisa (who had to be brought up from Godalming for fittings) and garlands for their hair.

A telephone call, concerning the decision as to whether or no the two mothers should wear gloves beneath the canopy, was interrupted by the appearance of a shaking Freda on Kitty's doorstep. It took two cups of coffee and a piece of Kitty's ginger cake to calm her down. She looked a wreck. Kitty's heart went out to her.

"There's been a summons," Freda said, taking a paper from her bag and putting it on the kitchen table.

Kitty read it. It was from the Magistrates Court on behalf of Miss Catherine Turnbull, an Affiliation Order naming Mr Harry Goldstien as the father of her child. It silenced Kitty who had privately thought that Freda's menopausal imagination and her childlessness had lent credence to the whole affair. She tore off a piece of kitchen roll and handed it to Freda for her tears.

"What does Harry say?"

Freda had watched him open the letter. He had looked puzzled then pale. She had thought that he was going to have a heart attack. Half-dressed, he collapsed on the bed and handed her the summons. She waited for him to speak. He picked up the envelope from where it had fallen on the blue waffle-nylon eiderdown and examined it. His face was ashen.

"There must be some mistake."

"I've known for a long time," Freda said.

Harry looked at her. "Known what?"

"About the baby. She wrote to me."

"Who did?"

"Miss Catherine Turnbull, I suppose. She never signed letters. How could you?"

Harry stared at her. He looked ill. "How could I what? You don't believe…?"

"It wasn't my fault," Freda said, "we couldn't have a child…"

"Freda…"

"Don't Freda me."

"You don't believe this?" He held the paper aloft.

"It's got your name on it."

"You must be mad!" Harry said.

And she was. She had gone made. She felt herself going. Things had been bad between them before the summons. Now it was a house of silence. Harry had tried to explain, tried to reassure her, but she would not listen. He was visibly shaken. Preoccupied. Freda knew that he had spoken to his solicitor with whom he played golf. Had consulted him.

"I'll divorce him," Freda said to Kitty, blowing her nose. "He can marry her if he wants. I won't stand in his way. I hope they'll be very happy."

Kitty had never believed Freda's stories about Harry. Now she was not so sure. She looked at Freda, thin as a stick, ugly with weeping. No man would have her.

"When's the case?" Kitty said.

Freda repeated the date which was engraved on her memory.

"Two days before the wedding," Kitty said.

Kitty did not know where the time had gone. Could not believe that there was now only a fortnight to go, and wondered what she had thought about, what she had talked about, before. She was as excited as Rachel, who sat in the car by her side on the way to Cupid of Hendon for the final fitting of her dress. More excited. Rachel herself seemed calm. It was as if having finished with her exams – the results were expected any moment – a great weight had fallen from her and she could concentrate on her marriage.

Kitty could no longer complain. Rachel had entered into the spirit of the proceedings and to Kitty's surprise had put all her energies into her prospective role as bride. Kindly, sweetly, willingly, she had penned her 'thank you' letters, supervised the fittings for the bridesmaids' dresses, helped Kitty to prepare the flat, and with the cooking for the *Aufruf*. She had spent a private evening with Patrick at the house of Rabbi Magnus – who had discussed with them, among other things, the sanctity of the union into which they were about to enter – and they had taken the Licence together with the *ketubah* – the Jewish Marriage lines – of both sets of parents, their birth certificates and their Hebrew names to the Office of the Chief Rabbi for his authorisation. Kitty (for Rachel) and Herbert (for Patrick) had accompanied them as witnesses – Hettie was spending the day at the hairdresser's for her wedding 'highlights'. Rachel had agreed to a haircut (quarter of an inch), chosen her 'going away' outfit (puce dungarees with a puce beret) and had trudged Kitty round a myriad different shops – making herself heard above the disco music, which deafened Kitty – for her wedding shoes.

"My nest will be empty," Kitty said, putting a hand over Rachel's as they negotiated the right turn at Hendon Central.

"Come on Mum!" Rachel said. "It's ages since I've lived at home."

"You don't understand," Kitty said. "Nor will you until you're a mother. I wonder if they remembered the blue bow for the underslip."

The dress hung, a white cloud, on the door of the fitting-room. Rika Snowman was as excited as Kitty.

"Take off your clothes, darling," she said to Rachel. "I can't wait to see what it looks like. The girls have really worked hard on it. There's only the hem to finish. Did you bring your shoes?"

ROSE OF JERICHO

The fitting-room was too small, for the flowing underslip, the layers of lace. Rachel put her arms out and Rika dropped the dress over them. Kitty sat in the salon, her heart beating, watching her younger daughter. 'Are you having her painted?' Maurice had asked. Even now, her hair in an untidy knot, Rachel looked like a picture. Rika smoothed the lace over the bust, the shoulders, struggled to fasten the long zip.

"Breathe in darling."

Rachel sucked in her breath.

"That's funny!" Rika frowned. "Have you put on weight?"

Rachel looked at Kitty.

"I never make a mistake with my measures," Rika said, examining the turnings. "We don't leave all that much. Not with lace." She ran her tape-measure round Rachel's waist then consulted her notebook.

"Twenty-two!" she said triumphantly. "I knew I hadn't made a mistake." She measured Rachel's waist again and showed the tape-measure to Kitty. "Twenty-five and a bit!"

Kitty, remembering with horror the Chinese take-away, looked at Rachel who lowered her eyes.

"Rachel!" Kitty said.

She was going to have another grandchild.

Twenty-four

Freda had never been in a Magistrates' Court. In any court. It
was the end of the road for her, the final confrontation. Sitting
on the hard bench, with the friends and relatives of those whose
cases were coming up, with an idle public whose curiosity took
them into the dusty amphitheatre of the courtroom, she was
vaguely aware that outside a sun was shining with a brightness
that was rarely seen in England, and that it looked as if it was
going to be a nice weekend for Rachel's wedding, for which she
had not even bought a new dress. She did not care. The last
weeks had been torture. Freda had carried the summons round
with her as an intimation, a reminder of her husband's perfidy.
Harry had tried to discuss the matter, but Freda would not
listen. After the court case, after the hearing, there would be
time enough for that. The house, Freda's home with Harry
where they had been so happy, where Freda had reared her
family of fictitious children, had become a prison in which they
shared a cell, although Freda slept at the very edge of the bed
and would not let Harry touch her. She no longer bothered to
clean it, letting the dust collect, and when Harry came home,
reluctantly now, sadly, he had to get his own dinner, for Freda
did not cook his meal.

The family had poked their noses in. Trust them. Mirrie, her
spinster sister, had begged to know what was the matter but
what could Mirrie know of the sacrament of marriage, of

infidelity? Freda had not confided in her. Lennie, the family doctor – at the instigation of Beatty, Freda was sure – had rung her up, tactfully, while Harry was at work, to enquire if she was feeling well, and whether he could be of any help. Nobody could. Not even Kitty to whom Freda unburdened herself. Her *fidus Achates* had always been Harry, by whom she had been betrayed. He was anxious, frightened, that much Freda knew. He had started to take tranquillisers – she had found the bottle when she went through his pockets – which she construed as evidence, if more were needed, of his guilt. What was going to happen to them, to their relationship, Freda did not know. She could not imagine that there was life beyond this day.

Her sister-in-law, typically, had offered to come with her to the hearing, but Freda would not let her, not wanting a witness to her shame. Besides, with the *Aufruf* tomorrow, the wedding on Sunday, Kitty had enough to do. Some people had happy times to which they could look forward. Freda had only despair. With the rest of the court she stood while the Bench – two women and a man – were seated, pulverised a paper hanky in her lap, not hearing while they dealt, the dust filtering the sun on to their heads, with a dishonest youth wearing an ear-ring, a violent husband who faced a wife with a purple eye. If the case against Harry were proven Freda would be violent. She would murder Harry. The knife was in the kitchen drawer together with the egg slicer and the potato masher. She had made her plans. They would put her in prison. It was all the same to her. Her life was finished. The seal would be put on it in this courtroom. "Turnbull v. Goldstien," the Presenting Officer called. Freda's life. On the Bench they turned a page. Harry – how handsome he had been when she married him – in front of the dock, was conscience-stricken, pale. Catherine Turnbull took the oath, held the Bible in her right hand. In her cotton skirt and blouse, this scarlet woman, this voluptuary, to Freda's astonishment, was little more than a child.

"This is an application," Miss Turnbull's counsel said, "under the Affiliation Proceedings Act, for Mr Harry Goldstien to be declared the father of Damien Russell Turnbull, born on the 27th December…"

Harry's child had a name. Freda wanted suddenly to rush to him, to protect him from the mob.

"Miss Turnbull…" In his well worn black Miss Turnbull's counsel adjusted the glasses which had slipped down his nose, waved an accusatory arm towards Harry.

"Is this man the father of your child?"

Freda's life was over. She had not lived it for this. She called upon her parents, long since dead, glad they had not lived to see her shame. Images invaded her mind, shameful, erotic, involving Harry and the waif-like Miss Turnbull with her spiky hair. From the witness box, where she had promised to tell the truth and nothing but, this girl gripped the pale wood with bitten nails. She stared at Harry. A puzzled expression crossed the homely face.

The court waited.

"I never seen this man before."

Freda was aware of a voice, seeming to come from far away, declaring, "I think, Madam, there has been some mistake in this case…" But she did not hear how Miss Turnbull's lover had been a man who called himself 'Smith': how she had found a football coupon in his pocket, made out in another name; how she had looked up his address in the telephone book and lit upon the wrong Harry Goldstein; because, like a sigh, in her summer dress, she had slipped sinewless to the ground.

"If you don't eat," Beatty said to the supine Leon, as if the soup, thickened with groats, with which she was feeding him, was in the British Pharmacopaeia, "you won't get better." It was a dictum in which she believed with a doggedness as thoroughgoing as her refusal to acknowledge that her husband's life – despite the marvels of modern medicine which were rapidly losing ground in the battle against his disease – was slipping away. "And if you don't get better I won't go to the wedding on Sunday. You want me to tell you about Rachel's wedding, don't you?" She looked at the high window, the other side of which the healthy were going about their business, with their arms, and their legs, and their circulatory and alimentary systems in working order, oblivious to the pain and tribulation of the eighteen men whose lives did not extend beyond the boundaries of the geriatric ward. Leon would not go on for much longer, the doctor had warned her. Beatty did not believe him. Fortified by her beef tea, revitalised by her custards, there would be no surrender. "You want me to wear my new dress, don't you?" she demanded of the unresponsive Leon.

She had already explained to him, with his sunken cheeks, his fleshless fingers, that the dress was apple-green – her favourite colour as a child when her hair had an auburn which owed nothing to the hairdresser and his bottle – embroidered with lurex thread. She had had her shoes dyed apple-green to match. "I'll be here on Sunday as usual to give you your lunch – I've cooked a bottom quarter, I'll mince it, you like that – then Sister will keep an eye on you. I'll ring up from the King Solomon Suite, she doesn't mind. Funny, Rachel getting married. I remember when she was born. Sydney was like a cat with two tails. Poor Sydney, he had no right to go like that – he was never ill. I think they should have asked the children. Austin and Brenda aren't a bit pleased. They're leaving them with Brenda's mother. For two pins they wouldn't have accepted, but they didn't want to upset Kitty. Poor Kitty all on her own. You have to take your hat off to her. I thought without Sydney she'd go to pieces. She's marvellous. Travelling on her own. I wouldn't have the nerve. Going to classes. It's like she's got a new lease of life. I told you about Carol's baby. And Sarah's. Kitty won't know which way to turn. I don't think Austin and Brenda will have any more. Not unless they guaranteed a girl. Won't be long before they can do that. No sooner turn round than they're getting married. I'll bring you a piece of wedding cake – crumble it up small – you used to like fruit cake. Remember the one I always made with the glacé cherries? Austin never could stand glacé cherries. Used to pick them out." Beatty scraped the last of the broth from the bottom of the jar and inserted it, heaving a sigh of relief, as if she had caught the last post, between Leon's lips. "You've done very well."

"Tea or coffee?" The disinterested ward-maid, with her trolley of pots and cups and sugar lumps, enquired from the end of the bed.

"He'll have coffee," Beatty said, and asked for an extra sugar as if the additional lump would be instrumental in turning the tide of the battle waged by the drugs.

In her kitchen Kitty, helped by Rachel, counted out the silver-plated forks, King's pattern, which had been her wedding present, hers and Sydney's, from Grandma Solomons, and wondered whether the salmon, which lay curled beneath the cling-wrap in the refrigerator, was going to be big enough for the luncheon following the *Aufruf*. She was serving it buffet-style – there were far too many people to sit round the dining-table from which the wedding presents had now been removed – and had been busy all day, helped by Addie and Mirrie and Rachel, scraping new potatoes, washing lettuce, and grating cabbage for the salad. Rachel had made the mayonnaise. She had been a great help.

She had been at home for a week now, living with Kitty. Kitty had insisted. She wasn't having her getting out of Patrick's bed in the council flat and going to her wedding. Kitty's rooms were full of flowers. People had sent them. The door bell had been ringing all day. Kitty had forgotten how exciting it was – Carol's wedding seemed so long ago. In the hairdresser's, to which she had popped out during the morning – although she thought it dreadful the way some of the women unburdened themselves to the stylists, nothing was sacred – she was unable to keep the elation from her voice. She watched tensely, anxiously, as she was combed out, and asked Jon if he didn't think her cut the least little bit too short, as if she were the bride. On Sunday Jon was coming to the flat with his heated rollers – her hair would be flattened after Saturday morning in her *shul* hat – and to put up Rachel's hair beneath her head-dress. The girl at the reception, with her scarlet nails, framed by the canisters of hair-spray, wished her *mazeltov*.

It was a *mazeltov*. There were several. Rachel had passed her exams, a second class degree which, Kitty thought, was well as could be expected considering the amount of work she had done – what she was going to do with it goodness only knew – and there was the baby. Rachel's trousers, as she grouped the forks into neat piles on the metal tray, were fastened with a safety pin. Kitty would not forget in a hurry the moment at Cupid of Hendon when the bombshell had been dropped. Not that anything had specifically been said, but Rika Snowman, tight about the lips, had summoned the fitter, and in between them they had worked out how best to deal with an insertion of lace into the 'gown'. "Better make it *four* inches," Rika had said pointedly. "There's still a few weeks to go!" In the car Rachel said: "I'm sorry Mummy" as if she were a child apologising for some misdemeanour. "I thought you had pills and things…" Kitty said. "I must have forgotten." "Do the Klopmans know?" Kitty felt as if it were a personal disgrace. Rachel shook her head. "They'd be furious with Patrick." "Thank God your father's not alive," Kitty said. She shuddered to imagine what Sydney's reaction would have been, and drove in silence as she thought about it. When she glanced at Rachel she was crying, slow tears drifting down her face from overflowing eyes. "What's the matter?" Kitty pulled up at the lights too close to the car in front. She didn't know what she was doing. Rachel scrubbed at her cheeks with what had once been a paper hanky. "I thought you'd be pleased!" she sobbed. God, children! Kitty

thought. She put a hand over Rachel's. "Of course I'm pleased."
It was only partly true. "You haven't even asked when it's due."
A car behind hooted. Kitty hadn't noticed the lights change.
"When?" "Five months," Rachel said. Within a few weeks of
Carol's and Sarah's.

Extraordinarily, then, as if she was glad the secret had no
longer to be kept, Rachel chattered on about her trip round the
world with Patrick which was going to be postponed until the
baby was three months old – when they would take it with them
on their backs – and meanwhile could they come anyway to stay
with Kitty? The baby would sleep in the room with herself and
Patrick, and she was going to breast feed, so they'd be no
trouble. Karl Popper and Wittgenstein had since been replaced
by books on natural childbirth – Rachel's baby would be
delivered on a birthing stool – and the wedding, if one were to
listen to Rachel, had taken a secondary and unimportant place.
Now, carrying the tray of cutlery into the dining-room, Kitty
watched her daughter. There was something she had been
trying to say to her. She waited until Rachel came back with the
empty tray.

"I've asked a friend to the wedding," Kitty said, cutting a
cucumber finely. She had left the cucumber till last as it was
inclined to go limp.

Rachel helped herself to a few of the slices as they dropped
from Kitty's knife.

"What's her name?"

"It's a man," Kitty said.

'Have you told Rachel about me?' Maurice had asked.

"A man!"

Her tone, Kitty thought, revealed that Rachel had considered
her mother to be of an age beyond friendship, beyond feeling.

"From the evening class?" Rachel looked at her watch. She
was expecting Patrick who would take her for Friday night
dinner at the Klopmans', to be introduced to Hettie's parents
who had arrived from Florida.

"I met him in Israel," Kitty said, an image flashing into her mind of Maurice, in his zippered jacket, his flat cap.

"You've kept him very quiet."

"There was nothing to make a noise about," Kitty said.

"Why on earth should he want to come to my wedding? He doesn't even know me!"

"He knows you."

Rachel got up from the corner of the kitchen table on which she had been sitting.

"I went to visit Daddy's grave," she said.

Kitty looked at her, surprised.

Rachel was at the door. "There were a few weeds. I pulled them out."

Kitty opened the kitchen door to Patrick who followed her into the kitchen.

"Excited?" Kitty said.

"I haven't eaten a thing for the past two days," Patrick said. "And God knows what I've been writing up for the patients!"

"Nerves," Kitty said, "Don't forget the ring!"

"I'll be glad when it's over."

"Don't let Rachel hear you!"

"It's worse than the finals!"

Patrick stood awkwardly by the sink.

"I love Rachel."

Kitty, covering the cucumber dish, looked at him.

"I should hope so!"

"I just wanted you to know. That I'll look after her…"

Kitty put the dish into the fridge in which there was no longer an inch of room.

"…I wanted to thank you…" Patrick said. "…For Rachel…"

Kitty put her arms round her son-in-law to be. "There's no need to make a speech," she said, her eyes pricking with tears. "Leave it for Sunday!"

When Rachel and Patrick had gone the flat was quiet. Kitty was glad, after the comings and the goings of the past week– the last of the presents, the flowers, deliveries of food and wine for the *Aufruf*, and dresses, Rachel's and the bridesmaids', and head-dresses, and telegrams of good wishes – to have it all to herself. Outside she was calm – "don't know how you cope with it all", Addie had said – inside was a maelstrom of emotions. She felt sad, conscious at every moment of excitement, every salutation of *mazeltov*, at the absence of Sydney, although somewhere she felt that he knew, exactly, what was going on; ambivalent about Rachel's baby, so soon, she was so young; excited about the wedding, but at the same time apprehensive lest the well laid plans, the long-standing arrangements, did not go right; in a state about Maurice. Rachel had not been interested. Kitty didn't know what she had expected. There had been another letter. A short one only. To tell her a final *Mazel Tov* and that he was counting the days until he would see her in the *shul*. The dining-room table had been set by Mirrie ready for the luncheon on Kitty's Madeira cloth which cost so much to launder. The sitting-room looked as it had not done since Sydney's death, decorated with anticipation, bright with flowers against which Rachel would have her photograph taken on Sunday. Kitty adjusted a bloom here, a stem there – how kind people were, Hettie and Herbert had sent an arrangement which took up so much room she'd had to stand it in the hearth – then shut the door on the heady perfume of the summer roses.

In Rachel's bedroom the wedding-dress – beneath its white sheet, on which Rika Snowman had pinned a horseshoe for good luck – hung from the cupboard door. Her case was packed. Case! A nylon hold-all, into which Rachel had thrown her trousseau – a new pair of jeans (maternity) and a few tops – which was all she had allowed Kitty to buy her, and a sweater of Patrick's. Kitty thought of her own trousseau which had, she remembered, to do with hand-made underwear, with pretty dresses, a fur coat bought by her father – not a piece of skunk from Camden Lock – and, how extraordinary it seemed now, with hats! She sat down on Rachel's bed and picked up the ragged bear, its glassy eyes sewn on more times than she could remember, that Rachel had kept from her childhood. It didn't seem long since it had been bootees and matinée jackets, which Kitty had knitted in a trice and threaded with pink ribbon. Soon she would start knitting for Rachel's baby. For all the babies! It was going to be a busy year. It was better that way. But at this moment, she would have given it all up, all the excitement, all the babies, for a quiet half-hour with Sydney.

Twenty-five

Kitty, in her turquoise dress, stood beneath the satin marriage canopy with its embroidered inscription from the book of Jeremiah – 'The voice of mirth, and the voice of gladness, the voice of the bridegroom, and the voice of the bride' – and waited for Rachel. She was trembling. As if she had not done it before. She had. But with Sydney by her side. This time she stood alone on the heels which were too high for comfort – the day had dawned clear and hot and already her feet were beginning to swell – on the bride's side of the *chuppah*, opposite Herbert and Hettie and Mrs Klopman, who, resplendent in purple silk, was sitting on a chair, and Magda and Joseph Silver who had flown in with their suntans from Florida. The synagogue was packed, the women fanning themselves with the white copies of The Marriage Service – personalised in silver with the names of Patrick and Rachel – the men, with their handkerchiefs, discreetly mopping their brows. The choir, in especially good voice, Kitty thought, were singing 'O Isis und Osiris' from *Die Zauberflöte* as Maurice had suggested. Kitty had to admit that it was beautiful.

From the corner of her eye Kitty could see Maurice. Taller than she had remembered him, certainly slimmer, in his tuxedo. Expecting the zippered jacket, the flat cap, Kitty had scarcely recognised him. He was a fine looking man and in his youth must have been handsome. This morning, in the midst of the hustle and bustle of getting Rachel ready – amid the panic and excitement of the timing of the preparations, the opening of telegrams, the dashings in and out of Addie Jacobs, the missing bridesmaids' posies – flowers had arrived from him. Kitty knew they were from Maurice, although there was no card. They were tall gladioli and palm fronds, their leaves tied in a knot, which took Kitty, for a brief moment, away from the wedding and back – how long ago it seemed now – to Avi in the Canyon of the Inscriptions. Maurice stood next to Harry, who did not recognise him and wondered – a palpable outsider – what he was doing on the Shelton side of the *shul*. Kitty's thoughts had wandered. The choir, against the background of the organ, was on to *Ma Tovu* whose haunting strains and minor key brought a lump into Kitty's throat. She hoped she would keep from crying. To preserve her make-up. Rachel had refused to wear any. Not even for her big day. It didn't matter. She was lovely enough without it.

Kitty had left her in the brides' room together with Carol, who was fussing over Debbie and Lisa – admonishing them to stand still during the Service – and Samantha and Lauren and Elaine. Kitty hoped that there was no last minute hitch, that Rachel didn't want to spend a penny, or anything, in her layers of dress. Patrick was already beneath the *chuppah*, waiting for his bride. Ghostly pale, holding his grey gloves with hands which, Kitty thought, must have been sweating, he faced the indigenous rabbi and the cantor – in their long robes, their velvet hats – and Rabbi Magnus, on whose presence Kitty had insisted. Rabbi Magnus gave Kitty a reassuring glance which acknowledged past memories of Sydney.

Suddenly the synagogue was tangibly quiet. There was an expectant shuffle. The doors at the back were thrown open and the congregation, turning towards them, rose to its feet. The music, *Baruch Haba*, 'Blessed be You', was heart-rending, the bride on Juda's arm, her bouquet of lilies trembling on the child she carried, magnificent. Kitty thought so. The lump

threatened to occlude her throat. She sniffed and caught
Maurice's eye, and it was as if they were alone in the synagogue,
as if he, of all the family and friends around her, could read her
thoughts and she his. The synagogue, in its wedding glory,
would not be consumed in the flames of a *Kristallnacht*, those
within it, in their wedding clothes, men, women and children,
would be spared the deprivations, the bestialities, the black
cloud, which had consumed Maurice's past. Among her unshed
tears for Rachel and her unborn baby, for Sydney, for this day,
Kitty shed a tear for Maurice's absent family and added a prayer
of thankfulness for her own.

Rachel, on the right of her bridegroom – 'at thy right hand
doth the queen stand' – was shaking visibly beneath her short
veil. Patrick discreetly took her hand. To Kitty's amazement
they had both fasted in accordance with the custom; to her
greater amazement, Rachel had also visited the *mikveh*,
immersing herself in the ritual bath – a symbolic purification –
before her marriage. What a strange child she was. What a mass
of contradictions. Behind their aunt, flanked by Patrick's three
cousins from Leeds, Debbie and Lisa – heart stealers in their
organdie dresses with their posies and their missing teeth –
stood sentinel, turned by their mother's threats to stones.

Mi Adir, the chant of welcome: the choristers were in full
and ecstatic throat. Kitty wished that she could sit down with
the rest of the congregation, as Rabbi Magnus stepped forward
for the address.

"My dear Rachel and Patrick. 'From every human being
there rises a light that reaches straight to heaven. And when
two souls that are destined to be together find each other, their
streams of light flow together and a single, brighter light goes
forth from their united being...'" Kitty had known that he
would do them proud. The congregation was silent, attentive, as
Rabbi Magnus – Sydney's Rabbi – followed the poetry of the
Baal Shem Tov with a few warm and personal words to Rachel,
whom he had known since her childhood, and to Patrick, who,

he had confided to Kitty, seemed a splendid and upright man. He referred to Rachel's upbringing, to Patrick's noble calling, and expressed his confidence that, together, they would create a home in the Jewish tradition. The *chuppah* beneath which they stood represented such a home, 'a symbol of good fortune that their descendants may be as the stars of heavens', at which Kitty avoided catching Rachel's eye. Despite the heat and her feet, the ceremony seemed all too short; the Betrothal Blessings after which Kitty lifted Rachel's veil and held to her daughter's lips the first cup of wine – which was afterwards handed by his father to Patrick – to remind them that henceforward they would share the same cup of life, no matter what it brought them; the hush, into which no one dropped the proverbial pin, when Patrick, in a quiet, clear voice, declared 'Behold, thou art consecrated unto me by this ring, according to the Law of Moses and of Israel' and placed the gold band symbolically upon the forefinger of Rachel's right hand; the reading of the *ketubah*, the marriage contract, in its Aramaic original, followed by an English abstract: '…I will work for thee, honour, support and maintain thee in accordance with the custom of Jewish husbands who work for their wives, honour, support and maintain them in truth…' The second cup of wine, which was offered as agreed – with much ado – by old Mrs Klopman whose unsteady hand was supported by Herbert; the Seven Blessings commencing with the blessing over wine, and going on to praise the Creator, who brought the world into being, created man in the divine image, instituted marriage and set the first man and woman into a life of Paradise in the Garden of Eden; the familiar and evocative sounding of the breaking glass, as Patrick stamped upon it, to temper the joy of the occasion with a reminder to the congregation of their tragic Jewish past, at which the cries of *mazeltov* echoed, inappositely, from the stained-glass windows of the *shul*; the Benediction, recited by the Rabbi, his hands raised high above the heads of the couple: 'The Lord bless you and keep you: the Lord make his face to shine upon you, and be gracious unto you; the Lord turn his face towards you, and give you peace.' And suddenly it was over. Rachel was Mrs Patrick Klopman. She kissed her husband – with what Kitty thought to be unseemly passion – and arm in arm with him went joyfully to sign the register. Hettie kissed Kitty, their tears mingling on each others' cheeks, then the best man – leaving an imprint of her lipstick – then the bridesmaids, and everyone else in sight until Kitty thought, for one horrified moment, that she was going to embrace the two Rabbis in her excitement. Against a joyful rendering of *Dodi Li*, My Beloved is Mine, they took their places: Hettie beside her husband (Kitty in a moment of aberration glanced round for her own), her parents, and her mother-in-law, and Kitty with Juda. There was a silent pause, then to the glory of Mendelssohn, and moist-eyed smiles and nods of approval from the pews on either side of the red carpeted aisle, led by Rachel and Patrick and their five bridesmaids, the procession swept in triumph from the *shul*.

From the top table in the Crystal Room of the King Solomon Suite, magnificent in its turquoise and gold, Kitty listened as Juda, in his splendid baritone, repeated the Seven Marriage Blessings which had been sung in synagogue, and looked out upon the culmination of the efforts – hers and Hettie's – of the past six months. So far so good. Everything – apart from the *Sorbet aux Citrons Verts*, designed to refresh the palate between courses, which to Unterman's mortification had got lost in transit – had gone according to plan.

Outside the *shul* the photographer had taken photographs of Rachel and Patrick, of Rachel and Patrick with the best man, of Rachel and Patrick with their best man and bridesmaids, of the wedding party with their parents, of the wedding party with their parents and grandparent, and of the wedding party with their parents, grandparent and the congregation who were finally released and surrounded them on the steps. The ushers, headed by Josh and Norman with white buttonholes of carnations, had courteously, efficiently, filled the wedding cars, shepherding the aged and infirm first into the larger models, and preventing Beatty, tactfully, from clambering into Herbert's beribboned Rolls beside the bride and groom.

On the steps of the King Solomon Suite, Unterman himself – the Crown Prince, in his impeccable evening dress – was there to welcome them. He ushered the two families into the ante-room where they would receive the wedding-guests and where he had thoughtfully provided refreshment for them, and Rachel and Patrick into a side-room where they would break their fast and spend a few quiet moments together in private – *yihud* – denoting their newly acquired status, as husband and wife, entitled to live together under the same roof. The line of parents, crammed to capacity in the foyer and snaking up the gracious staircase, seemed to Kitty to be never ending. Standing next to Rachel, who appeared to be enjoying the whole procedure, she shook hands, and kissed the cheeks of a caval-cade of faces whose names were announced with a sonorous majesty by the sergeant-major of a deep-chested, twirly moust-ached toastmaster, in his be-meddled red. From the corner of her eye, a solitary figure on the staircase between two chattering family groups, Kitty caught sight of Maurice.

"Mr Maurice Morgenthau!"

Morning Dew, Kitty thought and held out her hand, her pulse quickening, to the handsome figure in his tuxedo. Still clinging to her hand Maurice put his face to hers. His cheek was freshly shaven. They did not speak.

"This is Maurice Morgenthau," Kitty said, her voice unsteady, to Rachel.

"Your mother's told me about you," Maurice said.

Jostled by the next in line he moved on to Patrick, offering him congratulations on his bride. Kitty watched his receding back then turned her attention to the next outstretched hand.

When the staircase was empty and the last guest had been received and ushered through into the Reception – Hettie's hot spinach pastries and Danish tartlets filled with smoked roe – there were more photographs, posed this time, with infinite care, against the background of an improbably urn of flowers. Patrick smiled at Rachel, and the two mothers smiled at the bride, and Kitty, *sotto voce*, reminded Rachel to hold her bouquet in front of her.

The dinner, under the aegis of the vigilant Unterman with his army of white gloved waitresses, had gone smoothly, from the entry of the wedding party, accompanied by hand-claps, to the Grace After Meals – although in her excitement Kitty had only picked at the *Sole Dorée* and had not so much as tasted the *Caneton à la Bigarade*.

To the tune of 'The More We Are Together' played by the band, Patrick, standing – 'will the guests kindly remain seated' – had taken wine with his friends and relatives, and Rachel had followed suit. Herbert had taken wine with his business associates, Patrick with his medical colleagues – cheers and catcalls! – and the wedding party with all the guests who had travelled from afar and crossed the Atlantic to be with them, at which Kitty had drunk a silent toast to Maurice at table number ten, which had been intercepted by his to her. The words of the final Marriage Blessing – praying that the bride and groom might live a life of 'joy and gladness, mirth and exultation, pleasure and delight, love and brotherhood, peace and companionship' – winged round the room. Juda sat down to congratulatory cries on his performance, the toastmaster, importantly, adjusted the microphone and prayed silence – 'Reverend Gentlemen, Ladies and Gentlemen' – for the best man.

Kitty, her mind beset by a tumult of emotion, keenly aware of Josh by her side in the place that by rights was Sydney's, listened with only half an ear to the speeches. The health of the bride and bridegroom, proposed by Patrick's best friend, who was an obstetrician, ended with the hope that together, Rachel and Patrick would keep him in work – they'd made a good start, Kitty thought; Patrick's reply was short, able and from the heart. There were speeches by Herbert, who told three funny stores, but whose voice was affected by the excitement of the day and the acquisition of a daughter – by Hettie, who with raised glass thanked everyone for coming and making it such a wonderful occasion and by Mrs Klopman, who told Rachel publicly, what a fine husband she had got for herself in marrying Patrick. There were calls for Kitty from her family, but she found herself unable to speak, and Josh rose to his feet to say a few words on her behalf. After the reading of the telegrams and the representation to Rachel and Patrick of a certificate – commemorating the planting of trees in Israel in their name – presented by the secretary of the Joint Israel Appeal, as an acknowledgement of Herbert's unceasing work on their behalf, the toastmaster, beads of perspiration standing out on his forehead, called for Roy Grose and his band to strike up for 'dancin'' and the Bride and Bridegroom to open the ball. After the first few circumventions, during which Kitty, watching them, thought – with a pang for her own past – how young and beautiful Rachel and Patrick were, and how exciting it was to be starting out in life, they were joined by Herbert and Hettie, by Debbie and Lisa – partnering each other – and by Josh, who escorted his mother on to the floor.

Norman, to a Piaf tune – sung in a voice not too dissimilar from that of the *chanteuse* herself – which he had requested from the band, circled the floor with Sandra, ethereal in grey chiffon which billowed behind her as she moved in his arms. Her lips were close to his ear, into which she whispered: *'Ce n'est plus Madame Piaf qui chante; c'est la pluie qui tombe, c'est le vent qui souffle, c'est le clair de lune qui met sa nappe…'* Norman had never heard any words more beautiful, had never been happier.

"Sandra…?" he said into her hair.

'*La Vie en Rose-er*' The vocalist, in her sequinned dress, gave it her all.

"Mm?"

'*Quand il me prend dans ses bras…*'

"I love you."

'*Il me par-le tout bas…*'

"I love you…"

'*Je vois la vie en Rose-er…*'

"Will you marry me?"

'*Il me dit des mots d'amour…*'

"I thought you'd never ask," Sandra said.

Freda and Harry were almost professional dancers. In their youth they had won competitions. Now they swung and pirouetted in unison, expertly round the floor.

"Look at Freda," Mirrie, sitting at her table by the dance floor, eating a reception pastry, said to her sister Beatty, who was looking for a smoked salmon one among the sandwiches. "She's like a young girl."

"I was really worried about her," Beatty said, parting the two triangles of bread to make sure her find had been successful. "But whatever it was, she seems to have got over it."

"You'd think she was the bride," Mirrie said, momentarily wistful, as she was on these occasions, for her own maiden state.

"She could be." Beatty's mouth was comfortably full. "She's hanging on to Harry like she'll never let him go."

"I don't dance," Maurice said to Kitty against the deafening beat of the *hora* whose circular dance, arms around shoulders, Beatty was instigating. "Can we go somewhere quiet?"

It was the first chance they had had to talk during the long evening. Kitty led him outside to the bar where they sat down on a pair of gilt chairs. Maurice took a Tootsie Roll from the pocket of his tuxedo and gave one to Kitty.

"I can't tell you how happy I am to see you."

"I'm happy to see you," Kitty said.

"Letters are okay…" He looked at Kitty's turquoise dress, her coiffed hair. "You're beautiful!"

Kitty thought of the zippered jacket, the flat cap and regarded Maurice, distinguished, in his tuxedo.

"You too."

Maurice took her hand. "There's something I want to say Kitty. It won't wait."

The strains of the *Hava Negillah* from the ballroom took Kitty back to the dark journey from Beersheba, to Avi's lighted coach.

"I told you I've got two apartments, one is my studio, where I paint. Why don't I move the painting into my apartment? There's a bed in the studio, it has its own bath. I could fix it up, you'd be really comfortable…"

Kitty looked at him. She no longer saw the King Solomon Suite, heard the rousing beat of the music.

"Come to New York. No strings attached. We're not kids Kitty. See how it goes, for both of us…"

"New York!" Kitty said.

"Why not?"

Why not.

"I couldn't possibly," Kitty said. "There's Carol's baby, they're all coming to stay, and Josh's baby – Sarah's mother's not a bit of use – and Rachel's baby, they're moving in after Carol, and the Day Centre – nobody else wants to work in the kitchen – and the WIZO – we're planning a big function after *Succoth* – and Norman…"

Maurice took Kitty's hands in his, looking into her eyes with his own which had been witness to so much horror, so many obscenities, so much distress.

"Kitty…"

"I didn't thank you for the flowers," Kitty said.

Maurice refused to be deflected. "It's time you started living for yourself. The children have their own lives. They can manage without you. The Day Centre won't starve. Give it six months. We'll see how we get on…"

"When?" Kitty said.

"As long as it takes to pack."

"Now?" Kitty said. She thought she would faint.

"Now," Maurice said simply, and Kitty was about to speak when Beatty, escaped from the *hora*, arrived breathless, mopping her mottled chest.

"I'm not as young as I used to be…"

"Think about it…" Maurice relinquished Kitty's hands and stood up. "I'll call you tomorrow…"

"…I thought I was going to pass out." Beatty fanned herself.

"…Around eleven," Maurice said, leaving them.

"Who's that?" Beatty asked, as he walked away. She didn't wait for an answer. "There was supposed to be a sorbet," she said, delighting in the slip-up. "Hettie told me. I could do with an ice." She looked at the jewelled watch embedded in the bracelet of her wrist. "I'm going to phone the hospital. If I can find a phone."

"*Everyone* said it's the best wedding they've ever been to," Hettie said, contentedly, when the last of the guests had disappeared into the night and a wilted Unterman stood with them in the foyer, flushed with his achievement.

"I think it went very well," Kitty said as she waited for Josh, who was in the cloakroom, to take her home.

Upstairs the band was packing up, tables, denuded of their golden cloths, were being folded. Rachel, in her dungarees, had left with Patrick in their open-topped car. Before she had stepped into it she'd flung her arms round Kitty.

"Thank you," Rachel said.

"For what?" Kitty's face was wet.

"For my life."

With their departure the zest, for Kitty, had gone out of the party.

The foyer was deserted as if there had never been a wedding.

Except for Beatty who sat motionless in a corner.

Probably eaten too much, Kitty thought, going over to her. "Aren't you feeling well?"

"It's Leon," Beatty said. "He's dead."

Kitty would not let Josh come in although he had offered to. She wanted to be alone. She switched on the lights in the hall and went into the sitting-room where she kicked off her shoes. She stood before Maurice's flowers, the giant gladioli and the palm fronds tied in a knot, and cast her mind back to the desert heat, to the Bedouin. 'This is his way of saying "I love you",' Avi had said, 'Later on, is coming by his very dear one. If she does nothing, she is turning him down. If she opens up the knot…'

Kitty sat down on a high-backed chair – if she sat on the sofa she would not get up again – and slowly, carefully, starting with the morning sunshine which had flooded through her window – 'Happy is the bride that the sun shines on', she remembered thinking – she re-lived the day, saving Maurice's outrageous suggestion that she go to New York for the last.

There was something else, now. Beatty would need her. Hysterical – widowed while she danced the *hora* – Juda had taken her home where Mirrie, always at everyone's beck and call, would stay the night with her.

Kitty sat for a long time in the empty room, the wedding tunes repeating themselves in her head. 'I don't dance,' Maurice had said. He had nothing, really, to dance about. Kitty stood up and leaving her shoes where they lay – she was too tired to pick them up – switched off the lights until the room was illuminated only by the five branched candelabra in the hall. Its beam through the doorway fell upon Maurice's flowers. Deliberately, in her stockinged feet, as if she had just learned to walk, Kitty moved along its length. Her final act of the long day – which, she felt, was approved of from his chair by Sydney – was slowly, carefully, with hands which had never spared themselves, to untie – God help her! – Maurice's knot.

ROSEMARY FRIEDMAN

GOLDEN BOY

This is one of Rosemary Friedman's best-loved novels. Freddie Lomax is a slick, work-driven city executive, popular and sociable, other eyes always drawn to the magnetic field of his charm. Utterly without warning he is given two hours to clear his desk at the bank and he finds himself joining the ranks of the middle-aged unemployed. His confidence that a new job will appear proves unfounded, and with all the time he now spends at home his marriage to Jane begins to suffer...until, when he thinks he can go no lower, he discovers that he is not the only one with problems and he applies his talents to a last attempt to save his relationship.

'What a story! What a storyteller!' *Daily Mail*

LIFE SITUATION

Oscar John has it all: a successful author, he has been married happily for sixteen years. But then everything changes when he meets Marie-Céleste, an elegant French doctor. When his sexual curiosity turns into passion and an all-consuming love, he is completely unprepared...

Rosemary Friedman

Patients of a Saint

The doctor's practice, first introduced in *No White Coat* and again in *Love on My List,* is expanding. He finds himself buckling under the strain of an increased workload and the demands of his exuberant twins. His wife, Sylvia, persuades him to take a much-needed break and he realises that it is time to find an assistant.

This proves to be a difficult task, but once he has found the right man, the doctor has more time to devote to individual patients and to his family.

Into this busy environment arrives the doctor's alluring cousin Caroline. On a study visit from the US, she invites herself to stay for six months – a situation which causes much chaos and hilarity.

Proofs of Affection

One year in the life of a London Jewish family at a time of great change: Sydney Shelton's business is not doing too well these days, but he has provided for his future and his worries are not about trade but about his own health and his children, now young adults. Sydney's wife Kitty knows how ill he is – but they cannot talk about it. The children openly flout tradition and go against his wishes. What will happen to them if he dies?

With a light satirical touch and great sensitivity, Rosemary Friedman explores the tensions and deeper feelings of a traditional family facing the pressures of change in a non-religious society. A thoughtful and moving novel.

Rosemary Friedman

To Live in Peace

This novel pursues the story of widow Kitty Sheldon from Rosemary Friedman's delightful earlier novels *Proofs of Affection* and *Rose of Jericho*. Kitty has watched her beloved husband die, and her children grow to adulthood. She takes security from her role as family matriarch, but now her north London Jewish community is rife with dispute about the recent Israeli invasion of Lebanon. At the invitation of her gentlemanly suitor, Holocaust survivor Maurice Morgenthau, Kitty visits New York – where she learns to please herself and in so doing learns to *discover* herself too.

Vintage

Clare de Cluzac seems to have it all she could ever want – but underneath her confident exterior lie the scars of an emotionally brutalised childhood. When her authoritarian, philandering father threatens to sell the family château and vineyards, Clare takes a big risk and flies to Bordeaux to run them herself, even though she will have to learn everything from scratch.

As she fights to overcome the many obstacles placed (often deliberately) in her way, she confronts old ghosts and grows into her new role as the *chatelaine* – discovering on the way new knowledge and a deeper understanding of her own desires.

OTHER TITLES BY ROSEMARY FRIEDMAN AVAILABLE DIRECT FROM HOUSE OF STRATUS

Quantity		£	$(US)	$(CAN)	€
	THE COMMONPLACE DAY	6.99	11.50	15.99	11.50
	AN ELIGIBLE MAN	6.99	11.50	15.99	11.50
	THE FRATERNITY	6.99	11.50	15.99	11.50
	THE GENERAL PRACTICE	6.99	11.50	15.99	11.50
	GOLDEN BOY	6.99	11.50	15.99	11.50
	INTENSIVE CARE	10.99	17.99	26.95	18.00
	THE LIFE SITUATION	6.99	11.50	15.99	11.50
	LONG HOT SUMMER	6.99	11.50	15.99	11.50
	LOVE ON MY LIST	6.99	11.50	15.99	11.50
	A LOVING MISTRESS	6.99	11.50	15.99	11.50
	NO WHITE COAT	6.99	11.50	15.99	11.50
	PATIENTS OF A SAINT	6.99	11.50	15.99	11.50
	PRACTICE MAKES PERFECT	6.99	11.50	15.99	11.50
	PROOFS OF AFFECTION	6.99	11.50	15.99	11.50
	A SECOND WIFE	6.99	11.50	15.99	11.50
	TO LIVE IN PEACE	6.99	11.50	15.99	11.50
	VINTAGE	6.99	11.50	15.99	11.50
	WE ALL FALL DOWN	6.99	11.50	15.99	11.50

ALL HOUSE OF STRATUS BOOKS ARE AVAILABLE FROM GOOD BOOKSHOPS OR DIRECT FROM THE PUBLISHER:

Internet: www.houseofstratus.com including author interviews, reviews, features.

Email: sales@houseofstratus.com please quote author, title, and credit card details.

Hotline: UK ONLY: 0800 169 1780, please quote author, title and credit card details.
INTERNATIONAL: +44 (0) 20 7494 6400, please quote author, title, and credit card details.

Send to: House of Stratus Sales Department
24c Old Burlington Street
London
W1X 1RL
UK

Please allow for postage costs charged per order plus an amount per book as set out in the tables below:

	£(Sterling)	$(US)	$(CAN)	€(Euros)
Cost per order				
UK	2.00	3.00	4.50	3.30
Europe	3.00	4.50	6.75	5.00
North America	3.00	4.50	6.75	5.00
Rest of World	3.00	4.50	6.75	5.00
Additional cost per book				
UK	0.50	0.75	1.15	0.85
Europe	1.00	1.50	2.30	1.70
North America	2.00	3.00	4.60	3.40
Rest of World	2.50	3.75	5.75	4.25

PLEASE SEND CHEQUE, POSTAL ORDER (STERLING ONLY), EUROCHEQUE, OR INTERNATIONAL MONEY ORDER (PLEASE CIRCLE METHOD OF PAYMENT YOU WISH TO USE)
MAKE PAYABLE TO: STRATUS HOLDINGS plc

Cost of book(s): —————— Example: 3 x books at £6.99 each: £20.97

Cost of order: —————— Example: £2.00 (Delivery to UK address)

Additional cost per book: —————— Example: 3 x £0.50: £1.50

Order total including postage: —————— Example: £24.47

Please tick currency you wish to use and add total amount of order:

☐ £ (Sterling)   ☐ $ (US)   ☐ $ (CAN)   ☐ € (EUROS)

VISA, MASTERCARD, SWITCH, AMEX, SOLO, JCB:

☐☐☐☐☐☐☐☐☐☐☐☐☐☐☐☐☐☐☐☐

Issue number (Switch only):

☐☐☐

Start Date: **Expiry Date:**

☐☐ / ☐☐   ☐☐ / ☐☐

Signature: _____

NAME: _____

ADDRESS: _____

_____

POSTCODE: _____

Please allow 28 days for delivery.

Prices subject to change without notice.
Please tick box if you do not wish to receive any additional information. ☐

House of Stratus publishes many other titles in this genre; please check our website (**www.houseofstratus.com**) for more details.